THE COVERTON CHRONICLES

REFLECTED

THE COVERTON CHRONICLES

ISBN: 978-1-7324271-1-2

Disclaimer: This book is a work of fiction. There are a few historical figures, places, and events that truly lived or happened. The storylines and plots that have been created within and around the historical figures, places, and facts are completely fake and are not to be considered true. Refer to the 'For the history lover' page in the back of the book to see details of where and how the history and fiction meld together. All other people, living or dead, places, and events are fictional, and any similarities are completely coincidental and not intended by the author.

Credits:

Proofreader – With written express permission to name – Janna T. Chamberlin
Book Cover Designs, Illustrations, and Formatting – Melissa Stevens, Illustrated Author Design Services

Published by Ariz Brune
(POD) 2018

Family is everything.

ACKNOWLEDGEMENTS

I'll keep this short so you can get to the good stuff. Thank you to my husband, Marc, for believing in me, encouraging me to do this thing even though I bored you to death with the details – constantly, and for helping me slack on the housework. I have to give a shout out to my children and my bestest friend in the whole wide world for supporting me, even when they thought I lost my marbles. I didn't lose them. I strategically placed them in forgettable places, there's a difference. And to my beta reader that came in midway through the book and pushed me to finish when I was stuck, thank you for pushing.

Love, B

PROLOGUE

The cold stone floors were wet and sticky from the mead sloshing out of the tankards raised in celebration. Voices were bouncing off the walls giving way to echoed conversations from every end of the room. Men were shouting to hear over one another and their obnoxious laughter.

"Come, Eirik," Guthorm yelled at his half-brother as he entered the dining hall, "come eat and fill your vessel with the finest drink in the lands!" Eirik made his way through the boisterous crowd as women moved in and out between men and tables, refilling cups. A weight dropped into the open leather pouch slung across his shoulder as he passed a slender-framed redhead. He gave her a slight nod as he passed, just as he did many other maidens.

He sat on the hard bench in front of Guthorm, pulling his wife into his lap. "Where have you been hiding, my heart?"

"Ah. Here and there. You would not want to know the boring details of my day to days, would you? It is not nearly as exciting as swinging your sword all day long," Gunhild replied while he nuzzled her neck.

"Did you get the potion from the witch's sister?" she whispered.

"Is that what the hag dropped into my belt?"

"Possibly. Let me look." She slipped his belt off his shoulder, peeking inside when she eased it under the table. "It is. Make a toast in his honor. Do not fail me, Eirik. You must secure your throne. He has tried to kill you once, he will do it again. Keep your brother's eye whilst I add this to his mead."

She slid her hand into the pouch and grasped the small bottle, leaving the belt on the bench next to Eirik when she got up from the table. "Where are you going, wench?" Guthorm guffawed.

"No bloody where, you old donkey," she replied tartly with a smile. She made her way to the kitchen, grabbing one of the serving girls as she walked by, pulling her into the hallway. She shoved the bottle into the girl's hand. "See to it this gets in Guthorm's drink. Tell no one or your guts will be served at the next feast with the haggis," she pushed the girl back out into the dining hall, turning to find all three witches standing in the shadows watching. "I'll meet you in Eirik's chambers when it's done.

They will take the body there. It's closer to the hall."

BULGARIA: 1598

The sisters stood at the entrance of the cave watching the action unfold under the setting sun on the battlefield below them. It was one of many mild skirmishes that took place in Stara Zagora over the last few hundred years. The Bulgarians, Byzantines, Russians, and even a few Ottomans have made a stand at the foot of the Sredna Gora Mountain at one point in time or another. More often than not, they were against one another, but on a few occasions, they have stood together against the opposer, whomever it may have been at the time. The exception is always with the Ottomans, they seemed to be against everyone all the time.

"You realize no one has called upon us in almost a century, save the rare couples who were desperate?" Milena whispered as she watched a group of three men in lavish colors corner one man in a ratty uniform against a boulder.

"Quit whining, Milena," Mira ordered while she leaned closer to the precipice. She squealed in excitement, clapping her hands like an amused child when the man against the boulder was skewered under the chest plate with a sword. "That," she announced, pointing at the fallen soldier, "was my doing! His mother called upon us, remember sisters? She was the one who left us naught for an offering."

"You did that after we had woven his destiny already?" Mila screeched in astonishment.

"We are supposed to be better than that!" Milena yelled.

"Says the sister who is supremely neutral, having nothing to say, one way or another. And not a word from you either, do-gooder." Mira said, turning from Milena and pointing a long finger in Mila's face, "You never allow my gifts to flourish, always making them span over decades. I give them a quick and painless way to go, but you drag it out. Their wives, children, and grandchildren have to witness the demise."

Mila stepped up to her sisters, "Not a word? You are horrible with your gifts. You give them diseases created to slowly eat at their brains or crush them with fallen rock, torturing them with an agonizingly slow death. If I can help lessen those atrocities, I will." Mila glanced between both sisters before continuing, "I give them longer lives. I ease the sufferings the *both* of you bestow. I am not shallow enough to look the other way when one is doing wrong, only to give him a disfigured face or shorter limb to accommodate the other sister," she gave Milena a pointed look, voice raising an octave at each point until she was screaming, "nor am I cruel enough to make them die a miserable death just for my selfish amusement!"

"Is this what we've come to, sisters?" Milena asked, "Fighting amongst each other, refusing to see each of us play a vital part in the lives of humans? Not once have either of these things been an issue before and now we are fighting? I believe it is because of those fights," she gestured to the skirmish below, "that we are fighting one another now. The people who have called upon us for these several hundred years are being killed. We are not what we once were. We were treasured, revered, honored, and yes Mila, feared because of our gifts. People called upon us, giving us food and wine and jewels and trinkets. Now they do not even know our names.

"Why is that? Hmm? Did we go wrong somewhere along the way? Did we get too soft? Spare too many the heartache of what cruelty could have been? We have a cave full of treasures which are no good to us anymore. We cannot spend that which has no value. Our powers are not being used. Why? Tell me why, my sisters," Milena finished in a huff.

"What will you have us do then?" Mira asked looking back and forth between the two. "Would you rather just make everyone ugly, Milena? Have everyone live to the ripe old age of sixty and three, Mila? We can no longer go in their homes and weave their lives, we must gift them when we get the chance. We were created with these powers to use as we see fit. We have done it once before, what is so different now? I tell you, I dare not waste mine."

The sisters stood for a long while watching as men bled the last of their blood, exhaled their lifeforce, stared, eyes vacant to the night sky. They stood until the last soldier left bleeding on the field joined his ancestors in the sky.

"That worked out so well for us last time, did it not? There's nothing more here for us. Our fates will be written by the blood of the men that die on every side at the foot of this mountain. We must move on to blend with them until our time comes once again. Work with what you have, doing what you can within the boundaries of your gifts. We must find a life apart outside our home," Milena whispered before she gathered her silky white dress in her hands, turned to wisps of mist and swept away on the cool mountain breeze.

AUSTRIA 1914

"Are you sure you want me to come with you, Sophie? Your anniversary is coming up." Mila said, "It would be a great opportunity for you to spend some peaceful time with your husband."

Sophie scoffed as she folded her dress, "Do you honestly think I will have the chance to spend any quality time with a royal husband on errand for the crown, even if it is our anniversary? Ha. I think not. Yes, I am quite sure I want to have you with me. Orphanages and schools can only take up so much of my day. He will be in political meetings and dealing with those dreadful arse kissers. I suspect his free time will be minimal. I do have to have someone with whom I can make girl talk."

"Well, if you are certain. I have seen the way you are treated here. The pettiness of the royal court in regard to the two of you. You cannot even dine with your own husband. Certainly, things will be different once you get to Sarajevo."

"I'll not have it today, Mila. You will come with us. I need to have someone who can look from the outside in and make sure I do not overlook anything. You have not one thing to gain or lose if I forget something, so I expect your professional aid as much as I do your companionship when Franz is unavailable. We leave in two hours. Please be ready."

THE TEMPERATURE WAS MILD FOR AN early summer day, even if it was humid, which was to be expected. The rain had stopped days before the entourage arrived. The bomb thrown at the car missed killing the couple. Lives were lost, but thankfully not the ones who were to be left untouched.

"I said do not kill anyone," Carter demanded. "Who gave you the authority to throw a bomb into the car?"

"It didn't harm Archduke Ferdinand or his wife. Do not be irrational, Mr. Doden. You came to the Black Hand for assistance in catching her, not the other way around. If we accomplish what we set out to do and help you in the meantime, all the better for everyone, am I not right?" Dragutin drawled as he watched the proceedings from the window.

"Captain Dimitrijevic, I will not be part of your political games. I am paying you generously to —"

"Yes, I am well aware of our arrangement. I am not safe here and cannot stay any longer than necessary. I will see the events through, mine and yours. As far as your order not to kill anyone, you may want to go talk to Mira. Apparently, you do not keep her on a short enough leash if she is able to make her way to my men to discuss strategy." Dragutin turned from the window to the bar. He poured two fingers of rakia in two glasses, offering one after he downed the other.

"Hmm," Carter responded as he took the brandy. He studied the amber liquid as he gathered his thoughts. "She spoke to your men, you say? When was this?"

"The day before yesterday when we were getting into position." He pointed to the window, nodding for Carter to take his place.

Carter pulled the curtain back, peering down into the busy streets below. From this point, he could see the street and the procession making its way toward them. Mira was talking animatedly with a lanky young man who couldn't have been over twenty. He glanced up at the sky, noting the brightness of the sky giving way to nightfall. He thought about how lucky he was the sun had already begun to set— though it was still up, it had gone down far enough to enjoy this simple pleasure he had grown to miss over the last thousand years. Before he could pull away from the window, one car then another turned onto the street Mira and the young man were standing in. The man scrambled around pulling a revolver, aiming and firing at the couple seated on the open top of the convertible, then tried to turn the gun on himself as chaos erupted but was thrown down by a passerby. Carter watched as Mira ran to the second car flinging the door open, yanking a silver-haired woman out. For a brief moment, there was a blur of light and dark hair visible over the roof of the car as the two women struggled with one another. A few short moments later Mira was leaning on the brick wall behind her holding her stomach where the pale blue colors of her blouse were turning crimson. Mila was once again gone, the only trace she was ever there was a bloody knife lying on the ground and a faint mist quickly sweeping away.

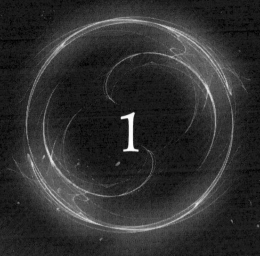

1

You are going to get us shut down," I told Miguel as he labeled his cup of apple juice to put in the fridge like he did each morning.

"Not if you don't say nothing to anyone," he replied for the umpteen hundredth time.

"Really? Do you think it's normal to have the same 'specimen' sitting in the same refrigerator day after day?" I asked, using the air quotes for the word specimen. "Somebody will eventually notice. Either that or one of these days you aren't going to be paying as much attention as you think you are and you're going to end up drinking someone's urine," I shuddered at the thought, trying to keep my vision steady as I looked into the microscope.

ARIZ BRUNE

Every day it was the same thing. Miguel would come in with his breakfast, put the food in the fridge, grab a specimen cup, pour his apple juice in it, label it like he would a collected urine sample with last and first name, date and time, seal it with the label, then place it in the refrigerator next to his food. Disgusting isn't the word I would use for it, more like bothersome. The secondary refrigerator was not typically the one we used to keep the specimens in, but it did catch overflow from time to time when the other fridge was full. On those days he would scarf down his food in the break room but would bleach the shit (no pun intended — we don't do fecal testing in this lab) out of the secondary refrigerator as soon as we completed the analysis on the contents so it would be ready for personal use the next day. He once told me his reason for keeping it in here was twofold; One, it kept Alexandria from stealing his food, which he had caught her doing more than once. Two, it was comic relief in an otherwise dull environment. He said there wasn't anything as funny as someone being in the lab when he pops the seal and drinks his juice. "The faces they make are hilarious! You have to be in here the next time I freak someone out, Lyssandra." Ugh. I would rather not. With my luck it would be my supervisor, a higher-than-me ranking affiliate of CMS or CDC, or somebody else much higher up the food chain at Biotech Chemlabs.

"Well it's a good thing you do all of the urinalysis and I stick with the hematology. Ha! D'you get what I just did there? Stick. Hemato—. No? Seriously." He huffed out a sigh, "I'm far less likely to drink the urine if I never touch it. Besides, if anyone were going to notice, or say anything, don't you think they would have by now?" he asked as he shuffled through the work orders on his desk. "I find it more likely you will grab my apple juice in attempts to find a hyaline cast or epithelial cells than I grab the wrong container." It did seem more plausible I would grab the wrong one before he did, but then again, it wouldn't hurt anything if I did grab his juice by accident. He, on the other hand, would be drinking piss. Another shudder rippled through me at the thought.

We quieted our banter, busying ourselves with today's work. I got lost in the repetition of pull slide, add blood, cover, observe, annotate, while allowing my mind to wander as I moved by rote. I could hear Miguel in the background humming a semi familiar tune as he trudged away at his own tasks. For most people science is either very boring or very exciting. I normally find it rather exciting, but today, it was just work. Before I realized how much time had passed, the centrifuge stopped spinning and the timer for the autoclave machine went off, marking the point when Miguel broke into the most upbeat part of one of his songs turning it from a simple hum to a belted verse of who knows what. He had this thing for making up words to

13

songs to see if anyone would notice. I suspect he did it because he didn't know the words, although sometimes it was entertaining.

We packed up our work, locked the lab, and headed out to the break room for lunch. Alexandria was already there rummaging through the food, tossing containers without thought or care as to who it belonged to or what it was. Miguel spied her and shot her a withering look.

"I'm just going to call it a day," I said, stepping back into the hallway, shaking my head at the cousins. Those two behaved like brother and sister more often than cousins and I had no interest in hanging around to get drug into the middle of one of their arguments.

"Wait. Why are you going home early?" Alex asked as she opened a container, sniffed it, and tossed it back in the door of the fridge.

"Meh. I got as much done as I could. There's only so much you can do once you run out of specimens to examine." And there really was. Before the lab opened this morning, I had already calibrated all the machines, restocked the supplies needed for all specimen procurements, disinfected all of the counters and equipment, ran all reusable items through the autoclave, prepped valid specimens for further testing in the lab one floor above us, and generally made the lab ready for Monday morning when we clocked back in after a quick clean once we were done with today's work. The rest was pretty much up to Miguel to clean whenever he finished up for the weekend.

"Oh, well shit, I'm coming with you," she announced as she slammed the door shut. "I'm finished with my stuff, too. I was eating the clock up in here until I decided what to do, but you made up my mind for me. You can drop me off at my house since it's on the way to yours. We can get all dolled up and go out tonight. There's a new club Mila was telling me about the last time we caught lunch, I think I want to see what's up with it. Mr. Can't-Remember-Shit over there can finally take Tia out and maybe get himself out of trouble with her for 'forgetting' about dinner with her parents last week."

"For the record," Miguel stated, "I really did forget about dinner plans with her family. When Abuela calls, you don't ignore her. You of all people know that, Alex. Other than the little issue with Tia being pissed and having to make up for it, going out does sound good. I'll just skip lunch," he commented as he strutted out of the room trying, and failing, to keep us from seeing how perturbed he was with Alex again. "I'll call her now to let her know we'll all meet up at nine tonight!" he yelled back down the hall.

Alex and I made our way to the locker room to get out of our scrubs and lab coats. There's nothing like taking all manner of bodily fluids home when the work day is over. Yuck. We were changed and in my car before another word was spoken.

"So, I guess nine it is," I told her as I started my beat up '83 Thunderbird.

My car was old but loved. I bought it when I was 16 with my own hard-earned money. I saw it sitting in a yard on my way home from school. The other kids on the bus were hyped up from a pep rally for the football game that night against one of our oldest rivals. It took me about three hours to talk my dad into taking me over to talk to the owner. When we got there, the guy took one look at me and laughed. Actually, laughed right in my face. He said there was no way I could afford his car. The typical selling price for it alone was more than what I could afford, not to mention all the additions that he'd made to it. Dad finally talked him into humoring me and at least pretending to take me seriously. When he finally did, we settled at six thousand dollars, and that was knocking off a grand and a half for 'shits and giggles since he was pretending anyway.'

If anyone who knows me can't say one thing nice about me, they at least can't deny I work hard and exceed at whatever job I do. I had already saved up almost five thousand dollars by the time we talked to the guy about the car. I worked at the library Monday through Thursday after school, at the grocery store two miles from home on the weekends, babysat a set of twins after I got off work from the grocery store on most weekends, and when they didn't need me at the library, I worked for Mrs. Lansworth across the street doing whatever odd jobs she needed done since her husband passed away. She paid as much for my help as my regular job at the library, which paid every two weeks. I busted my ass everywhere I could the next couple of months to scrounge the rest of the money to buy the car. We showed up at the guy's house on a Saturday afternoon and I drove away with a smile on my face, happy to know I would never have to ride the bus again.

It has the original silver paint job, which is more than overdue to be redone. Black vinyl or leather (I don't remember which, but it's the shit that sticks to your bare legs when it's scorching ass hot and feels like your skin will be branded for all eternity) seats with black dash and door paneling that keeps the heat trapped. The windows are hand cranks; no power windows for this girl. It even has an ashtray and working lighter. I know, Jurassic! But it's mine and I love the old dinosaur.

"Yeah, he didn't even bother to ask if we wanted to grab food first," Alex whined.

"He's probably going to take Tia out to dinner alone if he is still in the doghouse."

"Well, he still could have asked. I mean, it's the polite thing to do."

"Since when have you ever known Miguel to be polite? And since when is it polite to add yourself to a date?" I retorted with a snort.

"You have a point, but you know they aren't really a thing. They just pretend to be. Speaking of dates, are you going to be bringing anyone with tonight?" she asked with a sly grin.

"Uh. No." I kept my eyes on the road because if I gave her any more attention on the matter she would have me on a blind date with who knows.

"Well, I'm bringing Cason. I don't want random paws all over me while I shake what my momma gave me."

"And on that note," I said flatly as I pulled up to her driveway, "here you are. Are you going to be meeting him somewhere or will he come by and pick you up? You realize you left your car at work just to ride home with me."

"Yep. I'll have him pick me up about seven. You want to grab something to eat with us before we go to the club? See, that's how that works. I invited you. Even with a date planned."

"Nah, I'll eat at home. Mila probably has some massive dishes made up since she's been on vacation for the last week, but thanks anyway. And just to clarify, if the other party doesn't know about it, it's not a date yet. Besides, you and Cason don't date, you two go out and have fun together to keep unwanted people away." She stuck her tongue out at me and got out of the car. She headed towards her house as I drove off half dreading the night out.

I pulled in next to Mila's electric blue Charger and saw the living room window almost half open, meaning I was right— Mila had cooked so much the house needed ventilating to release heat. She's a stress cooker and she was probably stressing about her vacation being over.

As I made my way through the door, I was assaulted by so many smells wafting out from the kitchen. She had made food from all over the world again. Her favorite things to make were traditional dishes from Bulgaria, but she had a talent for cooking, so there were no limits on what she could prepare. Since we'd been roomies for almost six years I could decipher most of the scents. She had made everything from the savory, mouthwatering gyuvetch of her home country (which would be Bulgaria, if you didn't catch the hint) to Peru's sweet picarones, and everything in between.

"I'm home, Mila," I called as I dropped my lanyard and keys in the bowl on the table by the front door. Making my way towards the source of the amazing scents filling the house, "Alex has plans for us tonight. You interested in hitting up the club you told her about?"

I rounded the corner to find mixing bowls, pans, plates, cookie cutters, flour and other cooking supplies scattered all over the kitchen. Mila cleaned as she cooked. The mess made little sense, sending my hackles up. I searched for the energy that was all Mila. Finding a slight trace slipping away quickly, I followed the sig into the utility room. I flipped the light switch and pulled up short when I found the door hanging askew and half off the hinges.

2

I pulled my phone out of my back pocket and dialed Miguel. He answered on the fourth ring as I bounced in place with impatience. "Hey. You better not be trying to find a way out of going tonight. It's only been about thirty minutes since we made the plans, you fuddy dud."

"Huh? What? No. I need you to get to my house now. The kitchen is a wreck, Mila is gone and my back door is off the hinges. I need your nagual abilities. Or you. Whatever. Just get your ass over here," the words rushed from me as I tried to wrap my mind around what I was looking at. He grunted before my phone beeped to let me know the call disconnected.

I took a deep breath to calm myself, refocusing on the energies still lingering. I could feel a faint trace of her energy. It eased over my skin like electrified goosebumps only less intense than usual. I was accustomed to many different sensations supernaturals left on my skin, and sometimes the other strange reactions my body had involuntarily. Part of being a Reflector was the ability to sense others, no matter what they were. The catch was if you were looking for someone who was no longer around, their sig (which is what I call the energy signature) could be gone completely or dissipating, and Mila's was almost gone. There were three other sigs I had never come across before. I could barely feel them but could tell at least one of them was a vampire.

Now, I know it sounds confusing, but it's not. Let me explain a little further. Every being has a look, smell, distinct voice, right? Right. Well that isn't all. We each have our own energy and signature to go with it. The former is especially true for supernaturals. Our energies are stronger, more developed, I guess. Anyway, a reflector can read the energy signals given off. We feel them on our skin like goosebumps, a little jolt of electricity running along our bodies, ants crawling, name a physical sensation and I could probably tell you which supernatural is around you. Yes, I said around you. We're everywhere. We hide among you and you don't even know it. Does that mean every feeling you get is one of us? Of course not, don't be silly. Your body still responds naturally to your environment such as with temperature changes, pressure changes in the atmosphere, static electricity, wind and rain, the like.

Well, now we have a general description of my magic covered a bit, let's get back to the sigs. As I said, different signatures for different types, right? Yes, but also as individuals. Miguel, for example, is a shifter. He is also a Shaman. That last tiny detail alone will make him feel different from other shifters. He has more magic within his energy than most other shifters, but then again, all naguals (the Spanish word for a Mexican Shaman Shapeshifter) do. Alexandria and Tia on the other hand are just your everyday, run of the mill shifters. Yet, they have their own different sigs because, well, they are different people. Is your skin the exact same shade as your mother, father, brother, sister, cousin, or neighbor? Do you all smell the exact same? Have the same freckle in the same spot? Same principle. We're all different in our sigs, even if we are of the same species. And I feel enough of the sig, I can tell you he or she is a vampire. The feeling is almost like the tingly numb sensation you would get if your foot fell asleep.

I almost jumped out of my skin when the front door slammed against the wall in the foyer, making the pictures on the walls rattle. Miguel rushed into the kitchen, nostrils flaring. His Timberlands crunched glass I hadn't noticed on his way through. He sniffed a few select spots by the sink, stove, and refrigerator then inhaled deeply by the back door. "There were four here," he says as he inspects the door and frame.

"Can you tell who or what they are? Do you recognize any of them?"

"No. Yes. No," he replies dryly.

"And?"

"And what? What do you want me to do, Lyssi? I don't know who they are. Two were vampire and two were shifters, but I don't know them."

"Well any information is a start. I'm pretty sure I sensed a vampire, so thanks for confirming that. Why did they come for Mila? Do you think she might have got away?"

"I doubt it. Vampires and shifters are both fast. She's neither. Let me sniff around outside. They may have been waiting and watching for a while. If they did, their scents will be stronger and I may find a scrap of something and be able to locate them, or at least be able to identify them later."

"That sounds better than just sitting here. I'll call Tia. She can help with cleaning the kitchen, I'll have her bring Alex. They need to know what's going on and another fresh set of eyes and noses won't hurt anything." He studied my face for a minute, looking for any indication I was hurt or scared, I guessed, then went outside.

Tia answered quicker than Miguel had, saying she would be over as soon as she picked up Alex. I pulled a rag out of the drawer and started wiping the flour and spices off the cabinets. The counters looked like baking supplies had been flung by a T-rex at batting practice. I was moving methodically trying to piece together what could have possibly happened when Tia and Alex walked in.

"Oh daaayyyyyuuuum," Alex crooned, "You walked in on this? No one was here when you got home?"

"Yeah. I don't get it. Why would anyone come after Mila? It's not just a random B&E because they took her. Took. Her. Alex." I said, exasperated.

"Alright, Lyssi," Tia started, her light brown eyes shimmering with unshed tears as she looked over the room, "what do we know so far?"

"Not much, actually." I stopped for a minute to really take in the girls standing in front of me. Alex is taller than both of us at 5'6 and Tia is only an inch or so taller than my own 5'0. Where Alex has dark brown hair and eyes, Tia has light brown eyes and dirty blonde hair. We're all similarly built with lithe frames but couldn't be more different in almost every other aspect. I tried to fit Mila into the group of girls here, but physically she just didn't fit. Mila's hair is so blonde it looks silver, her eyes are a teal blue that looks like the popular image of the perfect ocean getaway. She isn't plump, but definitely full figured, and tall. She has the body most men drool over, acting foolishly to get her attention. She's also the mother figure of the group. Well, not really, but in personality. She's the mother hen that who made sure we all took care of ourselves and fussed over us if we didn't think before we acted. We were all close in age with Mila being 28, Tia and I are 27, and Alex, the baby, is 26.

Looking at my girls in front of me, I could see if someone had started trafficking women why Mila would have been picked. She is not a shifter like them, where someone would have a hell of a time not getting chomped or scratched to death attempting to capture them. She's not a reflector like me. She couldn't turn someone's own abilities against them. She's a... Well, we don't know what she is exactly. She has always kept it to herself and we've respected her privacy. I know it seems crazy, a reflector unable to tell you what someone is, but honestly. I don't go around testing everyone's powers just to see what's what and who's who. That would be just plain rude, not to mention exhausting. We can't pick up all their abilities and we can't pick and choose which we get when we do it the first time. For example, if I were to tap into Alex or Tia, I would get their strength and speed, as well as partially shift into their respective animal. If I were to tap into a vampire's I would get their blending, healing, and speed attributes. I wouldn't need to drink blood or stay out of the sun, but I would have to consciously absorb their energy to receive any of those abilities. Otherwise, I'm just a plain Jane human. Mila lives her life much like the rest of us. She gets up, goes to work, maybe goes out to lunch with a friend, comes home from work, doesn't draw attention to herself from the normies.

Alex snapped her fingers in front of my face, "Yoo-hoo, rock three to Lyssandra. Repeat, rock three to Lyssandra Trottingwolf."

I blinked several times to pull myself back to the here and now. "What?" I asked, trying to remember where we had been before my mind started running away.

"What do we know? About what happened here. What did you find and what did Miguel say when he got here?" Tia asked a little more impatiently.

"Oh, sorry, right," I stammered, the thoughts still bopping around in my head. "Not much. I came home from work and nothing seemed amiss. I came in, the house smelled amazing because of all the cooking she's been doing." I glanced around the kitchen seeing much of her prepared foods still left out, now ruined, from what the hell ever happened in here. "The kitchen was destroyed. The chairs were tipped over, flour all over the place like someone threw a bag of it as a last-ditch effort to evade or something. The back door was half hanging on the hinges and I couldn't feel much. I could feel a faint trace of her in here which lead me to the back door. I could also barely feel another energy that I guessed was vampire, and a few more I couldn't decipher because they were too faded already. I called Miguel and when he got here he did some sniffing around, confirming my thoughts on the vampire, saying there were three more with it. He said two vampires and two shifters came in, and they may have been lying in wait so he went

27

outside to have a look around. I was trying to figure out why Mila. Has she ever told either of you what she is?"

They gave each other a quick glance and shook their heads. "Not me," Tia replied. "Me, either," said Alex looking just as lost as I probably did.

"Okay, see if you can find anything Miguel or I may have missed. I'm gonna get the mess cleaned up then go find Miguel."

I threw all the food in the trash with a heavy heart. Mila would be furious to see all this food go to waste, but there was nothing I could do about it. I didn't know if anything else had been strewn across it all and I really didn't want to take the chance of something a bit more dangerous than unbleached flour and spices being consumed. I moved on to sweeping the floors, thinking about all the possibilities but nothing was coming to mind. I was just going to have to see what Miguel found since calling the police was out of the question. We supernaturals pretty much police ourselves, living by the unspoken rule to not expose the community to the normal humans. Even our children learn it at an early age and are home schooled or go to a private school if their parents can afford it. I don't mean a school for supernatural kids, like the X-Men and their school for mutant children, but a school ran by other supernaturals. They learn the same things that human children do, but if their powers get away from them, which can happen often, there's no need to explain what happened to the normies.

REFLECTED

By the time I finished cleaning, Tia, Alex, and Miguel were talking quietly in the living room. I rounded the corner and the talking stopped abruptly. "Give me what you've got so far, guys," I said, ignoring the pitiful looks I was getting. I flopped down on the couch, slinging my feet up on the table in front of me.

Miguel sat down beside my feet, taking care not to make it wobble any more than the rickety thing already did. "Look," he started quietly, "I don't want to scare you any more than you already are, but there's no easy way to—"

"Spit it out already," I snapped.

"Alright. We don't think you're safe here. We think you should stay with one of us," he gestured to the three of them, twirling his hand around in a circle. "Just until this all blows over and we find Mila."

"What makes you think I need to find somewhere else to go? What are you not telling me?"

Without saying a word Miguel pulled a bloody shirt from behind him.

3

Where did you get this?" I asked as I
examined the shirt. It was not Mila's. I
had no idea who it belonged to, but I could almost
guarantee Mila had not been wearing some man's
shirt. First of all, she didn't even have a boyfriend.
She dated from time to time, but she didn't settle.
Second, she's pretty. Okay, that came out wrong.
She likes to dress femininely with frills, lace,
ribbons, or cutesy-tootsie as my brother put it
when I went through that phase as a teenager.
She puts makeup on to go to the grocery store for
crying out loud.

"In the woods about a quarter of a mile
northwest of the house," he said softly.

"Alright. Whose shirt is it?"

"I don't know, but it's her blood."

"What?" I shrieked, standing up so suddenly that I bumped into him, making the table crash to the floor.

He grunted as he hit the floor with the debris. "This is why we feel you need to stay with one of us. We don't know why they took her. We don't know what happened to her, but she's hurt, Lyssi, or worse. Until we find out who did this, who broke into your home, you need to come home with one of us," he said, glaring at me from atop the mess I had caused.

"Shit. Sorry, Miguel," I held my hand out to help him out of the mess. "Okay. Slow down. The blood is Mila's but who does the shirt belong to? Does it belong to one of the assholes who destroyed the kitchen?"

"Yeah, we sort of do know. It was one of the assholes that destroyed the kitchen. No, I still don't know who they are, but we'll find out. I have their scents. The fucked-up part about it is that I have smelled this person before, but I can't remember where." I could tell he was perturbed with me by the tone in his voice.

"So, plans for tonight are still on. And we make plans to go to various places from here on out to track down who ever this is," Alex chimed in after a several tense seconds.

"Wait, wait, wait just a damn minute," sighed Tia. "We go on with life as usual until we accidentally bump into someone somewhere?

That is assuming the he-she-it-shit is from around here?"

"Have you got a better idea?" Alex popped back without hesitation.

"No," Tia deflated quickly, "come on, Lyssi. I'll help you pack and we'll figure out what to do with you either while we work or not long after."

"Oh, thanks. Like the puppy you can't take with you on vacation because Auntie What-the-fuck-ever is allergic to dogs," I groused, stomping my way up the stairs to the second floor where my bedroom is.

"That is so not what I meant and you damn well know it," she spun on her heels, rounding on me so fast I almost fell backwards over the banister that opened the second floor up to the first.

"Alright, alright. Put your finger down, missy," I said pushing her finger out of my face, "things are insane at the moment and everyone's on edge. I don't like the idea of not staying in my own house. I don't like the idea of going out to clubs. I don't like not being very active in looking for Mila when she's probably hurt and needs us."

"I know. Me too, but we have to start somewhere. And they're right, the best place to start is where you find the biggest group of supernaturals," she pushed my door open, stepping aside for me to enter my room.

I pulled my travel case out from under the bed and started sifting through my dresser. "Pick out a couple of things from the closet that I could go out in and grab me some work clothes while you're in there. I'm gonna get my shower stuff from the bathroom and be right back," I told her while I padded off into the bathroom that attached Mila's bedroom to mine.

4

The five of us stood together waiting to enter Effusion, the new club that opened not long ago. I think Alex had said it had only been open about a month or so. We could hear the music thumping inside and feel the pulse of it through our shoes. The wait wasn't long, not like if we had been waiting in line I'm sure, but Alex couldn't remember where she put her ID. She dug around in her clutch for a few minutes then stopped to pop herself in the forehead. "Duh," she said to herself as she reached into her top and pulled it out of what I could only hope was her bra. Yuck. Boob sweat.

We stepped up to the large black double doors and presented our identifications to the massive man standing guard in a black tee, which looked four times too small, and tight, black denim jeans. The overall look was typical for a bouncer if you ask me, which you didn't. . . so moving right along.

We squeezed our way through the narrow hall that seemed to last forever. It might have seemed so because there was every flavor of supernatural lingering in said hallway doing who knows what. Waves of energy rushed over me causing my skin to feel as if I were on fire one second, then chilled the next. I would certainly be limiting my alcohol consumption because I did not want to lose the ability sobriety gives me to block most of this out. The dark gray walls looked like marble with gold filament running through them and was lined with dimly lit wall sconces giving the hallway an added closed in feel.

Finally pushing ourselves out of the hallway and into the main room, which had an entirely different feel to it. Oh, don't get me wrong, I still had the heebie-jeebies from all the individuals, but this area opened up immensely.

Stepping out onto the landing we could see over the entire first floor. People were mingling everywhere but the dance floor. There, bodies were wrapped around each other, moving with the flow of the music. The bar started on the right wall and wrapped around midway along the wall directly in front of the entryway. Bartenders and mixologists were already moving quickly to attend or entertain the customers lined up along the lengthy bar.

REFLECTED

Waiters and waitresses of every shape and size were carrying trays between the tables scattered on the opposite side of the room. Booths lined the wall to our left and were divided by lattice partitions to give the illusion of isolation. I counted three doorways behind the bar, two more at opposite ends of the left wall and a hallway to our right just before the bar started. The hallway to the right marked the restrooms and a recovery room. The doorway at the furthest end of the room on the left wall indicated stairs which I presumed led up to the second floor that opened directly in front of us. The walls on the first floor appear to be black with Jackson Pollock style gold paint smattered everywhere, whereas the second-floor walls were lacking the artistic splashes. There were sheer curtains of light gold hanging in what seemed to be random places on the second floor, but I'm sure they were probably both for aesthetic and privacy reasons. The same style of sconces that hung in the entry hall were placed along the walls throughout the entire club.

Looking over the crowd of partygoers, I could see they catered to every type of personality. Men and women wore business attire, some people were wearing leather from head to toe with various colored hair, jeans and tee, and others dressed like your typical image of college frat kids.

"I'm going to get a drink. Someone grab us a table," Miguel stated as he took Tia's hand, pointing at the bar in front of us.

"Grab me something, anything fruity will ya, Tia?" Alex chimed as she made her way down the stairs, bouncing to the rhythm and catching up with Cason since he had already made his way down the steps.

Tia nodded to her and cocked an eyebrow at me, "You want anything?"

"No thanks, I'm good for a few. I'll find us a table."

I glanced over my group, then back over the crowd to see where we would blend in best. It looked like people were sticking to their own species. There were a few people lingering with others, but it seemed to be just a wandering individual here and there. We looked like your average club goers on a typical Friday night. Tia had on a short black skirt, light blue top that was lacey around the middle, black and blue chevron pumps. Her short spiky hair was streaked with pink highlights. Alex was wearing a mid-thigh neon pink dress, cut low in the back with matching heels. Her dark hair had been twisted up in a chiffon bun that would make my arms feel like falling off if I even attempted it. I had opted for comfort. Their makeup and hair were done supermodel friendly, whereas mine was just mascara, lip gloss, and a brush quickly run through the medium length of my straight black locks. My jeans looked like they were painted on, but were flexible and comfy. My top was a simple black crisscross sequin cami that was both pretty and comfortable. My tight, black knee-high boots were light and flat enough so if I needed to run, my feet wouldn't hate me later or get me killed. Why did I think about running when dressing up for a night out with friends? Well, we were trying to find my roommate. Who was kidnapped. And hurt enough to bleed all over someone else's clothing, making them opt for ditching them. Planning for the worst seemed to be a good idea. Miguel and Cason were both in butt hugging jeans making the female eye, and very likely a few male eyes, travel down south for the winter. Cason was wearing a plain white V-neck shirt, which went surprisingly well with his light skin and blonde hair. Miguel had on a hunter green colored polo, making him hard to see in certain places in the shadows.

I headed towards the tables behind the dance floor, which seemed to be where all of the groups started to meet together. If we could get a table close to the wall we would have the advantage of blending in with the frat looking crowd, but not appear to be eavesdropping on everyone else. As I made my way around the dance floor my skin started to feel slimy. No, no. No one had spilled anything on me yet, although the night was young. I could feel another reflector, which always makes my skin feel like sludge is dripping off of me. It's more disconcerting than any other supernatural energy because it reflects my own energies back to me. I quickly found a table near the back, leaving only one table behind us. I took a seat facing the crowd of people writhing on the dance floor, thankful I had found us a place far enough from the sweat, perfume, and pheromones that go with the territory of having bodies smashed together.

Tia and Miguel found me about fifteen minutes later watching the faces passing by. They set three glasses down on the table. Tia slid the tallest one over to me. I took it, arching an eyebrow and taking a whiff its contents. "It's just a Sprite," she assured me. Raising her voice to be heard over the music, she said, "You don't seem to want to drink any alcohol so I thought you were just being too polite to ask for something else. If you don't want it, I'll drink it in a bit when I finish my Sugar Daddy."

"No, it's fine, thanks. Where are Cason and Alex's drinks? Your what?" I asked through a laugh.

"My Sugar Daddy. And eh, they can grab their own," she said proudly holding up her glass of dark liquid.

"Rude ass," I said with a grin. "What the hell is a Sugar Daddy?"

"It's this drink," she held it up again as if I didn't see it the first time. "I think the bartender was flirting with me and trying to annoy Miguel, though."

"Really? What makes you think that?" I asked sarcastically. "The fact that you don't even know what you're drinking tells me he asked if you wanted a sugar daddy and you obliged." She shot Miguel a guilty smile that he just grinned and shook off. "You're okay with her telling some other guy she wants a sugar daddy?" I asked.

"We're not that serious, besides, I knew what she was getting into. I wanted to see how she reacted when he set the drink in front of her. It was quite funny really," he shrugged as he turned around to look over the crowd. "Where did Alex go?"

I pointed to the dance floor where I could see Cason's head bouncing with the crowd around him. "I think she's on the dance floor with Cason. She followed him down the stairs when I came to grab the table." He nodded, turning back around to survey the throng of people.

We sat in relative silence for a little while before Tia piped up, "Miguel, I want to dance. Do we have to sit here all night?" He looked at me and I nodded. He took her hand, pulling her up and to the dance floor.

Around four songs later Cason and Alex came stumbling and laughing over to our table, sitting down as a waitress walked up asking if anyone needed anything. She took their orders and left as quickly as she had shown up.

"This place is crazy," squealed Alex.

"Not bad, not bad at all," Cason agreed. "Coverton could always use new places to have fun. This place isn't exactly as busy as New York or Los Angeles."

"With good reason. We can't talk openly about being supernaturals in places high with tourism," Alex responded.

"I get that. I'm not saying we need to have a population of some crazy number like 4.6 million. All I'm saying is this town needs to have more than rock shops and zip lines. That's all."

"We have more than rock shops and zip lines, Case," Alex said, standing, "I want to go explore. I'm going upstairs. This place might have an outside balcony. Fresh air would be nice."

I waved them off and took a deep drink of my Sprite.

"I knew I sensed another slimy reflector," came a familiar voice from behind my head, leaning in close enough his breath moved my hair.

A giant smile spread across my face as I jumped out of my seat. I spun around and threw myself into his arms, squealing like an idiot. "Where the fuck have you been, Jaykob?"

"Around. Tell me you're okay," he said as he squeezed me back, pulling me in close enough to get a good whiff of his earthy cologne. "Miguel called me to let me know my sister's house was broken into and her roomie was kidnapped."

"Shook up. Worried. Frustrated. Scared for her. You know, clinically how I am supposed to feel."

"Well, all of that will all change soon enough. We'll find her, bring her home, and make whoever took her wish they hadn't even known her name," he said kissing the top of my head. "Let me look at you, I've been at the reservation for so long."

"I know. How's Dad?"

"He's great. He's still doing his thang. He's got a few more months before his spirit journey, so he's staying pretty busy working with the elders."

"He still isn't done with all of that? You'd think they would have some other young pup running around like a crazy person for them by now."

"Come on now. He's not that old yet. He still has many, many years left in him before he becomes an elder. And you know Mom keeps him on his toes. Anyway, enough reservation business, we don't live there anymore. Tell me everything, what happened?"

"Alright, let's find somewhere private to talk," I suggested. We found Tia and Miguel, letting them know we were leaving the table unattended. They left the dance floor while Jaykob and I went back to his car. I filled him in on everything we knew so far. He listened silently, nodding occasionally. The one thing I have always adored about my big brother was how good of a listener he could be. He never commented on how crazy I must be if it were something important to me.

"Oh damn, you've had quite a day. I'm really glad you're okay. Have you recognized any sigs since you've been here?"

I shook my head, "No. I don't know if I would in such a busy place with such a faint feel of it. If I had been home sooner I could have helped—"

"Stop right there. First of all, you weren't so there's no need to beat yourself up for something you can't help. You have to have a job. Food doesn't buy itself and we can't hunt our own food in hard times like a shifter can. Second, you could've been hurt, kidnapped, or killed if you had been home. You. Are. Safe. And finally, she has a chance to be found because of it. Don't berate yourself because you were not home when you normally wouldn't be anyway."

I hung my head to gather my thoughts, knowing he was right. "What do we do from here?" I asked trying not to sound as defeated as I felt.

"We start by identifying who came in your house. You have the sigs. Miguel, Tia, and Alex have the smell. This isn't the best place to start, but it is a start. They can filter smells better than we can, so let them sniff around, pun fully intended," he smiled at his own dumb joke. "Let me help you. Focus on the strongest sig you found. Let your head clear, feel how it flowed over your skin when you walked in."

I closed my eyes because this was Jake's thing. He had a body too many women fell over themselves for and a voice that could soothe the soul. He was just instant ease.

I knew the minute he started reflecting consciously. The vampire's energies intensified, the tingly numb feeling flashed across my skin. Though I couldn't name him or her yet, I would know when I found them. I stopped focusing on the vampire, turning my attention to one of the sigs I couldn't place. I may not be the best at using my magic, but I did it without missing a beat. A sensation of goosebumps slipped over my arms, warming my skin slightly at first, then growing hotter. It reminded me of slipping my arms underneath sun-kissed sand after spending all day in the air conditioner. It was a strange sensation to have goose pimples on warm skin. I stopped when Jake inhaled sharply, eyes snapping open.

"I know that sig," he explained quickly, "we have to find Miguel. Now!"

5

We rushed back inside to our table to find both couples there talking. Jake immediately called Miguel to the hallway in the back of the room. They were gone for five or ten minutes, long enough for me to fill the other three in on what just happened.

"I'm glad I didn't null your magic when we got here then. I mean, I know you're supposed to be trying to find those sigs, but I imagine it would be overwhelming trying to decipher one from the hundreds in here," Cason said sheepishly.

"Seriously?" Alex exclaimed, "you were seriously thinking about nullifying her magic?"

"I just thought about it, obviously I didn't. I don't want to be counterproductive. I was only thinking about what she's already been through today. If I could help ease her mind in any way, I would like to do something. It's not like I can do much in the way of anything else."

"Cason, I really appreciate the thought. I appreciate even more that you didn't null my magic without talking to me first," I told him honestly. "You're capable of more than you give yourself credit for. Look at me giving you the pep talk instead of the other way around. See, you've already eased my mind." I winked to boost the effect of the compliment.

Cason is what we call a Bland. He can null the magic of other magic users. He can't stop a vampire from blending or a shifter from shifting. He can't turn off heightened senses or anything that is part of their original self. Confused yet? Okay, it's like this; a shifter has two bodies. They have their human body with which they do everyday people stuff, like hold jobs or take care of their homes. They also have an animal body. There is no way (that I know of) to remove the animal from them. It would be like trying to physically pull the voice out of your head that won't shut up when you are about to do something dumb. The same goes for vampires. They have a second form we call blending because they can blend into shadowed areas. It's one of the main reasons you would almost never see them coming. Their bodies go into this misty, foggy looking phase. Sort of. Well, more like they turn themselves semi-translucent. From a scientific standpoint, they are the chameleons of our world. Their pigmentation, or lack thereof, can be consciously manipulated to a shade so thin and sheer they appear to have metamorphosed to mist or fog. Blands can't stop vampires from blending any more than they can stop you from wiggling your toes. My magic, however, can be manipulated towards another body, be it living or otherwise. Those are the kinds of magics a bland can null. They too can turn on and off their ability to make someone else what we call a dud. When they do, we know what we're supposed to do, but we can't.

"Time to fill everyone in with everything, Jake," I said when he and Miguel returned. "Who did the other sig belong to? I assume it had to be another shifter since you needed to find Miguel so fast?" Or at least it seemed logical to me. If it were a shifter, then Miguel would possibly know who we were dealing with, or at least had the means to find out rather quickly.

"No, actually. She's not a shifter. She's an elemental. She's dating or mated to a shifter, I'm not sure which, but it would explain why Miguel smelled another shifter. Her name is Selby McIntosh and she's an earth elemental," Jake explained.

"How do you know her?" Tia asked.

"We used to work together at the hospital until she got an offer to work at Biotech in the research department."

"In the research department?" Miguel and I asked simultaneously.

"When did that happen?" Miguel asked.

"We work in the research department, we would have seen or at least heard of her," I stated indignantly.

"She's been gone from the hospital for about six months now," Jake responded to both of us.

"Are you sure it's the research department she went to? I know they are always going through new recruits in the testing areas. People get transferred pretty quickly out of the research area because of how dangerous it's supposed to be." Alex offered.

Jake looked between the three of us and shrugged, "That's what she said. I can't tell you where she went after she left. I haven't seen her since, but I know her sig from having to work beside her for two and a half years."

"It's a starting point. Do you know who she's with?" Tia asked, "Surely in two and a half years you would have seen her partner, or at least heard her talking about him?"

"No," Jake shook his head, "not a clue. She did her job and went home. She didn't make any girlfriends to go grab a drink with or anything. She was a bit of a recluse, only interacting when needed."

"Well that may or may not be helpful," Cason chimed in sarcastically.

"True dat," Alex piped up.

Miguel hadn't said anything else but the look on his face meant the wheels in his head were turning. I looked around the club, trying to decide if we needed to stick around any longer. We hadn't gotten any leads from here unless you counted what my brother had pitched in, but we could have done a reflection anywhere. Before I could voice the question, a table flew by, crashing into the wall behind us. We all ducked down, turning to see where the commotion was coming from.

Bouncers rushed towards a group of four or five people who were throwing punches. A small woman with black spiky hair had grabbed a big, burly, and rather hairy guy by his throat, slammed him onto his back and was sitting astride his chest pounding his face in. Two more guys tried to pull her off the guy on the floor but got hit in the faces with her elbows every time she pulled back to take another swing. I couldn't tell if she was hitting them on purpose or if they were just having shit luck at grabbing hold of the wily little female. A woman stood off to the side looking like she wanted to run but was either unsure of where to go or too scared to move. I was trying to determine if she was with the brawlers or just happened to be walking past when the fight broke out.

Tia and Cason must have noticed her about the same time I did because they rushed over to pull her out of the way of the fight. She dug her heels in at first, refusing their help but relented quickly when she saw the bouncers lifting the woman off of the poor guy. All four of the participants found themselves being thrown out of the place rather unceremoniously and we turned our attention to the skittish looking woman.

"Hey, that was pretty nuts, huh?" Alex announced, attempting to direct the woman's attention away from the front door.

"What? Yeah, crazy," she replied while staring at the exit, "I gotta go."

"Wait, are you okay?" Tia asked quickly.

"Yeah, I'm fine."

"What's your name?" Alex tried again to get her attention.

"Um. I really need to go. Thanks for pulling me away from the flying tables," she said, turning to leave.

Cason was standing behind her which caused her to stall for a minute. "Are you sure you're okay Miss. . .," he gestured with his hand for her to fill in the blank.

"Milena. I said I was fine. I have to go. Thanks for everything," she snipped as she shoved her way around him. She made her way up the stairs, disappearing through the doorway.

"Her energy sig was familiar. Not familiar as in I know it, but I probably should," I said trying to place where I may have known her from. The problem was I worked with people every day coming in and out of the lab getting tests run for one reason or another. I could have taken blood and urine samples from her or someone in her family at some point. It seemed we were all having memory problems, first Miguel with the scents in the house, then myself with the odd woman.

"Well that wasn't weird at all," Tia noted.

"Not one bit," Alex agreed.

"She was probably afraid someone with her group was going to leave her. I wouldn't appreciate being ditched either. So. Now what do we want to do?" I asked.

"I vote for staying and enjoying the rest of our time here. If we happen to find something, great. If not, no big deal, Jake has already given us something to start with. It's too late to do much now," Miguel suggested as he glanced at his watch.

"That works for me," Jaykob said, kissing the top of my head again before walking off to where a lady with rich mocha skin was waving at him from across the room.

I rolled my eyes at him when he got about halfway to her and decided to start walking with swagger. "Well I feel like a bit like a third," I glanced around at the other four, correcting myself, "fifth wheel. I think I'm going to mingle for a while before heading home." I walked off before anyone could argue about me heading back to my house.

I found myself standing by the bar watching the latest show the mixologist was putting on. He had a tower of shot glasses filled with every color of drink imaginable stacked precariously in the center of the bar. The song blasting from the speakers had him moving to a rather seductive beat while he poured a clear liquid into the top glass.

The glass overflowed, trickling alcohol down to the tiers below. Before the flow reached the bottom row of glasses he struck a Zippo and lit the tower up making everyone around me ooh, ah, and cheer. He did a few fancier bottle tosses as the flames died out and when the fire was completely gone he began handing out the drinks that were previously aflame.

A gentle tap on the shoulder made me pause as I turned around to go explore another area of the club. I swiveled my head to see if it was deliberate or just one of the people in the overly excited crowd and was greeted with a bright smile and an alluring pair of the palest blue eyes, arresting my thoughts on the spot. "Hi," he said, with a husky, intoxicating voice.

"Hey," I nodded my head as I tried to turn away. How could I find a voice intoxicating after only hearing a single word?

"You're empty handed. Would you like a drink?"

"Does that line work often?" I asked sardonically.

"Oh. Um, I'm sorry? I didn't realize I was fishing," he said cocking an eyebrow up.

"Well, as they say, 'There are plenty of fish in the sea'."

"Yeah, that's what they say all right, but it seems most of them don't even make it to the dock. Are you in a hurry to get out of here or just looking for a breath of fresh air? I could use some friendly banter while I try to remove the perfume from my nose. I'll grab us a drink and we can take it to the balcony or step out on the patio," he smirked, tipping his blonde head in the direction of the back of the club.

"I could use some friendly banter," I finally decided after a few moments of glancing out to the dance floor and seeing the other two couples shift in and out of my line of sight while they danced carelessly. We went back to the bar where the fire show had been presented. I was impressed there were no visible signs of the pyro show only a few short moments before. I thought there might have been scorch marks, but nothing was there but polished honey oak shining brightly under the back-lights lighting up the bar.

"What can I get you two?" the bartender asked as we stepped up.

"I'll have a water," I said leaning in to be heard.

"Not drinking?" my new friend asked.

I shook my head, "Not tonight."

"Okay, then grab a virgin Bloody Mary or Sunrise. You don't have to stick with water to save my wallet."

"I wasn't thinking of your wallet, but I could use something refreshing." I told him, then turned back to the bartender. "Can I get a Peach Tea?"

"I'll have the dark draft."

The bartender quoted the price while he grabbed a glass out of the freezer and one off the shelf. We stood waiting, lost in our own musings until two full glasses landed in front of us on the bar. New Guy paid as I found the easiest path out to the back patio sipping my tea.

I stepped out into the Coverton cloudless night. The patio was inviting with warm lighting from the old-fashioned acorn shaped lanterns hanging sparsely along the posts on the fence line. Large potted plants dotted the borders of the open area giving the night a sweet floral smell. I sat on one of the wooden benches nuzzled under a trimmed weeping willow overlooking the small channel that branched off the river a few miles to the east. The soft cushions let out a small *whoosh* as I leaned back to enjoy the view. I could almost pretend I was alone out here if it weren't for the quiet chatter of other peace seekers or the loud music seeping from inside when the door opened to allow someone out or in.

"Hi again," New Guy's deep timbre floated from behind me. "Are you still alright with a little banter? You walked away rather quickly back there."

"Banter?" I looked up to into big blue eyes that seemed to give off a small glow. "Yeah, about that. On the way out here, I decided I didn't need any more friends so I decided to make you a stalker instead," I smiled.

"Ah. I'll take it as an upgrade then since I won't have to talk to you."

"Ha. That was good, but since you are still talking I guess it means you aren't quick enough to get the memo," I tapped my temple.

"I guess not, but then again the one who wrote the memo probably couldn't figure out how to send the message," he smiled when he winked.

"Well since neither one of us are smart enough, I guess that would make us good company for one another. Have a seat." I moved over to give him enough room to sit next to me without invading personal space. "I'm Lyssandra. Call me Lyssi. Who might you be? Calling you *New Guy* is all well and good in my head, but probably rather rude out loud."

"New Guy, huh? That's rather original. It's considerably nice compared to some other things I've been called. I'm Bobby. Call me Bobby," he replied with another wink as he sat down beside me.

"Oh, I bet. I've been given some pretty choice names as well. No use going into all of that though. Where you from?"

"A small town outside of Seattle, you?"

"Oklahoma. And here. We moved back and forth from time to time. My parents owned two homes. One was on the reservation in Oklahoma and the other one here was inherited when my grandparents passed."

"Wow. That must have been nice, bouncing back and forth all the time."

"Yes, it was. My brother got the house here when our dad decided the family needed to stay on the reservation, so when I turned eighteen I moved in with him while I went to college. There isn't anything on the reservation that could give me the opportunity to go to school for what I loved doing."

"And what was that?"

"Science. Medical lab technician, specifically. Have you got a career?"

"Yep. I'm a genetic engineer."

I let out a small gasp, "Seriously? Where do you work?" I realized I probably sounded like an airheaded fangirl so I toned down my excitement, "I mean, there is only one place your skills would apply in or around Coverton. Do you still live outside of Seattle? You visiting someone here?"

"No. I live here now," he chuckled, "and yes, there is only one place my skills are useful in almost a hundred-mile radius. I work at-"

"Biotech Chemlabs." I finished his sentence with him. "How long have you worked there?"

"I just got here a little over a month ago. I gave myself a couple of weeks to settle in before starting to work, so I've been there for only two weeks. Next week will be my third. Where do you work? Did you get a job as a lab tech somewhere?"

Laughing I told him, "I did. At Biotech Chemlabs." The surprise in his expression caused me to giggle. Giggle. I don't giggle. I was feeling a bit like a giddy school girl, which was starting to unnerve me a bit. I cooled my expression and tamed my giggles, "I was lucky enough to land a job right after I graduated college. I've worked at BTCL for almost three years now."

"You were pretty lucky. It took me that long to land a job after I graduated. I noticed the banter died off and turned into to a great conversation, but do you want or need to go check in with your friends?" he asked turning and glancing at the door.

I raised an eyebrow while I tried to decide how to respond. I guess he figured out how stalkerish that sounded because he quickly added, "I saw you with a couple other people when I walked in. You can see almost the entire floor from the landing and your table was right next to an interesting fight."

I nodded as I stood up, "That would probably be a good idea. Would you like to come too? Miguel and Alex work at BTCL, too. I'm sure it would be nice to meet another coworker or two."

"Sure, sounds great." We walked back inside where the music was still thumping loudly. Cason and Tia stood next to the table, Tia's arms waving wildly as she spoke with her typical vigor. Cason noticed us first as we weaved in and out of the crowd gathered around the dance floor. He leaned down, kissing me on the cheek so he could discreetly whisper, "You good?"

Nodding I said, "Yeah. I'm fine. Where is everyone?"

Tia did a little dance because, well, it's what Tia does. "They went to get more drinks. Alex tipped all four glasses over when 'her jam came on' and she jumped up like her butt cheeks caught a lit match," she said using air quotes to repeat what Alex said when she jumped up.

"Oh, okay. They'll get intros later then. This is Bobby," I said tugging at Bobby's shirt sleeve to usher him a little closer. "Bobby, this is Tia and Cason."

Bobby held out his hand for Cason to shake and nodded to Tia, "Hey, how's it going?"

"Not bad. Enjoying the new club. We needed something else to do around here," Cason replied, taking Bobby's hand and giving a polite, quick shake.

"Yeah? Is there not much else to do here?" Bobby asked.

"No, not a lot. Smaller cities are kind of like that though. Lots of what you need, but not much in the way of what you might want," Cason noted.

"True, true," Bobby nodded in agreement.

"How long have Miguel and Alex been gone?" I looked to Tia since Cason still seemed to be in a huff about the lack of entertainment in town.

"They should be back soon. They probably had to make a pitstop so Alex could clean her shoes. You know how uptight she is about them."

"I would not want to have her shoe bill," I agreed. "Well let's all have a seat then." I pulled out my chair and sat down. Bobby came up behind me, placing his hands on the back and helped me scoot the chair back in. He pulled out his own chair and sat to my left. Cason and Tia shot each other a quick look that said, 'Did you just see that?' while I tried to pretend like my cheeks weren't as bright as a tomato.

Miguel and Alex rushed up to the table not sparing a glance at the newcomer. "Hey, where are our drinks?" Tia whined.

Alex huffed out a sigh, holding up her hand like she was going to high five Tia in the face. "They're here," she blurted out. No one said anything before everyone exploded out of their seats. Everyone except Bobby, that is. He looked around with a confused expression.

"Hold up, guys," I said, stopping all motion from my group.

"What? What's the problem?" Miguel spouted.

"Just stop for a minute. Who is here?"

"The shifter from your house," Alex blurted, while Miguel shot her a look telling her to shut the hell up.

"Which one? And who is it, have you seen him or her yet?" I asked.

"What's wrong?" Bobby asked looking from face to face.

"Who are you?" Alex shot him a look of incredulity.

"Miguel, Alex, this is Bobby. Bobby these are the two I told you about who work at BTCL. Bobby is a genetic engineer at BTCL. Bobby, I've got some stuff going on that I really don't want to drag you into," I explained.

"Are you in trouble? I might be able to help. I mean, I know I'm new here and we just met, but it doesn't mean I can't help out somehow."

"We don't really know what is going on, so again, I don't want to drag you into anything."

"Cason, I need you and Tia to come with me," Miguel interrupted, "Alex, stay with Lyssi and her new friend for a minute. We're going to see what we can find out."

Without another word the three of them went in the direction Miguel and Alex had come from. Alex and I just stared at one another for a few moments. I wasn't sure what I could say that wouldn't make me sound bonkers. Coverton is a town rife with supernaturals, but again, we hide in plain sight next to the humans. BioTech ChemLabs specializes in the super community, so keeping what species we were a secret was probably moot. Especially since he was someone that picks apart DNA. He'd most likely seen it all. My thing was, I didn't know him well enough to know exactly how personal I wanted to get with him. Did he know Selby? Were they friends? Was he here on his own terms or was this some ploy to get to me, too? Or was I just being a skittish little shit? I was almost certain Miguel had already thought about these questions and would have warned me not say anything when I told him where Bobby worked. Since he could smell the other shifters there, I was almost positive he would have been able to tell if Bobby had been with them.

"I think we need to be careful," Alex said, giving Bobby a side glance.

"I thought that was the plan all along," I responded in kind.

He stood up with us and walked around the table to stand in between the two of us. "Ladies, if you're referring to me, I can just go if you want.

Lyssi, all you have to do is say so, but I would really like to help if I can," he repeated, shoving his hands in the front pockets of his jeans.

"I'm going home after we leave here," I told Alex, "and I want everyone there. If you're serious about helping, that goes for you too, Bobby. We'll wait on them to get back and see what's what, but then we go and figure out what to do from here. We won't be able to talk freely in such a public place anyway. My house is where it all started so it seems like the best place to keep it going. Bobby, if you can wait for a little while longer to get caught up, you're more than welcome to put your two cents in. If not, then maybe we should call it a night."

"Sounds reasonable. I can handle waiting," he nodded then moved behind me and held out my chair. "Why don't we get some water, soda, or something and we can talk about whatever you ladies want until they get back."

"What a good idea," Alex responded as she waved down a tall redheaded waitress a few tables away.

6

The constant buzzing had given Mila a headache. It wasn't a loud noise, but it affected her in ways she didn't want to explore. She knew it stopped her ability to pass from one place to another, which had been the first thing she noticed when the two vampires broke in her back door. The second was it scrambled her energy, preventing her from using her magic effectively. When she tried to throw them back out of the house, her magic shoved her backwards instead, as if she had run full force into an invisible wall. When the other two people stomped into the kitchen behind the vampire holding items she both did and did not recognize, she tried to pull the floor-to-ceiling shelf down onto them. The only thing that happened was its contents flew everywhere and hardly where they were supposed to go to begin with.

She sat on the thin, smelly cot lying on the floor as she yanked the chains secured to the floor next to her. The cuffs around her wrists were rubbing her skin raw. She thought back through the entire morning trying to figure out how they were able to capture her. She was confident she knew who had come up with this plan, but never in another million lifetimes would she have imagined it to have been successful.

Thinking back on one of the most painful days in Austria, she knew she would be hard pressed to find any peace. She had grown comfortable and complacent, knowing she had no one to blame but herself.

> *The bomb rolled off the car and toward the unsuspecting people standing in attendance to see the royal heir and his wife. They had almost come to the end of their business trip and were making one last pass through the streets before going back home to deal with the tediousness of royal politicking. Little did we know; the world would forever be changed because of my sister's insatiable need for death. When Mira appeared out of the crowd while we were on our way to the hospital, I knew then she was behind the bomb that was intended for*

the royal couple earlier in the morning. There was no way she would be working alone. I wondered to myself if it were her who caused our driver to make the wrong turn. She would use whatever advantages the era of time would provide; bribery, blackmail, coercion, or simply paying someone were hardly unheard of in those days either. When the young boy shot my dearest friend and her husband, I knew then she would be after me for the rest of our long, long lives.

She looked around at her surroundings. The unadorned cinder block walls painted the standard gray one would find in any basement, right along with the single light bulb hanging from the ceiling in the center of the room, were completely unoriginal. There were no windows and only one door at the top of the steps that creaked underfoot when the brutes shoved her down the old wooden stairs. The only other thing in the room aside from her cot was a cylindrical device sitting in the corner farthest from her. It was about six inches tall and three inches wide and was the source of the constant buzzing that made her head thump to its own disparaging rhythm.

She had not seen or heard anyone in several hours so she tried to gauge how much time had passed since she was taken, but without any source of natural lighting, it was difficult to tell. The dried blood on her forehead made her head itch, which distracted her mid-thought occasionally. Not needing to eat or use the restroom was one of the benefits of her existence. She just was. She had no mother, father, or familial parentage. She was a form of spirit, god-like, she and her two sisters.

She leaned back against the wall, closed her eyes in hopes to help alleviate the thumping, at the very least give herself some semblance of relief as time passed by in an agonizing dance through her forehead. Imagining the powers moving through her body, she pictured a light baby blue glow. Holding her hand out palm up, she concentrated pushing all of the magic into a tiny ball and moving the ball from the center of her hand to her chest. Nestling her powers between her breasts and locking it all down, she hoped if she minimized what was flowing freely, the electronic thing wouldn't be as disorienting.

It took quite a bit of effort to lock it all down. She was used to dampening her powers because of what she was since it would cause more problems than not to with people like Lyssi around. Mila thought Lyssandra was an amazing roommate; she always paid her share of the bills before the due date, cleaned up after herself, gave space or was attentive when she needed to be. She was a great person all the way around, but Lyssi was a reflector, and all people aren't good people. Some take advantage of others, so to prevent her powers from catching unwanted attention, she dampened them. Keeping them cut off almost completely was another matter entirely. It took more effort and was quite taxing; even if it didn't really limit the headache, it did keep her mind busy.

Several hours later the door opened, letting in a sliver of bright light that shined over her eyelids. She kept her eyes closed as slow footsteps made each step creak loudly. The person walking had made it down the steps, standing quietly for several seconds before finally clearing her throat. Mila kept her eyes closed.

"Miss. Dragov," a small voice called.

Mila cracked her right eye open enough to peek out, then closed it again. "Don't you know who you kidnap? Or is it common for you to snatch up random strangers?"

"It wasn't a question. Do you need anything?" the small voice asked.

Mila belted out a laugh, opening her eyes to see the no nonsense expression on the face of the petite woman standing in front of her. "You're asking me if I need anything? What could I possibly long for in these amazingly beautiful accommodations that you have not already provided? Food? Use of the facilities? Water?" her Slavic accent became more pronounced with each word. "What are you really here for, darling? We both know if you were going to be hospitable I would not be in chains and you would have offered refreshments or a restroom hours ago."

"You do not require food, drink, or a bathroom. We both know it, so don't try to play like you actually need them. You are not getting an opportunity to trick one of the lug heads that would be unfortunate enough to have to tend your needs. What we do need, however, is your cooperation. The sooner you give it freely, the sooner we can be done with all of this mess."

"Cooperation for what? What can I possibly do for you while I am chained to the floor? You do realize the common dog gets better amenities?" Mila's blue eyes flashed with power, causing the little woman with strawberry blonde hair to back up swiftly.

"I was sent down here to make sure you would agree to cooperate. I was not told with what or whom. Nor was I told what would happen otherwise, but I have seen plenty of things that make me strongly recommend doing as they ask," she stated, sounding braver than she looked.

"What is your name, child?" Mila asked seductively.

"Sss... Selby," she stammered, "Selby McIntosh." She jutted her chin up as she said her last name.

"Selby. Pretty name for a pretty little thing. What has my sister got over you? What has she promised you? Why do you do things that you know will get you killed if someone as powerful as me so much as thinks you dead?" Mila slowly stood up, towering over Selby's 5'4 stature. "You know I am caging my powers. You know that the thing in the corner is just an annoyance," she bluffed, "I am getting tired of my sister's games. She has been trying to capture me for well over 500 years now. Ever since I put a knife in her stomach almost a hundred years ago, she has been a persistent little bitch. Do you really want to be the one standing in between two bickering, powerful sisters who could shatter this world and recreate it with just a temper tantrum, Selby?" Mila stepped forward menacingly as far as the chain would allow.

Selby looked back towards the door. "What am I supposed to do?" she whispered. "This is not what I signed up for when I took the job, but I have no choice."

"Of course, you do. We all do. We may not like the choices, but we have them. Unlock my cuffs. That is all I need. I will not cooperate with my sister. You do not know what you are asking of me. It is safer for us all if I don't. Unlock my cuffs and I will protect you from her. I will walk up those stairs, out the front door, taking you with me. But you must promise you will stay with me. And you must tell me everything you can."

Selby stuck her hands in the pocket of the black pullover sweater she had on. She hung her head, squeezed her eyes closed, and blew out a long breath. Finally, she looked up to Mila, "I don't have the key, but I know where it is. I'll be back in about a half an hour." She quickly turned and went back up the stairs with attitude. She was determined the morons upstairs — the huge, violent, musclebound, hot tempered, shifter morons — would not scare her. If they did, she would absolutely not let them know it. She just hoped she could tame her fears well enough they couldn't smell it on her.

"I think I am going to like her," Mila told the empty room after Selby shut the door as hard as she had flung it open.

7

Selby pushed the door open with enough force that she knocked the wolf shifter behind it into the wall. "Hey, short shit! No need to go throwing a fit," Josh said, scowling at her.

"Don't stand so close to the door, you dipshit. You really aren't the brightest crayon in the box are you, Josh? What are you doing standing around anyway? Don't you have a grandma to steal from or a little boy to beat up?" She glared as she walked by.

"Kiss off, dumb bitch," he yelled as she rounded the corner in the hall. She shook her head as she entered the second doorway on the right. Her office was small, but it was hers. For now. She didn't bring anything sentimental here, but she did bring a few important items. She grabbed a box off the floor she had left under the window when she completed last week's genetics reports. Next, she grabbed a pen and notepad and began scrawling names. She wrote as many as she could remember from the last two or three weeks. Going through hundreds of files made it difficult to be able to remember every individual one, but she needed enough to validate sending for them. This part wouldn't be so easy to do if she were actually at the BTCL building, she thought to herself. She got about fifty names written down, picking a few random names off another notepad since she couldn't remember that many on her own. When she had what she thought would be a convincing enough list, she called for Josh.

He stomped in, not pleased with being ordered around, especially by her. "What?" he snapped.

"I need these files from the office. Take Dustin and Terrance with you to pick them up. I have some work I have to do, but I need the files to be able to do it. I've been given a time limit and I need to get started as quickly as possible."

"Is that so?" he asked with malice gleaming in his eyes and dripping from his words.

"Yes, that's so," Selby said as she leaned forward placing both fists on the table, "and if you take any longer than necessary to get those files to me, I will be sure to let certain authority figures know you had other pressing matters to attend, preventing me from doing my job as directed."

He deflated his puffed-up chest, grunting almost intelligibly, "Fine. Give me the fucking list."

She ripped the paper out of the notepad, tossed it in the box and shoved the box into Josh's chest. "Happy hunting!" she called as he left the room with a pissier attitude than what he'd walked in with. "I probably should *not* be goading him," she mumbled to herself as she changed out of the hoodie and into a black t-shirt. "Three down, only about twelve more to go."

She folded her sweater and set her small cactus plant on top of it. If she didn't already have the habit of taking it home every weekend, this would probably look strange. She didn't trust any of these assholes further than she could throw them, and an earth elemental leaving behind a plant she could turn into a weapon was not a good idea. She grabbed a few other things she had stuffed here and there that normally went home on the weekends, snatched her keys out of the top drawer and headed out to her car.

She got her things placed in the backseat, as per her usual routine. Breaking her routine, she went back to the driver's seat and removed the Black Chaos knife and holster from underneath. She strapped the holster to her outer right thigh. She pulled the blade's twin out from under the seat and repeated the process on her left leg. She snagged an elastic band off the gearshift and dropped the sun visor down, catching the pair of elbow length, black, palm-less gloves. Her tennis shoes were swiftly kicked off and tossed into the trunk. From there, she grabbed her thigh high, thick, lace up, steel toe boots. It only took about a minute before she had on both her boots and gloves, hair pulled into a tight bun on the top of her head, and was making her way back into the dilapidated office building to the security room.

She knocked on the door twice, paused, twice more, paused, then four times. "McIntosh," she stated and waited for the click to let her know the door was unlocked. Darrell had already made himself comfortable again by the time she got in and locked the door. Luckily his back was to her when she entered because she was pretty sure he would have hit first and bitched later. There would be no questions coming from him. He was the most down to business of all the shifters there. He was the one she had been most nervous about as she rolled the plan through her head.

"What brings you in here?" he asked as he turned his attention back to the monitor flashing between the front and back gates. She noticed the rest of the monitors were off, which explained why she was not greeted by a welcome party at the front door after changing.

"I sent Dumb, Dumber, and Dipshit to go get more files from the office. I was told since they don't always follow directions, I was supposed to inform whomever was manning the station from now on," she said as she quietly unsheathed her knife.

Darrell nodded, leaning back in the office chair, "Yep. They decided to take a detour and

check out the scenery the last time they were sent out to do something. I hate how we have to babysit those dumb fucks, but they have potential."

"That won't be your job anymore," she said as she grabbed his forehead with her left hand, snapping his head back while using her right to stab the knife into the side of his throat between his spine and windpipe. With the tip of the blade protruding from the opposite side of his neck, she twisted, severing the voice box and causing enough nerve damage to the spine, he was instantly paralyzed. His dying eyes remained open as she wiped her blade on his shirt. "Sorry, Darrell. Well, not really. I told you when you had my brother slaughtered and my sister kidnapped I would be the one to kill you, especially if anything happened to her. I even told you I would slit your throat when you least expected it, didn't I?"

She sheathed her newly cleaned knife, not expecting an answer as she dug in his pockets looking for the keys for Mila's cuff. She forcefully removed them from the left front pocket of his jeans. "Did you really have to wear tight pants today?" She picked up his cell phone off the table and slid it into her back pocket. As she left the room she made sure to lock the door behind her.

She crossed the hall moving silently to the door to the basement. She took her keys out of her pocket and slid the key into the lock. Mila was standing, waiting, by the time she made it to the bottom of the stairs. Selby tossed the keys for the cuffs to Mila then went to the corner the device sat in. Lifting her boot, she slammed her foot down on it, shattering it to pieces. The sounds of keys, then one cuff hitting the floor right after the other joined the sound of grinding metal as she stomped over and over until she was satisfied the thing was properly destroyed.

A sudden flare of power washed through the small room, bouncing and reverberating in their bones. Mila let out a moan almost making Selby feel like an intruder on an intimate moment. She stood with her back to Mila for a few minutes before she said, "He had my little brother killed and my sister kidnapped. He said he wouldn't hurt her if I cooperated, but he and a few of his packmates played too rough with her. She died a few days ago from her injuries. I was told I would end up the same as she did, *a pack chew toy* if I didn't do what I was told. I have been biding my time for the last several months. I didn't know how I was going to save her and make it out with my own life. Please understand if I did anything to harm you, that I had no choice until you offered me another one." She stood for another moment before she turned around to face her fate.

When Selby's light green eyes met Mila's bright blue ones, power rippled through them both. They both felt a connection snap into place. It wasn't one tying them together like a mate bond, but uniting them on the same side. Selby's eyes flashed a bright green Mila would have missed if she had blinked.

"How many are out there now?" Mila asked as she calmed her magic.

"I sent three out on a fool's errand, killed the head security officer, who also happens to be the pack alpha. He's the piece of shit that had my brother murdered and let my sister be torn to shreds. There are probably fifteen here on a typical day, sometimes more, sometimes less. I have been stuck in my office most of the day so I haven't seen who all has been coming and going. I would guess we have at least ten or twelve more roaming around, but I couldn't begin to tell you where they are."

"That's better info than what I had sitting in here," she replied with a smile. "We can work with that. I am guessing you actually know how to hold your own since you are dressed up so spiffy."

"Maybe a little," she winked, walking up the stairs.

8

They stood for a full minute motionless and
quiet at the door before Selby nodded to Mila,
signaling her to follow. Mila nodded back once,
urging Selby to open the door. The hall was empty,
but they could hear the obnoxious banter of men in
the rec room a few doors down. Walking silently in
the opposite direction, they hoped the guys would
keep themselves occupied long enough for them to
get out.

One of the men shouted, "stop them" causing
the Selby to spin around immediately. Not seeing
anyone they paused, waiting quietly to see if anyone
would intercept. When no one came and chorus of
cheers erupted followed by a loud "touchdown!",
they released a breath of relief. Selby unsheathed

her knives, resting the spines against the outside of her wrists. She relaxed her body as she crept up to the intersection leading outside if you turned to the left or further into the building if you went right. She stopped and peered around the corner. Before she could bring her head back around the phone in her pocket started singing *Dirty Deeds Done Dirt Cheap* by AC/DC.

"Oh, fuck," Selby sighed, dropping her head down. "He either had a dirty sense of humor or that song was just too damn fitting."

One of the guys walked out of the rec room. Staring at his phone he called out, "Hey Darrell, I've been trying to get into the security room for about fifteen minutes now. Where have you—" he stopped in his tracks, eyes going wide, surprised to see them standing in the hall. "Shit. They're escaping!" he yelled back to the rest of the guys.

Mila threw him up against the wall with a sweep of her hand. Selby ran up to where he was pinned to the wall, drew back and hit him full force in the face with the knuckle guard on the hilt of the knife. His eyes rolled back as Mila let go of her power. He slumped to the floor, but the damage was already done. Four more guys came barreling their way out into the hallway, the first not slowing and slamming Selby face first into the wall. The other three stood for a second to assess the situation. Two ran for Mila while the fourth yanked Selby up by her hair from where she had fallen to the floor from the force of the impact. Mila swung at the first one to reach her. She caught him in the jaw, head snapping back. His head whipped back to face her while she side kicked the other in his stomach causing him to double over. Both men stopped to smile at her, then their teeth and claws came out.

She took a quick glance at Selby who was back on her feet, standing free of the one who had jerked her up. She had both feet planted shoulder width apart, arms held loosely at her sides, blades at the ready. Mila's gaze switched back to the wolf shifters in front of her. Her eyes flashed bright blue with the power of her magic as her excitement accelerated.

"Well now, I haven't played rough in a while boys. Let me know if I hurt you," she winked at the one she had already jaw checked.

"Gladly, but I don't think it'll be a problem," the bigger, scruffy looking shifter said as he lunged, plowing into her midsection and sending them both into the wall behind her. The plaster cracked from the force of the hit. Mila grabbed both sides of his head and shot a quick pulse of power through his temples. His eyes widened as the shock of magic scrambled his brain for a brief second. She shoved him to the floor and leapt over him. The brunette stalked forward, throwing a punch in the direction of her face. She pulled back far enough to miss the punch, but not the set of claws he sliced downward across her stomach.

Selby shrieked, "Holy shit, do you have to hit like a bitch?" She ducked a swing from the shorter guy on the left, simultaneously stabbing him in the groin. While she was squatted down, she spun around doing a leg sweep, pulling the big one's feet out from underneath him. She quickly crawled up his sprawled body while he was flat on his back and punched him three times in the side of the head, catching him once in the ear, busting the eardrum, blood seeping out of his ear. He growled, trying to dig his extended claws into her shoulders as he attempted to throw her off. She thrust her arms hard upward preventing him from getting purchase, drew her elbows inward and slammed them onto his chest, causing him to gasp for the breath that she knocked out of him. Straddling him, she took advantage of being inside of his reach and sunk a blade into each side. She heard the thick suction pop when she pulled the blade out. He coughed up blood, wheezing, and she knew she had punctured at least one lung. She continued to thrust her blades into his chest in rapid succession until he lost consciousness.

Mila screamed as she unleashed a monstrous wave of magic, sweeping over everyone, knocking all of them three to four feet back from where they were. Her hair was disheveled, hanging in limp strands all about her face, sticking to blood trickling from her hairline above her right eye. Struggling to stand, she bent down to the guy with the dark brown hair, grabbing handfuls of his hair and pulling him onto his knees. She yanked his head back, forcing him to look at her. She gave him a quick kiss on the forehead and twisted hard. The crunch of bones reverberated in the quiet, echoing in the empty foyer. She dropped his limp body and turned to the scruffy guy who had plowed her into the wall. He staggered to his feet, leaning against the wall that sported a Mila-sized hole. She gently placed a hand on his chest. The disorientation in his eyes was obvious when he smiled kindly at her. She pushed a dose of magic into him, causing him to fall flat on his face, unconscious.

Selby turned to the last man who was struggling to stand, "How many others are on duty right now?"

"Like I'm telling you shit."

She stepped up to him, planting her left forearm across his chest, shoving him against the wall. She pushed a knife to the base of his throat with her right, nicking the skin enough to let a small trickle of blood ease down under his shirt, "I am going to leave you standing on your own feet, but you will deliver a message to Bossman" He looked back and forth between her and Mila, who had walked up to stand just behind her, hand extended, fingers bleeding magic. His eyes shot back to Selby and he gave a slight nod.

"Great, now answer my fucking question. How many?"

"Six," was his simple answer.

"Where are they all?" she pushed on the knife a little harder.

He gulped, causing another trickle of blood to flow, "One is upstairs and the rest are outside.

You won't be dealing with them though. They are preoccupied."

"Doing what?"

"Taming."

"Taming what? What are you talking about?"

"Like you don't know. You have access to all of the files," he snarled.

"I may have access to files, but apparently I'm not high enough on the totem pole to get a good view of everything. What in the hell are they taming?" she tightened her grip on his chest.

"I said I would deliver a message, either give it or I will say fuck it and finish this fight here and now."

"You can tell Mira," Mila interjected, "the next blade will not be in her stomach. I am done with her games. She can go ahead and pencil me into her schedule as the last appointment for the next millennia because I am coming after her sorry ass."

Selby shoved him again as she let him go. Mila quickly grabbed his wrist as if to help him catch his balance when he staggered and shot a light jolt of power through his arm. He slipped, landing spread eagle on the floor.

"Damn, Mila. I said I would leave him on his feet. What the hell?" Selby exhaled.

"You did. I put him on his ass. Now where in the fuck did you park the car?" Mila responded, walking out the front door they had almost made it to.

9

Carter roared as he threw the chair against the wall. The crack was resounding in the silence, causing the four shifters in front of him to flinch. "How in the bloody hell did an elemental get the better of a pack of wolves?" he screamed, enunciating the last word. The men kept their eyes downcast while he paced the floor in front of them. None of them dared look up for fear of catching his undivided attention.

Josh cleared his throat, looking up, "I don't know what happened after we left," he said pointing to himself, Dustin, and Terrance, "but it was a complete wreck in the hall and they were already gone by the time we got back."

"Do you think that clears your fucking name? Who sent you out? If it was anyone other than myself, Mira, or your alpha, you are in just as much trouble as the rest of those good for nothing mutts," Carter said stepping up into Josh's face. Josh's eyes went back to the floor immediately. "The question wasn't rhetorical, fuckwad. Who sent you out?"

He cleared his throat again, keeping his eyes to the floor, "McIntosh. She said she needed files from the office. Gave us a paper with a shit ton of names and everything."

"Really? So, she tricked your dumb asses into leaving. Did you bother checking with anyone to see if she could request said files?"

"No," Josh answered simply.

"What do you propose we do now? The suppressor was destroyed. It will cost more than money to catch her. I can have another one made, but do you think she will forget what it does? Do you think she will forget her magic was hindered? Do you think it will be easy to catch her again? You, Mr. I-was-just-doing-what-I-was-told, and your friends are on shit duty until further notice. You get to clean the cages. You get to do the feeding, watering, and general fetching like the bitches you are. If those two women who escaped had not killed our men and cut our numbers, your heads would be on pikes Vlad Dracul style. One more fuck up from you idiots and they will be, numbers be damned. Now get the fuck out of here and report to Dominique." Josh, Dustin, and Terrance darted to the door, tripping and shoving each other trying to be the first out.

"Full report, Tysen."

Tysen looked over from where his eyes had been planted on the bookshelf behind the desk since he was first pulled into the office. He told Carter about trying to get into the security room to no avail. He explained what happened from the point when he called Darrell and found the women in the hall to when he called Carter and Mira. Carter looked at Tysen's bloody shirt and pants and shook his head, "Well, I'm pissed at you, too, but I don't think I could stand up straight if I got stabbed in the balls either. Because you actually fought, so I'm not going to give you shit for it. Now that your alpha is dead, you will need a new one. I know how dissention will occur if you're all forced to just deal with a beta. How long do you think your pack will last before you have to fight?"

"A new alpha has about a week to step up. If the beta concedes, then the pack should be back to full strength within another week or two. If the beta chooses to challenge for the role of alpha and the pack wants someone stronger, then it could take much longer. If everyone is fine with beta taking on until an alpha presents himself, we have a month or more before the beta starts to lose it. Dynamics have to be met or we'll shred ourselves from the inside out. We'll be no use to you if we don't have an alpha, which is a role the beta can only fill temporarily."

"As a beta, I assume it is your responsibility to find another alpha?" Carter asked.

"In a way. There can only be one alpha in a pack. We will have to have time to leave, as a group, to search for someone if no one in the pack currently wants the position. Typically, an alpha is born and works for the rank when he comes of age. He will fight for his right of dominance. If one alpha kills another, the survivor gets the dead alpha's pack. It's not the same when they have no heir and are not killed by another alpha. Darrell was the son of our previous alpha and fought his way into position when his father abdicated. We have no basis to go on for our pack's dynamics with a new alpha. No one challenged Darrell. He had no heir. It may take a while to find a new one."

Carter absorbed this information. He stood with his arms crossed, his right hand stroking the blond hair on his chin. After a few moments he nodded, "It will take at least a month to get anywhere near ready to go after Mila again. There is no need to have runners here except for those that are needed for the tamers. Will five or six suffice for you to take care of business for now?"

Tysen nodded, "It should be. But I will tell you, I will not concede to just anyone."

"Fair enough. I'm a reasonable man. I wouldn't ask you to do anything less for your people than I would my own."

REFLECTED

"Would you like me to clear it through you first before I pull the guys or do I have to freedom to choose my best guys?" Tysen asked.

Carter squinted his eyes at Tysen, "I see what you did there. If I say no then it looks like I don't have the interest of the pack in mind. If I say yes, then I still don't have the interest of the pack in mind. Be careful of the mind games you play with me. We may both be a force to reckon with, but I've had over a thousand years to perfect the art of pain." Carter went to the chair scattered in pieces on the floor, staring for a moment at the mess he'd made, then turned back to Tysen. "No, you do not have to clear it through me before calling together the members you feel you need but have the courtesy to let me know which ones I'll be without."

"Fair enough. I am a reasonable man. I wouldn't ask you to do anything less for your people than I would my own," Tysen tossed Carter's words back at him with nod as he walked out the door.

Carter stood for several minutes staring at the doorway. "That dog will be nothing but trouble," he told himself as he busied himself, picking up the pieces of the broken chair to toss them into the hallway. Two out of three chairs still sat at the desk. One was behind the desk between it and the bookcase and the second chair was more at the side. Carter set the remaining guest chair back in front of the desk. The fake plant to the left of the bookcase had been impaled to the wall by a piece of the chair when Carter lost his cool.

He walked around the desk to yank the wood out of the plant and wall when he heard footsteps enter the room.

"Well then, I insist you put a leash on it before it bites the hand that feeds it," Mira chimed as she sauntered into the room.

"If I wanted your opinion I would ask for it, hag."

Mira tsked, "Ah. Ah," she said in her sing song voice, "careful Mr. Vampire. Remember who made you."

"Remember who killed me, you mean? I remember very well."

"Oh, I did no such thing. Do not start over reacting again, Love. You know it never works out well for you when you do."

"Did you not make the potion that killed my body?"

"That I did do, as you know. But I was not the one who put it into your tankard. You have your sister-in-law to thank for that."

"And you were supposed to prevent her from killing me! That is what I paid your filthy dues for," Carter seethed.

"But I did, at least permanently." She stepped up to him and ran a long fingernail down his cheek, starting next to his eye, moving to his mouth before trailing it down the length of his body. "Do not try to tell me you don't enjoy my gift. I see how you like to play. You enjoy being immortal. You learned so quickly how to sustain this delectable body. Just like you learned quickly how to use it," she grabbed his crotch and gave a little squeeze.

"I have never and will never touch you. Get that nightmare out of your head. Your sister escaped and I need her back. You have work to do. I suggest getting to it," he shoved her hand away from his nether regions, pushing past her, storming out the door.

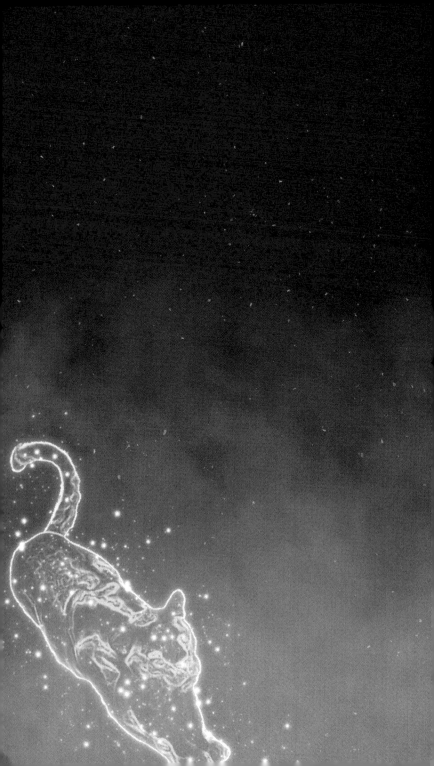

10

The food in the refrigerator had been spared the flour and spice shower from the day before. Cason guzzled down his third glass of Mila's homemade fruit punch while everyone else polished off the empanadas or butterkakas. For whatever reason, Mila always made desserts first, then the main courses. At this moment, it seemed to work for everyone because there was no mercy shown to the sweet delicacies.

We were all sitting around the granite top island in the kitchen on the high back stools that were supposed to be at the wrap around bar. On days like this where everyone was over, I was glad to have a large kitchen. It was easy to sit and talk without having to look around the person next to you to see who you were talking to.

"They vanished," Miguel said while he licked the powdered sugar off his fingers.

"They were in the hallway leading up to the second floor, but when we got up to the alcove, they were just gone," Tia explained after Miguel started making humming noises.

"Do you need to go upstairs for some alone time with your hand, Miguel?" Alex asked as she smacked his hand away from his face.

"Hey! Don't hate cuz you can't boil water without burning it," Miguel gave her a shove in return.

"You better not be hatin' on my skills in my kitchen," Mila announced as she and a tiny wisp of a woman walked into the kitchen.

I screeched as I jumped off my stool, "Mila! Holy shit, you look like hell. Are you okay? Where have you been? What happened?" I rushed to her and wrapped her in a crushing hug.

She returned my hug and pushed me back to arm's length. "I'm good. Stop worrying. I'm home and okay. First, this is—"

"Selby?" Jake asked, astonished.

Selby gave a meek smile and slight wave, "Uh, hi Jake."

Mila looked between Jake and Selby with a puzzled look, "Well, I think it would be an asinine question to ask if you know each other, so how about this one; how do you know each other?"

"Better yet," I interjected, "why don't we start at the beginning. Jake, grab a couple of stools and I'll grab more food. Tia, take Selby to my room and see if you can find her something to wear. She looks like she can use a shower. Mila, go find your Zen before we get started down here. We have more questions than answers, but I bet between the two of you, we can get a few things figured out. I have a feeling this will take a while, so you might as well be comfortable from the start."

Forty-five minutes later we sat around the island once again, though a little more squished together. Heat waves wafted towards the ceiling from the hot dishes placed in the center of the island as Bobby put plates, glasses, and sets of silverware in front of the two freshly showered ladies. Selby nodded her thanks and began piling her plate full of the steamy goodness of the world.

"This smells great," she nodded to me as she took a bite of the gyuvetch, moaning as soon as it hit her taste buds.

"Thanks, but this is all Mila. All I did was reheat it."

"Seriously?" she looked at Mila with rounded eyes.

"Yep. I am no cook, so you're lucky I learned how to work the oven well enough to reheat it without burning anything." I said while I washed my hands.

"From the beginning seems like a good place to start," Mila stated flatly, "also probably coming out with a lot of things I have kept secret for a while now. So, let's start with a simple question; who knows what I am?"

We all looked around the island at one another to gauge the reactions of each other. There were shoulder shrugs and head shakes all around. Bobby cleared his throat, "Hi. I'm Bobby. This is going to sound a bit forward, but does it really matter what we all are here?"

"Hi Bobby. Yes, it does. Why are you here?" Mila quizzed right back.

"Oh. Well. Alright, so it matters." he cleared his throat, "Lyssi and I met this evening, well, last night I guess. I'm a biokinetic. Lyssandra seemed to need help, I offered my assistance."

Mila nodded her approval, "Fair enough. Lyssi, do you trust him?"

I shrugged, "We just met. You were missing. The only identifiable sig came from a coworker at BTCL. He's either a friend or foe because he works there, too. It's best to find out on our terms instead of theirs."

"Logical. Dangerous, but logical," she said as she gave him another head to toe once over. "Well, since the reason I am in this pickle to begin with is now known to those at BTCL, there's nothing I can say that he could run and tell if he is one of the bad guys." She gave him a pointed look, to which he just dipped his head in polite acknowledgment.

"Okay, so the beginning is where and when?" Cason asked.

REFLECTED

Mila took a deep breath and leveled each of us with an intense look. She hadn't started eating yet, so she slid her empty plate further back on the table to rest her forearms in front of her. "You all know very little about me. What you do know is what I have wanted you to know. Knowing anything more would only put you into a dangerous position. I am usually moved on by now, not staying in one place long enough to establish any kind of roots or relationships. I never tell anyone what I am and let them think whatever they want. I rarely use my gifts or powers and when I do, I dampen my magic so it can't be read or reflected. I have been doing this for nearly 600 years now. However, my sisters and I are much, much older than that." She stopped for a minute to pick at the string hanging from the sleeve of her shirt. When she started back up again, there was a distance in her eyes meaning she was talking through memory rather than present conversation. "We were never born, not in the terms you know. We just appeared one day, full grown, full knowledge of what we can and cannot do, what we are and are not capable of. We hold the knowledge of the Earth within us. We were alive when the Cro Magnons and Neanderthals walked, as well as many others. There are many more types of human and subhuman species than you could imagine, and I am not referring to those of us who are supernatural or supposedly mythical." She stopped again to see everyone's reaction. When she started back up her Bulgarian accent was thick, "My two sisters and I go by many names. In Greek and Roman mythologies, we are the Fates, in the Norse the Norns, in many Slavic traditions we are Sudjaje, and so on around the world. We appeared in what is modern day Bulgaria, which is where I consider my country of birth because it's where we spent so much time in our early years. People called upon us from all nations and lands to weave their stories, hoping for power, love, fame, fortune. Some people believed we only read the past, present, and future like an oracle. Some thought we created the fortunes or misfortunes ourselves. There are too many versions to really detail each one, but all of them have a little snippet of truth within. We are oracles. We are creators of destiny. We weave life and death and fortune and misfortune. But we are much, much more than all of this. Words cannot ever be put together accurately enough to say exactly what we are. We are as much of life and death as we choose to be."

"Hold... hold on just a minute..." Cason spluttered. "Are you telling us you are... a... uh, one third of the triple threat? *The* trio of goddesses that could kill us with the snap of her finger?"

Mila snickered at his, and probably everyone else's, wide-eyed, reaction. "If you want to look at it that way, yes. But also no."

"Huh? You gonna hafta essplain yoself better than that, sista," Alex exhaled, "I'm confused as shit."

"Well that's not a far leap from some sort of normalcy," Miguel elbowed Alex, who turned her scowl to him.

"Shut up, jerkface," she told him before turning back to Mila. "How is it yes and no? It can be only one or the other."

Mila laughed a full bellied laugh ending in snorts and tears. "This is why I have not moved on like I should have," she gasped, "I love our dynamics here. I have never felt so at home anywhere with anyone quite like I do the six of you."

We beamed at one another from her admission. "All well and good, hoochie, but flattery will not get you out of clarifying for us," Tia announced as she filled the plate Mila had pushed away. "Eat while you explain. Did you eat while you were gone?"

"HO, blagodarya ti, I did not." She thanked Tia in Bulgarian for the plate and started shoveling food like she hadn't eaten in a month. "To be truthful, I do not have to eat to survive, but I do love to taste the flavors."

"While you eat, I can fill them in with a few of the more recent events," Selby offered, getting up to put her now empty plate in the sink. "So, I'm going to guess Jake filled you in with how he and I know each other," she looked to Jake who nodded, "but Mila doesn't know, so I'll start there. A few years ago, my parents were in a car accident. I had just graduated college but hadn't been able to find a good place to apply my research degree. I was offered a position at BTCL but I turned it down because I was trying to get out of this town. I had some so-called friends who worked there for a good six or seven months and they had nothing but great things to say about the place, but something kept niggling in the back of my head. I blew off the feeling for the most part but listened well enough to not take the offer. About three months later my parents were on their way home from dinner when Daddy lost control of the car, hitting a light pole. I'll save the details, but Mom was killed instantly and Dad was in ICU, expecting to make a full recovery when I got a call in the middle of the night saying he had flatlined. I had to rush to the hospital without my younger siblings. My brother was fifteen and my sister was thirteen, so I woke them up and let them know I got a call to go to the hospital because of some details in the paperwork. They wanted to go, but I wanted to make sure I was strong enough to help them grieve. I wouldn't be any help to them if I lost it in front of them. I told them I would come back to take them up there if it was that important, but they needed to try to sleep because they had school the next day." She turned away from us, wiping her face, under the guise of looking for a glass. We let her do her thing while we let her story thus far soak in. After a few minutes of searching relentlessly Jake got up from the island and stood behind her. He put his hands on her shoulders and turned her around to face him. She immediately buried her face in his chest, quietly crying.

Mila pushed what was left of her food around on her plate. Alex grabbed one of Miguel's hands while Tia grabbed the other and leaned on Cason's shoulder. Cason twisted his empty glass on the table with one hand and put his other arm around Tia. Bobby and I just sat quietly with our hands in our own laps. The mood had turned real somber, really quick. We waited in silence for her to gather herself. It seemed too rude not to.

Twenty or so minutes later she pulled herself out of Jaykob's chest. "I would normally apologize for taking so long, but I'm not going to this time. I have not allowed myself to stop and grieve for any of them. I was afraid I wouldn't be able to keep going if I did," she said as she wiped the fresh tears off her cheeks, jutting her chin out.

Jake rubbed her back while she finished gathering herself together. "No, no one here expects an apology, whether you have grieved yet or not. To lose one family member is hard enough," he gently guided her to her seat. He walked to his stool, pulling it to the other side of the island beside her. "Whenever you're ready, we're not going anywhere."

"Thanks, Jake." She smiled bashfully at all of us, wiping a few errant tears away. She inhaled deeply and continued like nothing had stopped her. "When I got to the hospital the charge nurse met me in the hallway and asked me to speak with her before going in to see my father. She said the doctor was requesting an autopsy be done. He wished to speak to me when I was done saying goodbye. He normally talks to the family directly but was called to an emergency and asked her to make sure I was aware of the conversation he would need to have with me. I went in and spent time with my dad, brushing his hair and all. I tried to be quick because I had left my brother and sister at home. I wasn't sure what all the doctor would need from me and I wanted to be available whenever he was done with his emergency so I could get home as quickly as I could." She took a big drink of water out of the glass Cason set in front of her when he got up to refill his own. "Thank you, Cason, is it?" He simply nodded and reseated himself to wait patiently for her to begin again.

"The doctor didn't take very long tending to what he was called to do. He met me in the waiting room and took me back to his office. As they all do, he opened with 'I'm very sorry for your loss.' Before I got a chance to acknowledge his condolence, he said, and I quote, *And I know it doesn't make this any easier, in fact, most likely more difficult to handle. I am sorry for that as well, but the death of your father was not due to his injuries, nor a natural cause such as a heart attack that we can tell at this point. I would like your permission to do an autopsy. Usually no permission is necessary when a death is suspicious, but your father was fully awake and coherent earlier. He was not on any strong narcotics, such as morphine, at his request. In fact, he was doing so well we only had to monitor him for another hour and a half, then he was being moved*

to a regular room. He also kept asking for his oldest daughter to look into it. He said you would understand.'
I couldn't help but nod and shake my head. I didn't know what to think, much less what to say. My father was possibly murdered and I was at a loss. I granted the permission for the autopsy, thanked him and left in a daze.

"A few weeks later the report comes in and they have nothing to go on. There were no toxins at a lethal level in his system. Morphine and other typical drugs used in the hospital were all at normal levels for one treated with extensive injuries, such as with a car wreck. The toxicology report came back clean when they compared the dosage chart to his autopsy report. The recordings from the machines he was hooked up to showed there was brief tachycardia, or rapid heart rate," she clarified for the non-medical persons in the room, "his pupils were uncharacteristically dilated, and his muscles were spasmodic. His oxygen level drastically dropped just before death. Blood work showed high levels white blood cells, but that's normal when the body is fighting injury because of exposure to infection and possible infectious elements from the surrounding environment. They did, however find certain anomalies in the blood as well as a few of his organs. For one, the ABG, or, arterial blood gas, tests results came back and his oxygen levels were severely below normal range. Lack of oxygen is backed up by the darker coloration of his blood, which tells us he was asphyxiated somehow.

But the strange thing is there were red splotchy and inflamed patches in his stomach, yet he had ingested nothing unusual before or after the wreck to notably cause the irritation. He also had venous hyperemia in the brain and lungs." She noticed the confused looks from Cason, Tia, and Mila so she went on in layman's terms, "That means he had engorged veins in the lungs and brain. It kind of ties into the spasms that were noted just before death. Certain parts of the body seized and relaxed, but the problem is there is no definitive cause for the spasms, engorged veins, and so on. The only feasible explanation is poisoning, but with the toxicology report being clean, that's hard to prove. That's how I ended up working at the hospital. I worked there for a couple of years doing the tox screens and other various in-house labs. If I found anything questionable it went to the state crime lab, where I worked part time."

"Were there ever any conclusive results?" Jaykob asked.

"No. There were never any determinable toxins in his system. The medical examiner closed the case as suspicious with notations to reopen if others with similarities came through the door."

"So, what happened to make you quit your job? Didn't you say you had originally declined an offer at BTCL? Did they give you another offer that would help you get the results you were unable to get through the hospital?" Cason chimed in.

Selby gave a bitter laugh. "You could say that."

"What do you mean?" Jake inquired.

"Well, you know Sam from administration? She asked if I would like to go out for a girls' night out one Friday night after work. I knew you were standing a few feet away so I told her no, I had plans with my boyfriend. You and I had worked together for so long I was hoping you would overhear and know something wasn't right," she sighed, "but it didn't work out that way. Anyway, it's no secret I'm an Elemental. She started asking questions about this elusive boyfriend. I gave her the details she wanted, but it wasn't a boyfriend I was describing. I was describing the shifter asshole, Dominique, who killed my little brother and kidnapped and tortured my little sister." She slammed her glass down after a long drink of water.

"Wait... he... your *boyfriend* killed your siblings?" Tia squealed in disbelief.

"No. He was never my boyfriend. I had been working at the hospital for about two years by this time. I came home from work one night to find my brother tied to a chair in the kitchen. My little sister's hands and feet were tied together like a fucking animal. She was laying on the floor at Dominique's feet with a rag shoved in her mouth. Darrell, the alpha who sent them, sent a message and said I had two choices: I was going to go into work, telling no one about what was going on, but give my notice saying I had a better job offer I was accepting or both of my siblings would be lying in a pool of their own blood and I would go anyway. I had no choice but to go along with it, so I told him I would tell them the next morning." She stopped talking again. She stood up and walked around the island. She put her hands together, her first fingers steepled in front of her mouth as she seemed to be gathering her thoughts. She paced back and forth for several moments before she stopped and turned to all of us once again, with tears in her eyes. "Then that fucking asshole slid a knife across his throat and told me it would ensure I kept my word on not telling anyone. The same would happen to my sister if I went back on it."

Immediately all the men exploded with anger, and I mean all of them. Miguel and Jake were the loudest, yelling about how they were going to hunt this Dominique guy down and kill him while Cason and Bobby fumed more quietly. Maybe not much more quietly, but they weren't exactly yelling like the other two. Tia, Alex, and I just sat there in stunned silence.

Who would do that to a child? Two children? Then my anger began. My magic tried to reflect off of everyone else's without me intentionally doing so. Almost as fast as it flared up, my magic went flat. That's the only way I can put it. It's like one second it's within reach and usable, then it's there but I can't touch it. I looked to Cason and nodded. He took control over the powers seeping from the outpour of sudden emotion. Miguel didn't seem to notice, but it was not surprising because his animal couldn't be dampened and he obviously felt a surge of protection for this female who had her whole family murdered. Children. Murdered. By shifters. Shifters normally held women and children in high regard and protected them fiercely. To assume Miguel was livid would be an understatement of the century if you wanted to go by the physical change he appeared to be fighting. Long black claws had popped out from his fingertips, black fur was erupting from his bare hands and forearms. His bones began popping as he flexed his hands. He was breathing heavily and pacing back and forth throughout the kitchen.

Without warning a sudden calm came over everyone in the room. Mila stood up from where she had been sitting quietly, patiently watching and listening. The tension left Miguel's face as he slumped down in a chair he was passing. His claws and fur receded back into his body. He ran his hands through his hair in what seemed to be an attempt to find the words to express what he just went through. Finally, he stood up, went to Selby, enfolding her into his arms. "I'm so, so sorry. I hope I didn't scare you."

The surprised expression on her face told everyone that scared wasn't what had been running through her mind. "Uh, no. It's ok." She reached up and awkwardly patted him on the back.

I stepped up behind Miguel to gently lay a hand on his shoulder, to which he replied with a growl. "Hey," I said softly, "she's alright. She is here at my house, Miguel. She isn't going anywhere any time soon. She's safe. You just met her so you cocooning her right now might be a little weird." He took another few seconds holding her before letting go. When he did she shot me a relieved look.

"Is everyone back to being calm?" Mila gave a stern look to everyone in the room. I don't know about everyone else, but the look accompanied by the heavy accent and parental tone made me feel about five years old. "Finish what you were saying, please, Selby."

Selby nodded and cleared her throat, "Well. Um… I did just what I was told to do. I went into HR and gave my notice. I only told people who asked where I was going. The only reason I could give was another job opportunity. So that was that. I did what work I could to make sure the next person in my position didn't have a mess on their hands because of me. I started working at BTCL as soon as my time was over at the hospital. I was sent out to a rundown building on the other side of town past the airport. They said they were doing testing there that could endanger the public if any of the test subjects escaped. It sounded too Dr. Frankenstein-ish for my liking, but then again, I didn't have a choice."

"What did they have you doing there?" Alex asked.

"Mostly comparing blood work. I would receive vials of blood to run the normal tests on and compare them to previous blood tests. If they were the base tests, I was to annotate any anomalies occurring naturally."

"Were the samples you received labeled by name or by number?" Bobby finally added to the conversation.

"Both, actually. I was given a few specific names I had been charged to keep track of. About 350 or so. I also had around 275 case files which were labeled by number."

Bobby nodded and immersed himself in his thoughts.

"Well, what happened after that?" Tia interrupted his concentration, turning it back to Selby.

"I went to work every day. They had me go to where they kept potential clients to make sure they had food and water. They also asked me to tag along on a couple of pick ups." She sent Mila an apologetic look. "As far as Darrell goes, he's dead already. I made sure of it this morning before Mila and I left." She pulled a bloody cell phone out of her back pocket and slid it on the table. "So, since part of it is all said and done, the questions left are as follows: What are they up to out there? What exactly did they want with Mila? And what are we going to do to stop them from hurting anyone else?"

11

Tysen called Tracey on his way home to gather the pack at his house. He had never had to call a meeting of this magnitude before and was not looking forward to it in the slightest. As he drove he tried to come up with the best opening to tell them their alpha was dead. There was no easy way to do it, so he decided to trash the script idea and just go with it.

He pulled up in his driveway to fifteen of his best friends and family standing around talking. He turned off the truck and got out, pocketing his keys as he limped his way up the steps of his plantation style house. He stood in front of the small group while their chatter died down.

"I really don't know where to start with this. This is one of the hardest things I have had to do, and I will be needing each of you to really step up right now and do your parts. Darrell won't be coming home. He was killed this morning." He stopped when the questions began.

"What happened?"

"Who killed him?"

"Who will take over?"

"Who do we kill to avenge him?"

All these questions and more poured out from the group below, but he couldn't single out any one person's questions. He let them go for a few minutes while he held the bridge of his nose in the vain hope of staving off the migraine he knew was coming on.

Finally, he held his hands up and shouted, "Enough."

Tracey came up the steps, taking a good long look at his attire. "Alright everyone. I am only going to say this once, so you better listen up. Tysen will answer our questions. He has more to say about what happened, I'm sure, but we need to think of the pack. Right now, our alpha is dead, which makes him in charge until we get a new one. Let's take care of him like he is. Let him get a shower and food, then we can sit and *listen* to what he has to say the way a pack should."

"Thanks," he told her as the rest of the pack turned around to go back to their respective houses. He dug his keys out of his pocket and unlocked his door. Tracey went to the kitchen as he headed up the stairs to shower.

When he came back down Tracey had a sandwich sitting on the kitchen table with a small bag of chips and a glass of orange juice. "I'm reheating the lasagna. Do you want me to throw the apple pie in after or do you want it like it is?"

"It's fine as it is, Tracey. You don't have to do all of this. I can make my own food, you know."

"No. I have to keep busy for now. We have a lot to talk about and if I let myself stop for a minute, I won't be any use to the pack."

He walked up beside her and placed a hand on her shoulder. She stopped moving for a minute, turned to face him. Her eyes were already rimmed red from the tears she'd shed. "It's ok to mourn your brother. You're supposed to."

"Not right now. The pack will be here in a few minutes and I can't show any weaknesses. Now is not the time."

"I won't argue, but know I won't think any less of you if you grieve when it's just us here." She nodded and turned back to the food.

Tysen had eaten half of the sandwich by the time the rest of the pack came bounding through the door. He stood leaning casually against the counter, one ankle crossed over the other in front of the sink. The light from the setting sun through the window behind him lit up his profile, making him hard to ignore.

"I know I dropped a bomb a little while ago. I plan to answer all of your questions to the best of my ability. I also know I am not the alpha, but I do expect you to act civilly during this discussion. I will not put up with any bullshit." He looked everyone present in the eye.

Dominique strolled in the front door as everyone found themselves a place to sit. Tysen gave him a brief nod of acknowledgement before continuing, "As many of you know, Darrell has many of the pack working at Biotech Chemlabs. I'll address my problems about it shortly, but for now, let's move to the main reason for this pack meeting. We've been working there for quite some time now and the jobs we have can be dangerous ones. This morning proved how dangerous when one of our co-workers killed him."

Outcries of disapproval erupted from everyone at once. He held up his hands in attempt to get their attention. When it didn't work, he stuck his fingers in his mouth and whistled. "Thank you for your attention. Again." He gave them a scornful look. "Let me fill you in a little more before you go running off to shred an entire building full of people. As I was saying, our job can be dangerous. We have to figure out what our priorities are going to be here, with the pack. What's more important? A new pack leader? Revenge? Pulling our pack out of BTCL? How do we go about all of this? Well, we get the facts straight." He shushed them again when they all started talking at once. "Yes, yes.

There are extenuating circumstances we will need to share here. There is more to this story than you all know. It's not like someone had beef with him over taking lunch out of the community fridge. There was a real reason for her to kill him. And if I had been in her position, I can't say I would have done anything differently."

"What are you talking about?" Eli, the youngest on the counsel, asked.

"For one thing, this dangerous job we have, though the pay is great, the moral code is all wrong. We were hired to do terrible things. When I was offered the job I refused, but because Darrell was alpha, he used his status against me and accepted the job. For all of us. The way we were initially approached was under the impression we would be bodyguards. As you know, it was nowhere near the line of work I was already doing. I was satisfied where I was. I had no intention of leaving my job. But Darrell had other plans. All he saw were dollar signs."

"What do you mean *'the moral code is all wrong'*? What do you really do if you aren't bodyguards?" Marcus asked.

Tysen stood a little straighter, "There are quite a few details to our jobs. One of them is to guard the facility and its inhabitants. Another is to acquire those inhabitants, and most of them aren't there willingly."

"That's enough bullshit out of you," Dominique said, springing up from his chair.

"Is that so, Dom?" Tysen retorted. "What do you have to add to make what Darrell signed us up for justifiable?"

"I don't have to answer to you. You aren't the alpha."

"Is that all you got? You don't have to answer to me because I'm not the alpha? Well, you are right. I'm not the alpha, but I am the beta. We don't have an alpha right now, which means you do have to answer to me until that changes. Are you willing to change it?"

Dominique stared Tysen in the eyes for several moments before leaving, slamming the front door behind him. Tysen ran both hands through his hair in exasperation. "Shit," he looked to the six shifters who made up the pack counsel. "I think this needs to be counsel business from here on out. I don't want any of you to be bullied by Dom or his buddies for the information that will be given here. If any of you do have problems, come see me or Eli immediately," he told the remaining eleven or twelve pack members, "I want the counsel to stay. The rest of you go home. We have a few things to discuss before we can initiate change of leadership. When that time comes, everyone will be called together, the way it's supposed to be."

Tracey patted his shoulder sympathetically as she passed him to usher everyone out. Low murmurs followed the small group out the door. The few remaining shifters sat in quiet contemplation while they waited for Tysen to start talking.

"I know we need an alpha. The problem I see with finding one right now is we have a moral dilemma to contend with first. The BTCL we work at is a testing facility. It's not the big institution down the road. It's hidden in the middle of no-damn-where in case their experiments escape, so the general public will one, have no knowledge, and two, not get hurt," he said as he ticked his fingers in the air to count his points. "Even many of the employees have no say in being out there. It isn't just the people they are testing on. The woman who killed Darrell, she was there against her will just like all of their test subjects are. Darrell coerced her to work there by killing her brother and kidnapping her sister. Tell me how that is morally sound."

"What the fuck?" Eli shook his head in disbelief.

"How in the hell are they getting away with that shit?" Marcus asked.

"People fear them," Tysen responded. "And rightfully so. They use creatures like us, who can be rather intimidating, to do their dirty work. I couldn't say anything while Darrell was alive. I tried. He would have banished me from the pack after beating me senseless. What good would I have been then? We have a problem with Dom and his little group of idiots, though. They like the work they do. We can't have them running and telling Bossman what is being discussed here because the entire pack will be at risk."

"You don't think we would be at risk anyway if you, or a new alpha, pulled what is left of our pack out of there?" Kendrick asked.

"Not if I handle it right, but unfortunately Dom heard me flat out tell you I disagree with the job, so more than likely, we won't have much luck flying under the radar now. I told the boss it would take about a month for us to find an alpha. I also told him the beta cannot become the alpha, which we all know is a lie," he motioned towards his packmates, "but I told him it was the beta's job to find a replacement if the pack was unable to produce a contender for the position."

"Okaaay." Eli drew the word out, confusion written all over his face.

Kendrick nodded his approval, "That should buy us time if Dom and the dipshits don't ruin it for everyone."

Marcus belted out a laugh, "Dom and the dipshits. Ha! That sounds like a bad 1950's bop group."

Eli scrunched his face, more confused than before. Shawn, who had been silent up to this point, threw a hand towel at Eli, hitting him in the face and said, "Don't hurt yourself, pup. The 50's were before your time." He turned to Tysen, as he rubbed a hand over his kinky, ebony hair, "What do you need from us? Where do we start?"

"I think the seven of us," Tysen said, looking to Damien and Chris since neither had said a word throughout the entire exchange, "need to go pay a visit to the lady whose house Darrell had ransacked yesterday by Dom. Her roommate was being rescued by the woman who stabbed me and killed Darrell. Maybe if we offer up a white flag, we can find that roommate of hers and put a stop to all of this. Bossman is without the device he needs to stop her powers, so if we can get to her before he does, we might have a chance to put an end to the abductions."

12

What do you mean I have to stay home from work Monday?" I asked. "I have to work. Not only do I have bills to pay, but we need inside information I could get."

"You aren't the only one who works there, hun," Alex said trying to sound sympathetic, "Miguel and I both work there, too."

"I'm not buying your pity routine, Alex. You have been trying to get me to take time off with you for a while now. It wouldn't surprise me one bit if you took a few days off with me just to torment me into doing whatever it is you've been trying to talk me into doing anyway."

"Look," Cason started, "we know you want to help, but you could be putting yourself in more danger if you show up."

"And staying at home is safer how? They know where I live because my address is on file in HR, like everyone else's. It's not like they haven't already barged into my house and kidnapped my roommate," I tried the logical argument.

"Exactly why you don't need to go walking yourself right into their front door," Bobby added, not helping my case one damn bit. "Sorry, Lyssi," he said when I shot him a look that should have vaporized him on the spot, but I don't have stupid laser vision, (Oh, you hush too, I can be pissy if I want.) "but they're right. You don't need to hand yourself over to the bad guys. They've already shown what lengths they'll go through to get what they want. Be smart about this. Don't give them a bargaining chip, which is what you would be, because I am certain Mila wouldn't be alright with the thought of you being hurt or killed. After talking to Selby, do you think they would care about you or her?"

I deflated with his words, because honestly, I couldn't disagree with him. If they were willing to kill Selby's brother in front of her very eyes, walking right into the lab Monday would be like saying '*My roommate ran away, but I'm the worm to re-catch your fish, come get me.*' I plopped down on the couch and crossed my arms like a spoiled five-year-old. "Fine. You win. I won't go in Monday." I received mixed reactions that varied from relief to excitement.

"We have company," Miguel said, pulling me out of my self-inflicted misery.

"What? Who?" Tia looked out the curtain to see what he was talking about, "I don't see anyone."

"They're coming up the driveway now," Alex said, her head cocked to the right so she could hear.

A few moments later three vehicles pulled up behind ours. The driveway was starting to look like a parking lot with all the various vehicles parked out there. When the new cars and trucks turned off, three large men got out of the first truck and two more got out of each of the other vehicles. The largest man, the one who was driving the truck, stepped a few feet away and held his hands up as if he were surrendering.

"Oh damn, I knew I should have aimed somewhere other than his nuts." Selby said under her breath.

"What? Are you fucking kidding me?" Miguel growled. "These are the assholes you two left alive?"

"What the hell are they doing here?" Alex asked.

"Let's go find out," Tia chirped, extending her claws as she made her way to the door.

"Here we go," Cason shook his head at her. "Can't I have normal friends?"

"Where's the fun in that?" I asked as I hip bumped him when I walked by.

Every one of us stood at the end of my porch steps, fanned out around Mila, forming a protective barrier. "What do you want?" I yelled to be heard over the shuffling of feet on gravel and wind in the trees.

"Just to talk. We mean you no harm. Quite the opposite, actually. Many things happened that we had no control over, and we are here to change the way things go. Can we talk? Please."

Miguel, Alex, and Tia growled low, menacing noises making the hair on my neck stand on end. I knew the shifters standing by the cars heard them because their muscles began flexing and twitching. It was typically a sign of an oncoming shift.

"Did Bossman send you to finish us off?" Selby asked.

"No. He doesn't know we're here. I want to keep it that way. Enough people have died because of him. He needs to be stopped."

"Why should we believe you?"

"Because your friend there behind you," he pointed at Mila, "doesn't need your protection. She could wipe us all out with the blink of an eye if she wanted to. She's who he is after, and she's who we are here to help protect."

"But if she doesn't need protecting, as you said," I chimed in, "why would you be here to protect her? You're talking in riddles. Get to the point. What do you want?"

He dropped his hands to his side, "My name is Tysen. My alpha was killed this morning by

McIntosh. Because of the binding power of the alpha, we cannot, physically cannot, refuse to follow orders of our alpha. Nor can we go against them. Now that he's dead, we have. . ." he paused to look at the six men with him to remind himself of his new status, "I have control over what is and is not done. We disagree with the choices the previous alpha made and want to do what we can to make things right. We can't do it without talking with you all first."

"Do you think he's telling the truth?" Tia looked to all of us to see what we thought.

"He is right about three things," Mila said, "Selby did kill his alpha this morning, he physically cannot go against an alpha once the alpha commands him, and finally, I do not need your protection. Let them in. Worst case scenario, there's another mess to clean in the house. Best case scenario, we have new allies." She turned and walked up the stairs, back into the house.

"Yeah, but she didn't have to clean up the mess the last time." I grumbled, following her up the steps.

13

Mira stood with her freshly manicured nails tapping against her hips, posturing like any bossy sister does awaiting a response. The minutes were ticking by while her patience was running thin. Her foot began hitting the floor in an annoying rhythm to prompt the answer she was becoming impatient for.

"What do you expect me to do?" Milena asked.

"For one, get off of your ass. For another, you could go get her."

"How am I supposed to go get her? She is as grown as you and I are. There is no making her do anything she doesn't want to do, which you should know by now," Milena stated as she got up from the plush chaise lounge she had been sprawled on.

Mira walked to the open double doors with a gorgeous view overlooking the Mediterranean Sea. "That is where you come in. You are the one she would listen to if she had to listen to one of us."

"Is that what you think? Do I need to remind you of the last time you had me talk her into something she wanted no part of?"

"Holy shit. Why does everyone keep bringing that up? He has turned out to be a wonderful creature. He is self-sufficient and sustaining. He has speed, strength, and intelligence unparalleled. He is a magnificent creation, if I do say so myself." Mira tutted.

"He is also a murderous parasite. He must feed off of the living to self-sustain, to retain speed and strength. He has the ability, and uses it, to create more parasites like himself. You are extremely lucky he didn't turn into one of those movie marathon monsters, the brainless twits eating everyone it encounters. You, Mira, are the only one who benefits from the death he causes."

"Don't act like you didn't know what he would be. Carter's blood lust, inability to walk in the sun, his life of solitude, that was all you. You knew what you were doing."

"Oh yes, that was me alright. It's my job to give struggles. But I didn't twist the spell at the last minute to prevent him from forever dying. That was you. You twisted the words to ensure he lasted as long as possible to create as much destruction as possible. Mila gave him the means to be able to live, the speed to catch his prey, the strength to maintain control of it so he could feed. You perverted the entire thing, using me to talk her into your dirty work. I can't blame her for refusing you for the last thousand years after what you did."

Mira whirled around, turning her back to the open balcony, "What *I* did? You self-righteous, pompous bitch! It's what *we* did. It took all three of us together to do that spell, so you are not going to put all the blame on me. Especially for what *you* presume was a failed experiment! He is not now, nor was he then, a failed anything! You need to get that into your obscenely thick skull. You also need to get it into our sister's even more obscenely thicker skull. She has blocked me from coming and going in her presence. It is really the only way I truly know where she is. If I can't pass to a specific location, that's where she is. It's been that way for too long now not to be her. At least since she was in Austria."

"Oh yes, the start of World War I when you had Archduke Ferdinand and his lovely wife Sophie killed to what purpose? Catch our sister's attention? Oh, you caught her attention alright. How does it feel to get stabbed in the gut?" Milena laughed at the anger spreading along Mira's features.

"I forget from time to time that you are the 'oh yes' sister. '*Oh yes, what a truly pitiful thing you did to the poor creature when you killed it. Oh yes, what was a pitiful thing, giving that man extended years.'* You play, oh what do they call it these days? Hmm, yes, devil's advocate. You don't take sides, but chastise everyone on every side so they may second guess their own abilities," Mira snapped. "But what of it when it's your abilities in question?"

"I don't care if my abilities are questioned. I know what I am capable of and I manage them well, until someone comes along and manipulates them." She gave Mira a pointed look, "and here you are again, trying to manipulate my abilities to round up our wayward sister, for I don't care what. I am not doing it. The last I heard, you had found a way to get close to her. Then you allowed a few idiots to screw it up. Why do you think I am way over here on the other side of the world? Did you not notice I am no longer in Coverton? She won't play nice this time when she gets her hands on you. I wanted nothing to do with your botched attempt at capturing her, and I want even less of her retribution when she comes for you."

"Yes, yes. The cowardly sister. The one who runs from everything. The one —"

Milena abruptly appeared in front of Mira, cutting her off mid-sentence. She stepped back, withdrawing the knife slowly. "Careful with your words, dear sister. I am neither one who runs nor am I one who is a coward. I removed myself from a situation I have no business in. Tell me, when would a coward place a blade in another in other than self-defense? *Oh yes*, she wouldn't."

MIRA SCREAMED HER FRUSTRATION TO the men in the room, "What is it with those blimey bitches and knives to my stomach?! Can't they think of anything more original than that?"

Carter covered his mouth in attempt to conceal his amusement. "You did call her a coward. What did you expect her to do? She was rubbing your nose into the mess you made. What was the purpose of your visit to her to begin with? To antagonize her or to get her help?"

"Oh, shut up," she muttered while she inspected her bloody shirt. "She has always been the passive one. How was I supposed to know she had a mean streak?"

"Did you just ask that? Didn't you say it was her doing that I can't go outside during the daylight hours? Isn't she the one responsible for me having to drink blood, of all things? Where did you ever get the idea she *doesn't* have a mean streak? Isn't it her reason for existence, to give people struggles?"

"Yes, it is, but technically it's not intended to be mean. Its intent is to '*build character*' or some such shite." She pulled her shirt over her head and dropped it to the floor as she made her way to the portable closet tucked in the corner of her tiny office.

She flipped through a few of the blouses she had hanging neatly on the left. Finding nothing suitable there, she moved to the top drawer under the shoes tucked away on the shelf below the hanging clothes. She whipped the white tee shirt off the top of the pile and slipped it on. "Where are we with the test subjects?"

"Would you like specifics or overall?" Dustin asked shyly.

She rolled her eyes and said, "Whichever version will get you the hell out of here faster."

Josh snorted a laugh which immediately earned him a death glare from Carter. "Right. Sorry," Josh cleared his throat, "specifically, there are two who can't control their shape, one either can't control her bloodlust or loves to rip everything apart we put in her cage, and a handful who are too lethargic to move once they have been fed."

"And that is why we need my sister." Mira sighed.

"Anything else?" Carter asked.

"Well, umm, there is the issue of my packmates…"

"What issue with your packmates?" Carter leaned forward on the small metal desk in the center of the room.

Terrance slowly shook his head at Josh, "I'm sorry, Bossman. We don't know exactly what the problem is. We only know Dom called and told us there were issues on the pack lands we would need to be home to deal with soon."

"Would this have anything to do with McIntosh killing your alpha? This is a problem already known."

The three shifters shrugged. "That's all he said," Dustin replied.

"Go find Dominique and get his ass in here. We'll deal with the rest later."

14

A lithe redhead appeared in the middle of our living room with blood dripping from her hands. A static electricity zap tingled over my skin, the hairs immediately standing on end. I couldn't quite place why, but the woman looked familiar and the sig she sent skating across my skin was similar to Mila's. It took me a moment to pull out of my shock to realize I did know her. Sort of. She was the skittish woman in the club.

"Oh, what the hell? Is it community service day at the Trottingwolf/Dragov house?" Alex huffed, throwing her hands in the air.

"Who are you?" Cason asked.

The woman ignored them both, finding Mila sitting on the couch. "Having a party?"

"If I were, there was a reason you were not invited," Mila countered quickly.

"Hmm. I should imagine so." The woman looked at her bloody hands, holding them up for all to see, "You mind if I use one of your sinks. This is turning quite sticky."

Mila rolled her eyes and pointed to the kitchen.

"Thanks," she turned in the direction Mila pointed, "oh, before I forget," she spun back around, "here's your knife back." In the blink of an eye, a knife was sailing across the room towards Mila. No one moved. We all sat or stood there in shocked silence while we waited to see if she would catch it or get impaled by the flying blade.

Mila caught the knife and let out a low chuckle, "Oh how wonderful, I haven't seen this in almost a hundred years."

The other woman let out a boisterous laugh, "I'll fill you in, in a moment. But first to wash away the sticky icky," she said holding both hands up, wiggling her bloody fingers. She turned once again and headed off into the kitchen this time. "Not a word until I get in there," she called from the other room, "I love a good suspense story as much as the next person."

Mila rolled her eyes again, this time with a smile on her face.

"Oooh, looky, looky. It's my hero," the woman chimed as she sashayed over to the seat next to Cason a few minutes later. "Mind if I sit by you, handsome?" She plopped down on the loveseat beside him without awaiting his answer.

"Heeey! You're the woman from the bar. Melanie, right?" Tia cocked an eyebrow up at the end of her question.

Mila and the woman giggled at Tia. "No, it's Milena, sweetheart," she said with a chuckle. "What's the gathering for, sweet ones?"

"You popped in on us," I announced, "is there something we can help *you* with?"

"You must be the lovely Lyssandra our dear Mila has been enraptured with these past few years," she said turning to face me. "Is there something special about you that has kept her tied to you? I can't quite tell."

"Who in the hell do you think you are? Popping into someone's house uninvited, throwing knives at people, insulting the other half of the people here?" I blurted.

"Now, now. That is no way to treat a guest," she smiled, "I did not throw a knife *at* anyone. I threw a knife *to* someone. If you are insulted by my question, and you alone are not half the people here by the way, then maybe it is you who is the clingy one of the situation. Whatever that may be."

"Tut-tut, sister," Mila cajoled, "you do have a way of saying things to sound one way and mean another. Don't start your drama here. We have enough going on without you bringing any nonsense in as well."

"Sister?" half of the people in the room spluttered while the other half opened and closed their mouths like gaping fish.

"Actually, that is exactly why I am here. Our dear sister paid me a visit today. I left Coverton this morning after the fiasco at the compound and she shows up at my Grecian home wanting to drag me into whatever nefariousness she is concocting. I was simply doing my sisterly duties by informing you she isn't letting things go."

"I figured as much," Mila sighed. "She isn't one to give up so easily. What were you doing here in the first place?"

"Oh, you know. A little of this, a little of that."

"No. I don't know, which is why I asked." Mila said, her Bulgarian accent becoming more pronounced as her agitation grew.

"Uh-uh. Don't start your maternal shite with me. We are the same age. We've never needed a mother. Don't pretend to be one now." Milena chastised. "She is up to no good again. I am sure you have noticed the spikes in power around here. If I could be drawn here because of it then surely you have felt it."

"Yes, I have. I do know a little of what is going on. There are others here who know even more than I do. Now, if you don't mind, we have some things to discuss."

"Aye. We do have things to discuss," Milena said with a sudden Irish accent. "And honestly it starts with Ms. Life-In-The-Box." She pointed a tiny finger at me.

"What did you call me?" I asked, bounding up from my seat. Bobby and Miguel grabbed an arm each and tried to pull me back down. I yanked my arms away from them, "No, seriously. What did you call me? Why would you call me that? What the fuck does it even mean?"

"Look, honey," she sat up to look me in the face, "I know about every single one of you here. And you are the weakest of them all," she waved her hand around the room at everyone. "I am not saying this to be cruel, but it is the honest truth." She stood up and stepped in front of Cason. "You are a bland. You may not have the ability to shift, make dirt form a wall, blend, or even run super-fast, but you can physically fight and you can block certain powers." She walked to Tia, "You are a coyote shifter. You grew up fighting in your own pack, so to say you can throw a punch would be an understatement." She slid over to Selby. "We all know what you are capable of, Elemental. Some of us saw it firsthand this morning. Right in the nads, isn't it so, Tysen the wolf shifter?" she shot Tysen a gleeful look. Tysen's gaze went out the window. The set of his jaw told us he didn't particularly care for the reminder. "And you, Reflector," she said as she stepped up to my brother, "why have you not taught little sister to fight or get her hands dirty if she needs to? She is going to need those skills if she is to survive what is coming."

"What's coming?" Alex asked, trying to not bounce out of her seat. I swear, if I had half of her energy.

Ignoring Alex, Milena made her way to Bobby. "You are an interesting thing. You have yet to tap into your full potential. You have the physical capabilities to fight, as well. You trained enough in… your past. You need to be her first trainer," she nodded her head at me, then sidestepped to stand in front of me. "And you darling. So, what? I get the silly American phrases wrong. What I mean is you always have to do everything so-so. Stop being so damn by the book or it will get you killed. You need to train with everyone here. Quit being so polite and nice, use people's powers against them. Tap into them without permission. Get some blood on your hands. Don't be afraid to break a bone, theirs or your own. No more working in a lab. You must learn to be alone. If you show up for work Monday, you are dead."

"Milena, what is all of this? It is not like you to come in and start throwing information and advice about." Mila looked puzzled by her sister's behavior.

"Since when? Am I not the Sudjaje of Misfortune and Dysfunction? Just because the misfortune or dysfunction isn't yours, doesn't mean it's not someone's," she winked, then a pool of mist was in her place, leaving us to look around at one another more confused than when she popped in.

15

After the shock of Milena's visit and announcements wore off, the room exploded into a cacophony of 'what the hell's' and 'what is that supposed to mean's.' Voices kept raising to be heard over another until no one could hear anyone else. Tysen let out an ear-piercing whistle, putting a stop to all talking.

"If she's to be believed, then we need to get to it," Tysen said once everyone quieted down. "I suggest we sit down and start sharing what we know. The more informed we are, the better the plan we can come up with."

Several of the guys grunted either disapproval or agreement, I'm not sure which. "Back to the kitchen. I need to feed everyone to make sure there are no hangry temper flares. Too many shifters for it not to happen," Mila pushed her way through the small crowd gathered in the living room.

Once we all were situated as best as possible in the now cramped space, Bobby got the conversation rolling, "Where to start? Tysen, how long have you and your pack been with BTCL?"

"Five years."

"Really? A long time." Miguel said.

"It is. And remember it wasn't by choice for many of us," he quickly added when he got scowls from Tia and Alex.

"Well, lucky for us it helps. It means we have plenty of information to start with," Jake commented.

"That's true," Cason said, "Selby's job was to run blood tests. Miguel, Lyssi, Alex, what do you do there? Exactly? I mean, I know, but we have a lot of new people here."

"We work in the main building lab, Lyssi and I do. Alex just eats everyone's food out of the fridge in the break room." Alex grabbed a spatula off the hanger next to her head and smacked Miguel hard. "Ow. We run blood tests and UAs. Once in a while, we'll fill in for someone in another area, but usually we stick to our own." Miguel laughed at his really old and really dumb joke, rubbing his shoulder where she hit him.

"You got jokes, don't you? Too bad they ain't funny," Alex tried to hit him again until Mila snatched the spatula from her.

"Don't use my kitchen utensils to hit the animals, Alexandria. It's cruel and unsanitary," Mila winked at Miguel, handing Alex a small frying pan.

"Oh shit!" Miguel squawked as he darted to the other side of the room behind Tia.

"Hey, no hiding behind me," Tia squealed, sitting in a chair and leaving Miguel to fend for himself.

"For real though," Alex started (which came out 'fo-reyal-doe') "I work in the endocrine and metabolic studies part of the clinic. If there are questionable spikes or drops in hormones or metabolisms, I'm the one who gets the patient files to study and hopefully help fix," she finished sounding more like the professional Alex we worked with instead of the laid back Alex we knew at home.

Bobby nodded, "I work in the lab on the top floor. We work with DNA and RNA. We try to locate the genetic codes to determine how illness and disease progress in some species yet lay dormant or are nonexistent in others."

"Well now we know what everyone does there, what's next?" the youngest looking shifter in Tysen's group asked.

"According to Milena, she" Cason pointed at me, "has got to start learning a few new tricks. And you," he aimed his finger at Bobby, "are supposed to start her torture — OW — ok, ok her training." He too was rubbing his shoulder where Alex whacked him, this time with the frying pan. "Did you really have to give her that thing, Mila?"

Mila didn't say a word. She just smiled and kept chugging along doing whatever she does when she gets into her cooking zone.

"How about we get introductions from the wolf pack over there? We got so wrapped up with all the excitement we forgot to ask who all you are," Tia offered.

"Yeah, right. Sorry guys," Tysen said pointing at himself then to each man in turn, "I'm Tysen. This is my pack's council. This is Marcus, Eli, Damien, Chris, Shawn, and Kendrick." They each gave a wave, wink, or thumbs up when they were pointed out.

"Lys, I think you and Bobby need to go outside to get started. We don't want Alex knocking the trainee or trainer out with the pan she is so happy to swing." Cason said with a grin, still rubbing his shoulder.

"You're either very brave or very stupid to talk such big talk next to a woman with a pan," Jake laughed.

"Meh, what's the difference?" Cason replied with a shrug.

BOBBY AND I WERE STANDING A FEW feet apart facing each other in the backyard looking like a couple of idiots, in my opinion. "Okay. So, what now?" I asked.

"Well, for starters, what did Milena tell you?"

"Which part? She said a lot of things."

Bobby nodded, "She did. But what did she tell you about tapping into other people's powers?"

"She said to tap into them without their permission."

"And," he motioned to keep going.

"And use them against them."

"Right. Have you tried to tap into anyone's powers yet?"

"No. She just told me to. We've all been a little preoccupied since she Jeannie'd her damn self out of here," I huffed.

He shook his head, pinching the bridge of his nose. "Lyssandra, take the hint and start tapping into my power."

"Oh. Um. It's called a sig. It's an energy signature which tells me wha—"

"Stop stalling. I don't need to know what you call it. We can talk about it after you have tapped it."

"Fine. You don't have to be an ass about it," I grumped, adding under my breath, "I wish Mila had given me a pan."

Bobby burst out laughing. "Oh man, you're adorable when you're acting like a baby."

"I am not acting like a baby. And who are you calling adorable, you ass?"

"You're right, I'm an ass. And you are acting more like an overindulged, whiny five-year-old."

"Over... You seriously—"

"Yeah, yeah. I know, I'm an ass. It seems to be your favorite name for me, but for the record, I like it better than *New Guy*. At least this one matches my character and tells me what you like looking at so hard," he winked.

"Oh, you…" I swung my right arm aiming to slap his cheek. I have no idea how it happened but the next thing I knew, he grabbed my wrist, twisted us both around, I was lying flat on my back behind where he had been standing seconds before, and he was nose to nose with me.

"You're cute when you're mad," he winked again. "First lesson is never let your emotions control your fight. Not the physical, the supernatural, or verbal fight. You will be too sloppy and make mistakes. Every time," he poked my nose once before pulling me to my feet. He. Poked. My. Nose.

I slapped his hands away. I was fuming and embarrassed. Heat rose in my cheeks, making me even more pissed. "Do you think this is funny?" I asked him as I stood back up.

"Should I? Probably, if I were an ass. But as it is, no, I don't. Well, sort of. Okay, I'm an ass."

"Yes, you are. I can't believe you just threw me on the ground and sat on top of me."

He stepped up to me, "First of all, you swung at me. Out of anger. If you had not swung at me, you would not have ended up on the ground so quickly. Second, I gave you the opportunity to start with the energy thing you do. And again, you swung. Third, I did not sit on you. But I will make a point to next time because you're letting your emotions rule your actions. You're also not paying attention to your opponent's movements at all times or you would have known exactly where I deliberately placed my body. Situational awareness will get you pretty far, too."

"What makes you think there will be a next time?" I thrust my chin in the air.

Within seconds I was somehow thrown on my back again. This time my wrists were pinned above my head and he was straddling my hips. "What made you think there wouldn't be?" He left out the humiliating nose pokes when he got up. He also left me lying there close to tears. He didn't walk away, which I was kind of thankful for because, because, well, I don't know why. It just seems wrong to walk away while someone you are supposed to call a friend is on the ground, and that is what someone who offers to help is, right? Yeah, I know, not always. But. (Sigh.)

"Do you want to continue the physical training or do you want to try your energy tapping thing yet?" He offered his hand. I slowly took it, fully expecting to be jerked to my feet. It didn't happen, so then I had all these mixed feelings. I was pissed because he tossed me around like a rag doll. I was humiliated because he tossed me around like a rag doll. I was confused because, yeah, you guessed it, he tossed me around like a rag doll.

"I think I should tap into your sig. Jake has a gym room he'll let me use for physical training. He's invited me over a few times to use it," I said, acting like I found a couple of leaves on the tree a few feet away rather interesting.

"Hey," he said, placing a hand on my shoulder, turning me around, "I'm not going to apologize for knocking you down. Things seem like they're going to get intense quick. We need you to be okay with conflict and ready to defend yourself at any cost. More importantly, we need you to be able to walk away from said conflict alive. Right now, luck will be what keeps you safe. I want you to have better odds than what lady luck says you can have."

Tears welled. I know it sounds stupid, but everything in the last twenty-four hours was finally starting to sink in. First was Mila's kidnapping, then the emotional ups and downs at the club with finding out one of the kidnappers was a former coworker of my brother's, the others finding a scent of one of the other kidnappers just to lose it, then Mila coming home all beat up and with one of her kidnappers, with terrible news of other people being hurt and killed, shifters showing up out of the blue, Milena popping in telling me I was going to get killed if I didn't shape up, and then being thrown around by a guy I actually kind of liked. It was all beginning to be too much for someone who was used to getting up, going to work, coming home to shower and eat, sleep, repeat.

"I've been up for over thirty-six hours. I'm tired. I want to go to bed soon. Let's get on with it," I sighed.

He shoved his hands into his jeans pockets, "I know, me, too. I haven't been through what you, Mila, and Selby have, but I can imagine you're exhausted. Ok, then do whatever you have to do to get my sig. We won't work on manipulating it tonight. Then we'll head back in and wrap up the activities inside so you can get some sleep."

I nodded then closed my eyes, which promptly got me a light thump on the forehead. "Don't close your eyes. It gives a false sense of security and prevents you from being able to see what's coming."

"Ugh. Would you stop touching my face?"

"Maybe. Have you got my sig yet?"

"Working on it." And I was. I began to get the sensation of bugs crawling on my skin. It wasn't the creepy, crawly, awful one, but more like the little tickles from a ladybug or butterfly. The feeling intensified as I concentrated harder. About the time it started to get uncomfortable, Bobby's hand appeared in front of my face and I pushed it away before he got a chance to touch me.

"Good. Your face was doing this funny thing making you look constipated," he chuckled, "I'm guessing you have my sig figured out?"

"Yeah, you feel like bugs all over me." I countered.

"Ha!" he leaned in and whispered, "stop trying to imagine what my hands all over you will feel like. I promise you bugs won't even cross your mind when the time comes." He turned away and went back in the house leaving me to my now

151

completely corrupt thoughts. I stopped for a split second. It took a few seconds, but I realized he said 'when'. Well, if that didn't add to the already dirty thoughts crossing my mind.

"Such a dick thing to do," I told myself as I followed him inside the house, not sure if I was referring to my mini-tantrum or him purposely giving me sweet, nasty images.

I drug my feet across the kitchen floor and flopped down on the kitchen chair closest to the door. Food was being set on the table, making many stomachs roll and growl. Jake brought a stack of paper plates and plastic utensils to the table. He pulled out the chair next to me and put his arm around my shoulder.

"Hey, sis. How you holding up?"

I answered with a grunt.

"That good, huh?"

Another grunt.

"This is new. You normally have much more to add to the conversations," he jiggled my shoulders.

I planted my forehead on the table in a not-so-soft manner, "Yeah? Normally I've had sleep, food, and no stress compared to this." I turned my head in his direction to look him in the face. "Don't think you've been a horrible big brother because she insinuated you didn't do your brotherly duties."

He looked me in the eyes, forehead wrinkled like he was trying to come up with the right words. Finally, he said, "I don't think I was horrible, but she was right. I could have been a better big brother."

"Stop your shit right there," I sat up, shoving my finger in his face. "There is no way you could have possibly imagined any of this. It's not your fault I don't know how to fight. I never had an interest in it. You can't force someone to like something they don't want to like. You have always been an amazing big bro. You've always made time for me, even if you thought whatever I needed you for was stupid. Out of everyone here, there is not one person I can trust or love or respect more."

"Aww. You're so sweet, Lab Rat," he said using his nickname for me since I fell in love with science in sixth grade, "but I really could have done more. I didn't teach you how to defend yourself. I did it for you because I knew you didn't like it. And it didn't help you in the long run, whether this crazy stuff happened or not. Think about it. If you were on your way to your car after working late one night and some jackass tried to mug you, what would you do? Give him your stuff and hope it's all he wants? No. It's not good enough."

"He's right," Eli chipped in. He looked back and forth between me and Jake a few times, "Sorry to interrupt, but he is right. Not everyone just wants your wallet. I'm not saying he's been a bad brother, but now you have an opportunity to change a few things, like learning self-defense, and now's the time to do so. I train the pack members to fight hand to hand. I'll be glad to step in and show you a few things."

I slumped forward again, letting my head thump back down on the table. "Ugh."

"I'd take the offer. He doesn't offer to train with anyone outside the pack," Shawn said, wiping the sweat off his forehead. "Is it me or is it hot in here? My gorgeous chocolate skin is going to melt if I get any hotter." He looked at Selby and blew her an air kiss, making her roll her eyes.

"Jake, she said you have a gym room?" Bobby piped up, trying not to laugh at Shawn's blatant flirting. "Do you think we can utilize it tomorrow?"

Shoot me now. I shook my head violently while Jake got this horrifying grin on his face, "Yeah. I'll give you the address. She'll be there early in the morning cuz she's staying the night with me tonight. Six sound good to you?"

"Sounds perfect," Bobby smiled an equally scary smile.

Seriously. Shoot. Me. Now.

16

It was five after six when I walked into Jake's wreck room. Well, that's what I was naming and calling his home gym. Because all I could see was my life being wrecked in this room. Room of doom? Nah, too cliché. The 'wreck room' it would forever be known as.

It was a typical home gym, I think. Exercise mats lined the center of the floor, weight sets, a treadmill, some gigantic rubber band thingy, and several other unnamable torture devices looked strategically placed around the room.

"You're late," came from the back corner in the room.

"Or you're early," I answered back.

"Nope. Pretty sure it's you who's late. Jake's out running. He left about an hour ago, so that only leaves you to rock the foundations with those earthquake forming snores."

"What? That's mean. And bullshit, I don't snore."

"Oh yeah? Let me guess, you stayed awake to find out."

"Shut up. You know that's impossible. Why do we need to be here so early? I doubt this is what Mila's crazy coot sister was talking about when she said to train."

He let out a soft chuckle, "She left it open to interpretation. Do you know the proper way to do stretches?"

"Of course, I know how to stretch. Everyone does," I crossed my arms over my chest.

"Uh huh. Do you have anything other than the baggy t-shirt you're wearing? It's going to hinder your movement," he pointed at me.

"I am not working out in a bikini or anything. You can get it out of your head," I scoffed.

"You put the thought in my head and then tell me not to think about it? You are a cruel woman," Bobby said as he stood up from where he was laying on one of the benches. My eyes didn't want to stay on his. They wanted to roam up and down, staying more down where his chest was already glistening with sweat. "And now you ogle me, after insinuating it's why I want you in something less baggy. My eyes are up here, ma'am," he snapped his fingers in my face.

"What? Who said it's why?" I asked, my face flushing.

He let it go and gestured to the mat, thankfully. "We'll start over there. I'm going to help you stretch, then see how hard your strikes are, and see if you have proper form when throwing a punch."

"I don't like you already," I grumbled.

"I know. I'm an ass," he shot me the first wink of the day.

I rolled my eyes at his antics. I sat down on the mat and reached for my toes.

"Yep. That's what I thought," he mumbled.

"What? What's what you thought?" I clipped, knowing he was already bitching about who knows what.

"I'm going to have to teach you how to stretch properly so you don't rip something. Reach for your toes again. Slowly." He squatted down next to me and placed his palm in the center of my back. He gave a gentle push, making my spine straighten. "Keep your back straight. If you can't lean all the way forward, it's okay. You'll get there. Keep your legs on the floor, don't allow your knee to bend, toes up."

I cut my eyes at him, glaring my most vicious glare. At least it's what I was going for. He just laughed at me. "How long do I do this?" I asked.

"Hold it for the count of ten. Do each leg ten times, then we'll move to the next set of muscles."

We stretched for about thirty minutes. Let me correct myself. *I* stretched for about thirty minutes

157

while he fussed about every part of my posture or movement being wrong. By the time I was done stretching I wanted to go back upstairs to do something productive for a Sunday morning, like watch senseless TV. But nooooo, we moved to the punching bag to see how hard I hit and so he could gripe about my form.

I stood in front of the bag while he stood next to me. "Aren't you supposed to be on the other side holding it or something?" I gave him by best version of the evil eye.

"I don't think it's going to be going anywhere just yet. Take your stance, but don't swing."

"Well, that's encouraging. Am I the first person you've ever trained? Cuz I am getting the impression you would have a hard time keeping a trainee around long enough to actually do any training."

My question only earned me a nod towards the bag. I turned, planted my feet shoulder width apart, held my fists up in the 'protect your face' pose I'd seen in the movies. He immediately popped the back of my hand, causing me to poke myself in the face under my eye with my thumb and punch my own nose.

"Ow! Son of a bitch, that hurt. Why did you do that? You were supposed to correct my pose if it was wrong."

"You won't hold your hands up like that again, will you?" he shrugged. "Some things are better self-corrected. Are you right or left handed?"

I rolled my eyes, "Right. Why?"

"Because you need to stand in a position to give your dominant hand the most force when you swing." He stood behind me with his hands on my hips. My body instantly flushed from the contact of his stomach against my back. I lost all train of thought until he tapped my right pelvic bone. "Pull this leg slightly back, turn your hips where your center of balance is, here," he then tapped my stomach. "Tuck your thumb in front of the other four fingers so you don't break your own bone when you hit. Elbows down to protect your sides, but not so wide your stomach will be an easy target. When you put your hands in front of your face, keep them away from your face, your arms taut, and your wrists straight. Now, punch."

I did. It. Was. Pathetic. The bag barely moved. "Ugh. Don't I need tape or something on my knuckles?"

"Why? If you have to fight hand to hand with someone one, are you going to say, *'time out, I need to tape up,'*" he said using the most horrible mimic of a girl's voice I'd ever heard. "If you're getting ready to fight in a life or death situation, you won't have time to worry about it. We'll tape you up when your body goes to stance automatically. Until then, you just need to focus on keeping your posture and form correct."

After another thirty minutes of bitching, moaning, groaning, and sweating, mostly from me, he decided the next round of torture needed

159

to be sit-ups (which I could do correctly, like two of them. But I did those two correctly, so it's a win in my book.) Next was pushups, then to the bar thingy he made me do pull ups and chin ups on. When I finished whining about how cruel and heartless he was, we did squats and leg thrusts. By the time this horrible, terrible work out was over, I stunk. My huge shirt was sticking to me, making it harder to move, which was difficult with my jello body anyway. I half crawled, half body drug myself to the stairs. I fell onto the bottom step and looked longingly at the door leading to freedom.

"Come on, Cookie Dough. You can get a shower in a bit. You need to rehydrate," he said helping me to a sitting position and handing me a bottle of water.

"Cookie Dough?" I arched an eyebrow at him.

"Yeah, it's what you said you wish you had been doing instead of training, right? I believe your exact words were *'I'd rather be eating cookie dough and watching senseless TV than looking at your face, right now.'*"

"Oh," I tried to avoid eye contact after the reminder because I remembered saying it.

He put his finger under my chin and tilted my head towards him, "It's all good. I was actually impressed you came up with something other than *'you're an ass'.*"

"No, it was a horrible thing to say. I'm sorry."

"Nuh-uh. The other thing Milena said is you need to stop being so nice. That's part of it. I know you don't really hate me, so we're good."

"She said you've yet to hit your potential. Do you know what she meant?"

It was his turn to look away. After a few beats he turned back, "You need any more water or are you ready to hit the shower yet?"

"Oh yes," I moaned. His eyebrow shot up, but other than that his expression didn't change. "I'm going to go get my stuff and shower. Will you still be here after I get out?"

"Yeah, I brought food for you to replenish your energy."

I nodded then headed up the stairs.

When I got out of the hottest shower I ever remember taking, Bobby had loaded the kitchen table with so much food, I initially thought Mila had been over. He had yogurts, boiled eggs, grilled chicken, fruits, veggies, whole wheat bread and bagels, fish, juices, and had somehow managed to get a shower before completing the smorgasbord of food prep.

"Where did all of this food come from? Jake eats at our house or does the take-out thing. There is no way all of this came from his fridge," I pondered.

"Nope. I brought it," he answered simply.

"Do you have a girlfriend or wife you normally cook for? This is just way too much for one person."

"Ha ha, no. I don't have a girlfriend or wife. This is from my house. What I didn't have I got from the store on the way here. I don't know what you like, so I figured I would get several things to choose from. You need protein and carbs after a good workout. Nothing here is bad for you." He got a confused look on his face for a minute. "Well, unless you're allergic to something. Do you have any allergies? I didn't even consider that when I brought all of this stuff."

It was my turn to laugh, "Yep. I am allergic to the rigorous workout you put me through."

With a wicked smile he said, "Well that's too bad. We do the same thing tomorrow morning at six sharp again."

I groaned as I pulled two plates out of the dishwasher. I set them down on the table and found several serving utensils mom and dad had left, along with a couple to eat with. "Really? Isn't it bad for the body to go so fast so quickly?" I hedged.

"Not as long as you do it right. Tomorrow will be cardio." He took a plate and loaded it with enough food to feed an entire football team.

"Holy shit, where is all that food going to? Tomorrow? You have to work tomorrow." I grabbed a boiled egg, a bagel, and some fruit with yogurt.

He patted his stomach, "All of this goes right here. Don't worry, you'll be eating quite a bit soon, too. I still workout every morning, whether I work or not. I'll just work out over here instead of going to the gym. You need to build a routine. I'll help you until you have the confidence to do it on your own, then you can meet me at the gym or we can work something else out."

I threw a blueberry at his face. It bounced off his nose, landing in his tuna. He shrugged, scooped up a forkful and shoved it in his mouth. "That," I said pointing my half-eaten egg at his plate, "was nasty." He gave another shoulder shrug and kept eating. "I think I am going to go home after I eat. I need to find out what the plans are."

"Sounds good. I'd like to talk to Miguel and Tysen. Do you think they'd be up for another meeting?"

"Maybe," I shrugged. "I think we need to talk to Selby and Tysen to find out what all really goes on out there at the compound. I mean, aside from experimenting on people. What kind of experiments do they do? Who do they experiment on? Are they using normies, shifters, elementals? What are they trying to accomplish?"

"Those are all really good questions. I think you're right about getting Selby and Tysen together. Maybe they can collaborate and fill in the blanks the other may not think are relevant." He stopped eating for a minute, "Did you just say *'normies'*?"

Jake walked in the back door, saving me from having to answer his question. "Wow, all of that did not come from my fridge." He snatched a boiled egg, tossed it in the air and caught the whole thing in his mouth like a piece of popcorn. "I'm hitting the shower then I am coming down to eat, so get what you want now," he said as he took off up the stairs.

Jake was back down in less than ten minutes dripping water everywhere. "Dry your hair,

163

Pocahontas," I said when he leaned over to grab some food, trailing water all down my arm. He pulled a handful of his hair around from the back and wrung it out on the top of my head. "You could use another shower. You got yogurt all over your lap," he pointed at my shorts.

"Ugh. Neanderthal." I yanked the towel off his shoulder and used it to clean the yogurt *he* pushed off of the table and onto me. "What are you doing today?" I asked, handing the towel back.

"I was thinking about going out to meet Tysen's pack. Cason and Tia want to go out there to see if there are any others who can shed some light on what's going on."

"Is that wise? They don't really know anyone out there." I asked.

"Yeah, it's cool. Cason and Eli seemed to have a bromance going on after all the serious stuff was over with last night."

"Have you talked to anyone this morning?" Bobby asked while handing out new bottles of water. "I want to meet up with Miguel and Selby today. I need to have some idea of what to keep an eye out for when I head back into work tomorrow."

"Not yet," Jake answered, "Miguel said he'd be back to Lyssi's by eleven. I think Selby stayed over there. She didn't want to go home since she started all the chaos. She figured it would be one of the first places they would look. She also said being around Mila would be one of her safest options right now because she broke the only device that can suppress Mila's powers."

"Have you tapped yet today?" Bobby nudged my foot to bring my attention to him.

"Yeah. A couple of times, but you said I couldn't tap out since we weren't wrestling." I stuck my tongue out at him.

"Ha. Ha. You know what I mean. You should be trying to figure out what you can do with my talents without my permission."

"That's sexual harassment," Jake snorted.

"Ugh, Jake," I smacked his arm, "not cool."

Bobby shot me a devious smile meaning he wouldn't have a problem with it.

"No. I need to know a little about what you are capable of doing before I try to utilize your abilities. I don't want to accidentally hurt someone."

"No, you don't," Jake said. "All you need to do is tap the sig and root around the energies you get. They'll be pretty self-explanatory as you sift through them."

"Since when?" I retorted.

"Since when you know what you're doing," he snapped back.

"Have you ever tapped a biokinetic?" Bobby asked.

"Nope," Jake answered.

"Give it a go then," Bobby said.

A few seconds later Jake no longer looked like Jake, but exactly like Bobby. My jaw went slack and all I could do was to stare. Bobby, the real one, clapped his hands. "No wonder you stare at my butt. It looks pretty good."

"Dude, it's still my ass you're checking out," Jake said.

I burst out laughing. "That is wrong on so many levels."

"You should be happy. You have two of me to check out now," Bobby said as he stood up and struck a pose to show off his behind.

"Eww. No. He's my brother. That's just nasty," my face twisted in disgust.

Jake returned to his normal appearance, "It's pretty easy, Lab Rat. You know how to sort through Miguel's energies. It's the same principle. You can control what parts of yourself shifts when you tap his sig. You can do the same with Bobby's."

I nodded and returned to the food on my plate. I finished off the fruit and yogurt and put my plate in the sink. "I'm heading home," I announced. "Hopefully someone will be up and ready to talk."

"Hang on, I'll drive you. I still want to catch Miguel." Bobby stated, "You got this?" he nodded to the food.

"Oh yeah, I got this alright," Jake said while piling more food on his plate. "You'll have to bring more tomorrow cuz this will all be gone before lunch."

17

Neither one of us spoke on the way back to my house. The silence had a comfort to it that would probably be uncomfortable for most people. I was finding I didn't have to fill the air with useless chatter with Bobby. I was also realizing I liked it. There aren't many things worse than awkward silence.

I took the quiet time to sort through the waves in his sig, making myself familiar with them. I could pick out a few and identify what the purpose was, but understanding how to manipulate it was another story altogether. I didn't feel comfortable trying anything in the car. It's not like with Miguel or Tia's sigs, I knew I would grow claws or sprout lengthy teeth if I wanted. For all I knew my head would swell up or I would turn my skin some weird shade of green.

"What are you so thoughtful about over there, Cookie Dough?" Bobby asked.

"Huh?" My thoughts were pulled to the here and now, "Oh, I was sorting through your sig trying to understand which waves of your sig does what."

"And?"

"And I would love to find out, but don't want to shrink down and get blown out the window or blow up and be stuck in your car."

He chuckled. "Reasonable. We'll go out in the backyard after we get back to your place if no one is up. If they are, then we'll head out there after we get done with the other stuff."

I preoccupied myself the rest of the way home with internal arguments about whether or not I should have further interest in where things could go with him. I couldn't figure out if one of us would be friend-zoned and, if so, which of us would be the one to zone the other.

We pulled up in the driveway and parked next to my Thunderbird. "Whoa, whose ride?" Bobby asked.

"Mine."

"Yours?" astonishment dripped from his voice.

"Yeah, my first car, actually. I bought it when I was sixteen and have had her since."

"That's... wow, that's awesome. Most of these beauties aren't running anymore."

"I know. I've dropped a pretty penny into keeping her on the road," I said as he inspected my car.

"Mind if I take her out for a spin later? It's been a minute since I've seen a classic quite like her."

I shrugged, "Shouldn't be a problem."

I walked into the house. The lack of conversation and laughter was a major contrast from the sounds of the night before. No one was up and about downstairs, so I went to my room. I threw last night and this morning's dirty clothes in the hamper, got a couple more sets of clothes ready to take over to Jake's house. If I was going to be on time for the training sessions, there was no way it was happening from my house.

"Hey. Hope I'm not intruding," Bobby said from the doorway.

"Nope, just getting a few things ready to take back to Jake's."

"Ah. You change your mind about the baggy clothes yet?"

I gave him another glare, "Yeah. I don't have much more than scrubs and jeans. I don't exactly plan on having my ass handed to me on a regular basis."

He laughed, "Nobody plans to get their asses handed to them, but it's what we're training to prevent, Cookie Dough."

I shoved a few more clothes in my gym bag rather aggressively. I hated the idea of being forced into training. I was not a physical person.

I wasn't one of the kids who liked to go play ball or one of the girls who insisted on cheerleading. I have always been more at home in a lab. Exploring the intricate details of the unknown. So many things made sense when you looked at the tiniest pieces of the most fundamental bases underneath a microscope. You can see why things function the way they do when you know what it takes to make them work. Information is what has always kept me moving forward. Not lifting heavy stuff just to be able to lift something even heavier. Not running for the sake of running. That stuff isn't pointless, but it's not me.

Bobby stood silently against the doorframe watching, hands in his pockets. "I feel like this is a repetitive question, but what's going through that pretty head of yours?" he asked after several minutes.

I slipped down on my bed and put my head in my hands. "I don't know. So much has happened, but not enough, ya know? Just a few days ago we find out there's some really bad guy out there doing all this bad stuff, aiming for someone close to me. We've more than likely, unknowingly, been part of it because of the general nature of our jobs. We don't even know who this bad guy really is, what he's up to, who he's hurting next, or how to stop him. Does that sum it up?"

"Yeah, it does." he sat down on the bed next to me. He folded his hands together, seeming to concentrate hard on his interlocked fingers. "I'm mixed about returning back to work. I know I would be of better use there to get information, but I don't want to go back and continue to help with experiments. After talking to Selby about how they process and label the work I've been part of, I am positive I've had a hand in those experiments. I didn't know what we were doing any more than you did. I don't want to go back and help hurt more people."

I blew out a deep breath readying myself for the rest of the day when Alex appeared in my doorway and yelled back behind her, "She and Bobby are up here in bed." I aimed to hit her in the face with the throw of a pillow, hitting her in the stomach instead.

Miguel came stomping up the stairs saying, "Really? They just met. It's about time she got out of her comfort zone." He was met with an attempted pillow to the face, too.

"Hey guys. Whatcha doin' up here?" Alex asked as she flopped herself down on the chair swing.

"Getting stuff to take to Jake's," I replied.

"Oh really?" she waggled her eyebrows like a teenage girl.

"Yes, really," I deadpanned.

"What you doin' in here, Bobby?" she asked in the same conspiratorial tone.

"Watching her get stuff to go to Jake's."

"If that's it, you two are boring," she sighed, letting her head fall back.

"Do you think either of you two would be allowed in here if we were doing anything else?" I asked them both.

Miguel shrugged and Alex remarked, "I don't know. Some people are into some freaky shit. Who knows what you two are into?"

"What we're into? Holy hell, woman. We've not held hands, hugged, or kissed. Don't be tryin' to throw us into bed together. We haven't known each other for forty-eight hours yet."

"Looks to be your loss, sweetheart," she looked at him like she was ready to take a bite, lip licking and all.

I swear my face turned every shade of red possible. Miguel had the whole knee-slap-snorting laugh going. Bobby either wisely or fearfully stayed silent. I'm not sure which because my face was buried in one of my many pillows.

"Oh. My. God. Get. Out, Alex. Take happy oinker over there with you. I'll be down in a minute."

Neither of them said anything when they left, but they didn't have to. They were making enough faces and hand gestures to do a twelve-year-old boy proud.

"I'm so, so —"

"I hope you aren't about to apologize for someone else's actions," Bobby interrupted me, trying to keep a straight face.

"Um. Well, yeah, I was. They were horrible."

"No, those were true friends. Part of it is the immature stuff we do to get under each other's skin."

"Not like that." I said waving my hand towards the door. "We aren't preteens anymore."

"Apparently you didn't get the memo. It sure looked like *that.*"

"Are you encouraging them?" I asked.

"Are they here to encourage?" he replied quickly. "Look, Lyssi. I've spent less than forty-eight hours with you, as you pointed out. So far, I see a good-hearted person who always tries to do the right thing, say the right thing, and be as responsible as possible. It's not a bad thing, but you should learn to go with the flow and live a little without those worries in the back of your head all the time. It's one of the things Milena was talking about. I can help with those goals."

"Is that so?"

"I think so," he scooted closer. My heart started to beat a little faster, my mouth dried up. Our physical contact had been limited up to this point and I was not sure how much of it I wanted to remain the same. I looked down at my hands not realizing I clasped them together when he sat down. I tried to keep my mind on anything other than our legs touching. One of his large hands engulfed both of mine, preventing me from wringing them more. It was all the contact my heart needed to run its own marathon. I'm not sure why I suddenly became so nervous, like I said, we aren't preteens anymore. I've kissed. I've had sex. But I wasn't looking for any kind of relationship. There were other things needing to be dealt with. There was a psycho out there kidnapping people, killing children, experimenting and torturing on only gods knows who. With the sobering thought I pulled my hands away. I got up, grabbed my bag and headed for the door.

"I'll see if Selby and Mila are up yet. You want to see if anyone has Tysen's number so we can try to get him over here?"

He nodded and followed me down the stairs.

By the time we made it downstairs, Mila, Selby, Alex, and Miguel were deep in conversation. I leaned against the counter, listening to the details of not much. As usual Alex and Miguel were turning a semi-serious conversation into something light. I guess Selby could have used the tension breaker. It had been nothing but chaos for her these last few days. Soon enough, Miguel and Alex were hitting each other and name calling. Selby was laughing and Mila stood in her favorite spot, at the stove with a smile on her face. Bobby leaned on the counter beside me and took the bag off my shoulder. He set it down on the floor next to the doorway, reached over and slipped my hand into his. I froze as all banter and laughter stopped. I expected hoots and catcalls from at least Alex, but no one said anything. The silliness and jokes began back up as if nothing had happened.

"Whatcha cookin', Momma Mila?" Alex asked.

"Eggs, bruschetta, ham and turkey rolls, to go with the Greek yogurt with berries."

"Ooooh, yummy," she rubbed her stomach in appreciation.

"Anyone get Tysen's number?" Bobby asked a few minutes later.

"I did," Miguel said, "he said he'd be over after Cason and Tia had the proper pack introductions. He wanted to make sure some guy didn't start shit just because."

"We already ate after training this morning. You guys eat. We're going out back to get some practice with the whole energy tapping thing she does," Bobby tugged on my hand, leading me outside.

He let go once we got out to the oak tree occupying the middle of the yard, sitting down and leaning against it, "What do you need help with? I may not know exactly what you do, but if you can explain it the best you can, I might be able to guide you in the right direction."

"Sounds fair," I sat down in front of him and concentrated on his now familiar sig. I still got the feeling of tickly legs, but it wasn't the awkward feeling it had been. I searched the waves and found most really were self-explanatory like Jake said. I began to pull and twist the energy until I had a firm grasp on a few strands. The best way to explain it is like this: if you have a blanket with large patterns sewn on it and a few of the strings are loose and hanging, you can take those strands, braid them or weave them together to create a new design. The blanket may not look the best, but the strands are still there, still functioning. This is similar.

I pulled one of the strands, wrapping it around my right arm where I wanted to attempt changing some physical aspect. I thought about what I wanted to change. I tried to think about building muscle, to make my arm thicker. The tingly sensation of change spread up my arm. My muscles burned as they stretched, bones cracked, snapped, and popped uncomfortably as they reshaped themselves. Not the results I wanted. Oh, my arm got thicker alright, but it turned into an elephant leg instead of a well-toned arm. Wrinkled, gray, calloused, extremely thick, no individually separate metacarpals — uh, fingers — but now thick metatarsals — um, toes — the whole shebang.

I let out a scream, probably waking the dead in every cemetery within a hundred miles. And damn, the thing was so heavy I couldn't lift it. It thumped the ground with so much force it put a hole in the earth. Bobby fell over laughing, holding his stomach.

"Stop laughing and help me," I shrieked. "What did I do? How do I change it back?"

I tried and tried to get the image of my own arm in my head, but no matter how much I visualized it, nothing happened. Okay, I lied. The horrible happened. Here I am, perfectly not fine, in the midst of a panic attack, and my left arm decides it wants to be like the right one. The tingly feeling spread over my arm, just like it did a few moments before with the other one. The same sensations followed, then I didn't have one, but two elephant legs instead of arms.

REFLECTED

I don't think there are words to accurately describe the noise coming from deep within my lungs and out of my mouth. After a good solid three or four minutes laughing, with tears rolling down his face, Bobby got himself together enough to be some sort of help. With a hand on each cheek, he coaxed me to a semi-calm state.

"Calm down, Cookie Dough." I violently shook my head in disbelief. "You have to calm down before you give yourself an elephant trunk or rhino horn," he said calmly.

"A trunk or horn?" I squeaked, tears slipping down my cheeks.

"Shhhh," he chuckled, "chill out a minute. Get your breathing and thoughts under control. You're still tapped. I'll walk you through it to get you back to normal. What did you think of when you tried to change?"

"I... I thought about making my muscles thicker," I sniffled.

"I figured it was something along those lines. When you first start off, you have to adjust the outside appearance. The internal characteristics, traits, and physiology will do what needs to be done on its own. Once you have mastered the general appearance of what you want, then we will move to the internal manipulations. Take a deep breath, keep your eyes on mine and picture yourself the way you're supposed to be."

I shook my head again, stopped, realizing I was telling him no and nodded instead. I took a calming breath, then another. When my breathing returned to somewhat normal, I tapped his sig again. I pictured myself on a good day. My arms tingled for a couple of seconds then became lighter as they began to shrink, the bones return to normal, cracking and popping.

I flexed my fingers in relief. I let out a happy shriek and launched myself at him out of joy. The force of my launch sent us both sprawling on the ground, with me laying on top of his solid body.

"Ooh, I'm sorry," I rolled off him as quickly as I could.

He kept one arm around my waist, "No need to be."

I pulled away and sat up. I offered my hand to help him sit up, but he brushed it away. "No thanks, I'm good right where I am. Why don't you try another look. Elephant arms really aren't your thing."

I giggled, "Okay, so you do it. Walk me through what you do to change appearance."

"It's like I said," his body rippled a little, then I was looking at a Miguel double, "think about an outer appearance and let your cells do the work. It's easier for me if I've touched a person." My face scrunched in confusion, so he explained, "Take Miguel for example. I've shaken his hand, so I can transform into his shape. I will even carry his birthmark if he has one. Now, if I have never touched the person, say Eli," I blinked and an Eli duplicate was laying in front of me, "I won't be able to generate a perfect match. I'll only be able to change to what I've seen. And then I might still get it wrong. I picked a random eye color because I don't know what color his eyes really are and I didn't have his cells in my database." He tapped his temple for emphasis and returned to himself.

"Alright, so if I wanted to duplicate someone I have never touched, could I do so using your database or do I have to touch them myself?"

"I'm not sure. I've never coached someone like you. What are you called again?"

"I'm a reflector."

"Give it a try. Try to copy someone you are familiar with, though. It will be easier."

I reached for his sig again and pictured Tia, short pink spikes included. I wanted to see if I could manipulate things that were not natural, like her extreme hair colors. Tingles swept over my body as I began to change.

"Well, that... is different," he said.

I looked down at myself. "Well shit."

"What did you think about this time? Last time I saw Tia, she was not pink."

"That answers my question."

He laughed again, "What question?"

"I wanted to see if I could also mimic unnatural things on a person. Tia's hair is not naturally pink."

He arched an eyebrow and did this head nod thing back and forth, "Reasonable, but I think you over shot it a little."

"Ya think?"

"Hey, Lyssi," Miguel called from behind me. Without thinking about how I looked, I turned around and immediately heard the 'click, click, click' from his phone camera.

"Dammit, Miguel," I yelled as I got up and took off running after him.

He ran inside where I was greeted by a room full of friends and shifters who stopped what they were doing to stare.

"Somebody put dye in the pretty smelling bath bombs?" Kendrick, I think his name was, asked.

"Miguel Alvarez Ballesteros," I huffed, "give me that phone. Or so help me, I'll—"

"You'll what?" he teased, holding the phone out of my reach, "turn me green like the hulk? I can dig."

"Miguel, you shouldn't tease her like that. Can't you see by her skin color, her bp is already up?" Alex snickered.

I took the small frying pan Mila suddenly appeared with and the chase was on again. As I went by I smacked Alex on her shoulder, "It'll be Shrek, not the Hulk."

"Ow. Damn, heifer. That hurt," she yelled as we went out the back door again.

"Bobby," Miguel called, "grab Princess Poppy before she gets into trouble."

"Who?" he looked around trying to find this Poppy person.

"Her," Miguel pointed back at me.

"Who the hell is Princess Poppy?" Bobby mused, laughing.

REFLECTED

"She's the princess troll in the movie *'Trolls'*. How do you not know who Princess Poppy is?" Miguel chided.

"The question is how in the hell do *you* know who she is?" I asked, stopping with my hands on my knees to catch my breath — hey, it's a big yard.

"Disney and Pixar movies are the best. How do you live with yourself not knowing what our youth is into?" Miguel asked, stopping behind the tree to catch his.

"You two are nuts," Bobby said.

"Watch it, buddy. I got Alex with this already," I brandished the pan, "he's next. I'll start a full-blown list if I need to."

He held his hands up, "You want to return to normal so I can take you seriously or do we have to Netflix Trolls?" He turned, whispering to Miguel, "It is on Netflix, right?"

Miguel shrugged, "I think so. I watched it with Cason's niece a few months ago. I didn't know you could watch a movie 157 times in one day."

A few seconds later Alex snatched the pan out of my hand, swung the damn thing like a baseball bat and hit me in the ass. I shot up in the air with a screech, holding my tender backside. Both men fell out laughing while Alex started in on me, "Don't hit me with my own weapon."

"Your weapon? That is Mila's pan, which she gave to me."

"She gave it to me first."

"It came out of my house."

"I'll show you what comes out of your house if you hit me with my own munitions again."

"Oh, for fuck's sake. Take the damn pan, Babe Ruth. But if you hit me with it like that again, you're gonna need surgery to remove it from your ass."

She turned and strutted her not-so-happy-self back into the house.

"You're gonna ass-shake yourself right off the planet," Miguel called to her, which promptly got him more butt wiggles and a middle finger from Alex.

Bobby gasped for breath as he said, "I don't think I could've done anything more entertaining today. What is it with you guys and the name calling? You come up with some crazy shit."

I shrugged my shoulder, "It's our thing. We've been doing it since we were kids. And you seem to be falling right in with us." I gave him a pointed look.

"I think I am. It's catchy." he said, wiping the tears off his face.

I took hold of his sig and pictured myself like I did earlier. The tingles sliding over my body brought a mental comfort I hadn't experienced before. I looked down to find myself back to normal once again. "I think I'll stick to practicing the natural looks for now."

"It would probably be the smartest choice you've made all week," Miguel called, still hiding behind the tree, hopefully deleting those pics out of his phone.

"Who's next on your list to try?" Bobby asked.

"I don't know. I hadn't made it that far in my planning. The plans keep getting spoiled by some weird effects."

"Wait, you mean you've already had at least one other body flub up?"

I shot Bobby a look telling him to shut it, "You could say that."

"And you didn't call us out here?"

"No. What's the other guy here for?" I shifted the focus of the conversation from myself.

"Huh? What other guy?" Miguel gave me a puzzled look, "Oh, Kendrick?"

"Yeah, him. Did Tysen come with him?"

"He was in the living room when I came out here. I think he and Selby are comparing notes or something."

"We need in on that conversation," Bobby said as he got up off the ground.

All three of us went back into the house where the smells of Mila's food were overpowering. My stomach growled in response. I pulled a piece of bruschetta off the top of the pile and made my way to the living room.

"— are not left without tamers." Tysen was saying when we walked in.

"What's not left without tamers?" Miguel asked.

"The test subjects," he replied.

"Is that what they're being called? The asshole. What are they testing and who are they testing it on?" I asked.

"I don't know what they're testing, but they're testing on shifters, elementals, vampires, blands, and whatever else they can get a hold of. I don't think they are being picky," Kendrick told us as he shoved a forkful of eggs in his mouth.

"Why are the guards being called tamers? Do they train the subjects to be controlled like animals?" Mila asked.

I pictured people on leashes like dogs earning body part treats from the suggestion of her question, shivering with the thought.

"I think it's because it sounds better. So far, we haven't been able to control anyone, but it sounds better in public to say tamer instead of guards." Tysen sank back into the couch.

"Obviously BTCL is behind this, but who is behind BTCL? My sister is smart, but she's not build a multi-million-dollar company to get what she wants smart. That takes work and she's allergic to it." Mila pointed out.

"We don't know. We know the man who runs the place is called Bossman. We all know Mira. She's tried to fuck half of the men there and manipulate the other half to kill the ones she slept with," Kendrick said.

"The CEO of the company is some guy from Europe, and he's not been to the main building since I've been there," Alex told us, "and I'm pretty sure I've been there the longest of us."

"Do you think the corporate heads know what is going on?" I asked.

"I don't know, but I am pretty sure it's not just my imagination that things are getting out of hand. I overheard Josh getting reamed by Dom about how the test subjects are needing more injections. Something didn't sit right with me about it. I was sent down to talk to Mila and when I got back upstairs, Josh was standing too close to the door for coincidence. I think someone is taking liberties with whatever they are injecting them with. Dom wasn't smart enough to come up with a plan to fuck it up all on his own." Selby explained.

"Even if Dom was smart enough, the job paid too good for him to want to fuck it up," Tysen added, "he's already let us know he doesn't approve of screwing up the deal Darrell signed us all up for."

"So, who else is pulling strings over there? What's the end game of all the players?" Miguel asked.

"Who in the hell are all the players?" Kendrick chimed in.

18

Are they ready?" Carter asked as he dropped his jacket on the back of the chair.

"Not yet, sir." Josh kept his gaze to the floor.

"Then why are you in here?"

"I was told to inform you the injections will be ready late this afternoon. The second round didn't go so well."

"Did he say what time this afternoon?"

Josh pulled his eyes from the spot on the floor to peek at Carter, "He said no earlier than 4:30 or so. We also had instructions on how to prep the subjects. Do you want those details?"

"No. Come find me at four. I'll decide then if I want to watch. So far you have all been a disappointment. I won't continue to tolerate it."

Josh nodded his head and made a beeline for the door.

Carter rolled his sleeves up and made his way to the holding cells. There was a certain individual who required his undivided attention. She wouldn't be going anywhere, but the sooner he introduced himself, the better.

"How has your stay been?" he asked her. She jumped, letting out a timid squeak. She pushed herself into the wall, trying to get as far away as possible, whimpering and covering her bruised face. He sat down easily next to her, causing the mattress to groan its disdain. He gently pulled her hands away from her face, taking care with his hand not to hurt her while inspect the damage done. "We'll get you all fixed," he said, biting into his wrist. She cringed and jerked away, eyes wide. He grabbed her jaw, digging his fingers slightly into her cheeks. He eased her head back to hold her mouth open enough to allow the trickling blood to drip into her mouth when he held his wrist above her. She tried to close her mouth which only resulted in her biting the inside of her cheeks.

Her bruising began fading and he pulled his wrist back to lick the wounds. "There. You'll be good as new in a few minutes when the blood is done working."

She sat back with a horrified expression across her face, "Why would you do that? What do you want? Why am I locked in here?"

"Slow down. One question at a time. Which do you want the answer to first?"

"Why am I here?"

"Because you will be an excellent leverage tool."

"For what? What do you want?"

"Oh, it's nothing to concern yourself with yet. Are you eating? Are they treating you well?"

"In comparison to what? The punching bag in the gym? The chew toys given to puppies?" she barked out a bitter laugh.

"Mmm. You have spunk. I like you. If you behave, I will see about releasing you to roam freely in the room," he tugged one of the chains bolted to the floor, "then we can work on leaving the room."

"Right. Like you plan on letting me live."

"I have no desire to kill children. I don't know where you would get such an idea," he cajoled.

"Your fucking monsters killed my seventeen-year-old brother and threatened to kill me," she screamed, "they used me as a chew toy for those… those… things out there in cages. How can you say you have no desire to kill children?"

Carter's face instantly shifted from one of false sympathy to detached coldness, "Is that so? Who killed your brother? Who threw you in the cage?"

"Like you don't know," she stated flatly.

"If I knew, I wouldn't ask," he bit back, fangs descending.

She shrunk back again, confused by his switch in demeanor, "Dominique, Josh, and the other one that follows them. I don't know his name. They never used it or I was too scared to pay attention."

"If you were too scared, how do you know the others' names?" he asked harshly.

"They talk a lot," she whispered.

"Mmm, that they do," he replied before speeding out of the room.

Carter slowed his pace while he schooled his features. He took the twists and turns blindly, lost in thought as he made his way to the cages. Many hundreds of years had taught him the element of surprise was a wonderful means to instill fear.

"Josh," Carter called out to the room where cages upon cages were lined up. The first row of cages held nothing but shredded mattresses, upturned buckets, and discarded bowls that once held food or water. Cages rattled and shook the further into the room they went. Several rows in, the occupants became more hostile than the previous rows where fear, melancholy, and depression dominated their demeanor. The warehouse smelled of fear, anger, excitement, piss, and shit making him thankful he didn't have to breathe like the shifters who worked here.

Josh popped his head out of the doorway at the end of the room, "Yeah, boss?" The room he was in was supposed to be for supplies, but the dumb asses brought a television and small stereo, which both could be heard at the other end of the warehouse, even if only because of his enhanced hearing.

"Who went with you and Dom to pick up the girl?"

Josh's face scrunched in thought for a moment, "Oh, it was me, Dom, and Dustin."

"Get everyone out here. We have a few things to discuss," Carter walked to a space large enough to hold everyone working.

"Dom still hasn't made it back, but you got it, Bossman," he disappeared back behind the door frame.

Carter stood with his hands clasped behind his back while the shifters crammed themselves into the small area. The rattling cages and screaming occupants sent a shiver or two down a few backs. Carter was taking in every detail of each shifter. The wolf shifters looked everywhere except at him, while some of the cat shifters took in everything about him. Some of the others shifted from foot to foot, obviously not wanting to be standing there.

Josh and Dustin were standing next to each other at the front of the group. Without warning, Carter sped to where they stood, grabbed Dustin by the throat and Josh by the jaw. Holding Dustin in place, he swiftly jerked Josh's head to the side and bit. He drank deeply, drank down all his blood, and dropped his lifeless body to the floor with a loud thump. Fangs still extended, face covered in blood, he turned to Dustin. "Who killed her brother?"

"D-d-dom,"

"And who threw her in the cages?"

"J-j-j-josh,"

"And what was your role in her torture?"

"I... I... I only held her. I held her while they... did what they did."

Carter's elongated nails dug into the side of Dustin's neck, "Sounds fair to me. I'll only hold you while it does what it does."

Carter shoved his way through the small crowd of shifters to the end row of cages dragging a screaming and kicking Dustin the entire way. He walked to the third cage from the end where a particularly small but feral looking woman was screeching. Her hair, face, hands, and arms were covered in dirt and dried blood. Her dress was torn, the patterns and colors were unrecognizable. His voice barely above a whisper, "Move back," he commanded her. She quieted slightly and stepped back until her back hit the bars behind her. Dustin's screams became louder as Carter jerked the cage door open, breaking the lock. "A free meal," Carter said as he shoved Dustin into the cage, still holding him by his throat. The woman's fingers stretched out as she screeched, launching herself at the shifter who was fighting to pull away from the death grip holding him in place. It took her only minutes to rip his body enough to where the shock quieted his screams and stilled his flailing body. Carter held him until the light fled his eyes, then dropped him as carelessly as he had Josh's limp form. The woman fell with Dustin, all of her focus on the fresh kill before her. Turning to the shifters who had followed quietly he said, "Let that be a lesson to any of you who feel you have any bright ideas of your own. If I send you to do a task, do that one task as directed. Don't make your own deviations or ad lib. When she is done eating," he pointed back to the woman, "get her into another cage. And someone find me that fucking scientist!"

CARTER SLAMMED THE DOOR WHEN HE entered the office. He stood for several moments with his hands on his hips attempting to reign in his anger. He knew he would eventually have to do something about the idiocy that had been allowed to linger in the employees, but killing all of them would mean starting over, which took time. Time, he did not have.

He snatched his jacket off of the chair and pulled out his phone. The woman answered before the third ring, "Speak." Carter let out a low growl, showing his disapproval. She made no sound to indicate his tone bothered her.

"I need you to be back by the end of the week. I have someone I need you to bring back to me."

"Bring back? You had them and let them go? That doesn't sound like you, Guthorm."

"How many times do I have to remind you of what will happen if you continue to use my given name? These shifters are a problem. Their incompetence is causing more problems than they are worth. I don't know why I listened to her."

"Oh, posh. You already killed me once, making me do plenty of the unthinkable, what more can you do to me? You'll continue to put up with it as long as you need me. I told you the shifters were no good. You should have hired my vampires to begin with. One of these days you will learn to listen to me."

"May I remind you, you are the reason the witches killed me first? What's the new saying? Payback's a bitch? They are not your vampires, as your sire, they are mine. You forget your place, Gunhild," Carter snapped.

"Emilia, Carter. Do you want the same two as before?"

"Yes, and two more with you. And you better know, if you bring me morons, I will rip their heads off and have you sitting with my test subjects for a week. Do not push me."

A light laugh filled his ear before the call was ended.

19

The next week sucked just as much as I thought it would. Monday morning (and every stupid morning thereafter) Bobby was at Jake's house at the buttcrack of dawn as promised to start training. I complained in hopes to discourage him, to no avail. He still dragged me out of bed by my feet. I still shuffled in misery to the wreck room.

I was already miffed about not being able to stay at my own house, but the fact Mila was staying with Alex, and Selby was staying with Tia made the hit to my ego a little less bruising. Too bad I couldn't say the same for my poor body. The hour and a half of physical training in the mornings had my muscles, some of which I didn't even know existed, hurting like a mofo. I had bruises defying explanation.

True to my begrudging word, I didn't leave Jake's house without someone with me, nor did I try to sneak back home for anything when we did leave the house. Every morning Bobby brought breakfast and each evening Alex and Mila provided dinner. Gods knew if it were up to Jake to bring in groceries, we'd have starved to death or had a massive heart attack from the fast food garbage he ate.

Throughout the week I found various things to occupy myself between hours of boredom. I reread the BioTech Chemlabs handbook front to back looking for clues as to who the main proprietor was. I snooped through all of the drawers in the house to see how long it would take Jake to notice I was messing with his stuff. You know, my sisterly duties. Laundry was not my chore of choice but working out with Bobby every morning left me with no options if I didn't want to smell like an overused gym sock every day. One chore usually led to another until the whole house was cleaned, and with how many shifters were in and out so often, the floors and dishes seemed to stay dirty. After all the cleaning I would make time to try and read something that might help figure out what we needed to do, but the only thing Jake had around the house to read were instructions on the back of the cleaning supplies. I was lucky Bobby had started BTCL such a short time ago and still had his paperwork from HR that included a handbook. Mine had long since disappeared somewhere in my closet ages ago. The funny thing was, I didn't really allow myself time to watch senseless TV like I complained about wanting to do.

We had all agreed to meet back up here at Jake's house on Friday evening to share news before going out. I was beyond excited to finally have a few people to interact with. Even though I kept myself busy, the house got rather quiet and boring after Jake and Bobby left for the day to go to work. I was developing cabin fever, further driving myself stir-crazy. I enjoyed the meals we shared together in the mornings and evenings, but everyone rushed off so quickly it wasn't enough to fill the gap that had sunk deep within my chest. I was accustomed to getting up and going to work every day. I don't know how people stay at home, I would lose it if I had to. Or I would be too excitable for civilized conversation and get myself thrown in the looney bin.

Everyone, including Tysen, Kendrick, and Eli, showed up between 5:30 and 7:15. Mila, as expected, brought enough food to feed a small nation. Of course, there were hardly any leftovers once all the shifters dug in. All in all, though, it was a great way to start conversations.

"Not a damn thing worth mentioning happened at work," Alex announced.

"Nothing to really discuss on my end either," Miguel added, "unless you want to count having to run the same person's blood three times a day and urine five times every other day."

"Why? Were the results off or the machines not calibrated properly?" I asked.

"No, the machines were fine. Every time I ran the sample one or more of the numbers fluctuated."

"By how much?" I wondered.

"Enough to wonder if it was the same species, let alone the same person."

"Same species? What do you mean? Why don't you think it wouldn't be the same individual?" Bobby perked up, now fully interested in the conversation.

"Yeah, no. I meant the same species." Miguel looked at the confused faces and proceeded with an eye roll, "Okay. So, it's like this," he cleared his throat, "running blood tests means that we do a CBC, or complete blood count. Each species has their own normal ranges. For example, female humans have a normal range of red blood cells valuing anywhere between 4.2 to 5.4 million per microliter and male humans are ranged from 4.7 to 6.1 million per microl— OW. What was that for?"

"We don't need the nerdy end of it you ass, just get to the point. This isn't a damn classroom," Alex said as she smacked him on the back of the head twice.

"So help me woman, if you hit me one more time," everyone but Alex drew back from the look he was giving her.

"Alright, normal ranges for each species..." I prompted to get him back on track.

With one last go-to-hell look at Alex, he turned back to the conversation. "As I was saying before I was so rudely interrupted, each species has its own normal red and white blood cell range. For dogs, the RBC is on the bottom at around 5.5 to 8.5 percent per microliter. Cats are slightly higher at 6.1 to 11 per microliter and a human's is in the 40 to 45 percent range. Now, as shifters, those numbers are going to be essentially similar to our animal's, but higher than both. Myself being a jaguar, my normal range is going to be around 18.5 million per microliter. Tysen, being a wolf, would have a norm of 14.6 million per microliter. With me so far?" Those of us who are familiar with lab works nodded our heads while the rest of them gave solid no's.

"Okay, I got this for a minute, Miguel. The best way to simplify what he is explaining is to say because of a shifter's animal, his or her blood cell count would be higher than a normal human's. The type of animal they are would determine how much higher the blood count is. But no matter what he or she is, there's a set range for their particular species, whether it be feline, human, canine, or shifter." I looked to Miguel to make sure it was the message he was trying to relay. He gave me a single nod, so I took it as my cue to continue, "I'm assuming since you had to run multiple tests, on the same individual, several times in one week, the numbers did not fit within the normal range of the species he or she is supposed to be?"

"Bingo," Miguel yelled, jumping up and knocking his chair over. He continued, pacing the floor, in the zone, "now, the blood I tested multiple times showed values belonging to different species. Let's say the blood tested in the normal range for a dog. Odd right, since we work with humans and shifters only? I would rerun the same blood test, on blood from the same tube, and the test results would have normal ranges for an ordinary human. I reran the test again, same tube, shifter ranges. Yet again, different species. How can I have three species from one tube?"

"Why didn't you just say so?" Alex added with a smirk. It was Miguel's turn to smack Alex, though he was nowhere near as rough and way more playful.

"Well what's the significance in that?" Tia asked shyly. She was never one who really cared to engage in shop talk. She wasn't stupid by any means, but occasionally we accidentally talked over her head.

"It suggests they need a scientist back at the warehouse if Miguel is getting the blood work I used to be doing," Selby answered. "They are not going to want fluctuating test results out there for just anyone to read, but they still have to have the results ran to know where they stand with the stability of whatever they are injecting. Were you able to pick up any foreign traces in the blood or urine you ran?"

"No, I was doing the typical tests. There was no reason for me to check initially. By the time my suspicions were like ding, ding," he gestured around his head with a finger, "the blood samples were no good or all used up."

"It also means the tests are either inconclusive because the results were not steady or the injection had not finished doing whatever it was designed to do." Bobby added.

"Is there a way to get a sample of the injection to Miguel or Bobby," I asked Tysen.

Tysen, Kendrick, and Eli all shook their heads, "Not as long as we're all out on leave. I was going to try and catch Josh or Dustin when they got off work, but Terrance came home Monday afternoon rattled all to hell. He was talking in circles for days about things eating and none of it made any sense until Tracey could calm him down enough to talk right. When she got him settled, he said the day before Bossman had torn into Josh's throat and fed Dustin to one of those things alive. We don't have any more shifters there from our pack other than Dom. We know a few other shifters who may be able to help, but they won't exactly be jumping in line to be the first if Bossman is feeding the tamers to the subjects and ripping out throats."

"Wait," Jake held up his hand, "Is this Bossman a shifter, too?"

"Nope," Eli said with a loud pop when pronouncing the 'p', "he's a vamp."

"Oh, for fuckity shit's sakes," Cason exhaled. Conversation stopped as we all turned to look at him in disbelief. "What?" he continued, "those things are bad news. I can't do anything against them, and how bad is this son of a bitch if he can kill one shifter with his damn teeth and feed the another one to a caged thing all in the same day? You shifters are not easy to kill. And he took out two of you."

"Holy hell, Cason. Did you have a bad day?" Tia asked.

"Sounds more like a bad week," Alex chimed in, "Boo, you need to go get some booty rubs if you gonna be all crabby."

"Make fun of me if you want, but I am telling you. This dude is not going to be easy to bring down. I'm not saying it just because he is a vampire, but really, think about what all he has going for him. He has a major company, which screams financial backing. Not only does he own, or at least half own, a major company, but it's a biogenetic company and also means the technical advances, some we probably don't even know about. Which brings me up to another point, if he is a partner, who is the other partner? Is Mira involved in the company or is she just hanging around for the benefits? What is her role in this? She is a fucking goddess for fuck's sake."

Mila moved away from her normal place by the stove and approached Cason. He was a bit on guard and flinched back when she did. She gently placed a hand on each cheek, turning him so they were eye to eye. "Cason, darling. Calm down." As she said the words, her hands lit up a light blue. The tension seemed to dissipate almost instantly; his shoulders slumped, back slouched, arms relaxed, fists unclenched. "You seem to forget, one of the triplets is definitely on your side, and quite possibly a second. Even if Milena doesn't take any further direct action in this, she has already shown she will not stand against us."

He closed his eyes as he pulled her into his arms, "Thanks, Momma Mila. I guess I needed your reassurances."

She harrumphed as she untangled herself and went back to her favorite spot. "Although the panic could have been left out of it, he does bring up very good points. Is this Bossman running the show alone or will we have someone after us after he has been dealt with? I can handle my sisters. You guys don't really need to worry about them. But we do need answers. So," she clapped her hands, looking around at all the faces turned to her after she was done consoling Cason, "Who's up for a night at Effusion? It seems to be where the lackeys like to play, so let's go play."

TWO LARGE BOUNCERS PROTECTED THE oversized double doors like last time. They didn't look to be the same guys, but I didn't really pay much attention then, either. I wondered briefly why there had not been a line that night, and the lack of a line again brought the thought back. I guess there was technically a line now since twelve of us stood waiting for them to allow us entry.

"If you must do another cavity search for your ID, Alex, get to the back of the line," Miguel nudged her with his elbow. I swear, these people have no respect for personal space.

We were all dressed to the nines, me included. I have no idea what possessed me to let Tia do my hair. Well, yes, I do. She'd asked nicely. She'd been hounding me forever to play with my hair. I'm fine with it being left down, but apparently it isn't 'club worthy' when I do. Or at least according to Alex. Anyway, I digress, we were all looking pretty good, but every one of us were also in comfortable clothes. We all wore something we could easily move in if we needed to fight or run.

Everything inside was the same as last time; people were divided into cliques, dance floor was packed with flushed and sweaty dancers, patrons were lined around the bar watching the bartenders who were giving a show, lights pulsing with the thump of the music. More than one head started bobbing and few hips began swaying as we made our way down to find a large enough place for all of us to hang out.

It was taking everything I had to not let the sigs overwhelm me. I do not like being left alone, but man, in an area this crowded, whew. It tested my mental strength. I thought it would be good practice to learn to sift through the various sigs, so

I picked a few people and made the mental note to 'get to know them' later.

We made our way up to the second floor where we could overlook the crowd. I claimed the empty settee at the furthest end of the room. It held the greatest viewpoint and closed us off on two sides. With my back to the wall and the balcony directly to my left, the only vulnerable points were straight ahead and to the right. No one objected as they followed, making themselves comfortable in the corner I picked.

We took a few minutes to look around the club from this new vantage point. It didn't take long for the ambiance to start getting to Alex, Tia, Miguel, and Eli. It looked like they were straining to not move to the music, which I found funny. I tried to hide my amusement by turning to look at the people moving about below, only to be caught laughing at them by Jake and Tysen.

"They can't help themselves, can they?" Tysen asked.

"Nuh-uh," I smiled, watching my closest friends.

"Who wants a drink?" Eli shouted, a little too loudly.

Half of us raised our hands, the other half offered to go.

"I'll take a Mango Margarita on the rocks," Mila said.

"That sounds good," Selby and I said together.

"You guys want your usual?" Eli asked Tysen and Kendrick.

"I guess I'll go and carry some of this shit back," Jake sighed. "You want anything, Bobby?"

"Yeah, grab me a Corona," he pulled a few bills out of his pocket, handing them off.

They all went down to the bar and the rest of us took a minute to talk about what we thought we should be keeping an eye out for. Since Kendrick, Tysen, and Selby worked at the warehouse, they had the best chance of spotting someone from there.

"What kind of shifters work there?" I caught myself asking before I could stop. It seemed rude, but Kendrick answered anyway.

"Mostly wolves and large cats. He may have a bear or two, but they mostly stay to themselves. They really aren't the kind who work well under another's thumb. Birds and smaller animals don't seem to interest him. I think he wants the bigger animals that are more prone to naturally bend to someone else's authority."

"Seen anyone yet?" Mila asked. All three of them shook their heads.

I decided to take a minute to try to find those sigs that had caught my attention earlier. I found them quickly considering the number of people present. The first one I tapped was a shifter of some kind, going by the pins and needles feeling I was getting everywhere. I didn't try to do anything with the sig, though the familiar itching of claws wanting to come out of my fingertips accompanied the prickly sensation the shifters always seemed to have one me. I resisted the urge and sifted through the other parts of her sig. There wasn't anything I was unfamiliar with, so I moved to the next person. The second one was much the same. The third sig sent chills down my spine. The tingly sensation of the vampire was alarming, even though this was what we were there for. We were there with the goal of finding someone who worked at BTCL, either openly like Miguel, Alex, Bobby and myself or behind the scenes like Tysen, Kendrick, and Eli. I was peeking over the guard rail trying to locate the owner of the sig when our drinks arrived.

"Mango Margarita on the rocks," Cason said as he tapped the back of my hand with the glass. "Lyssi, what's wrong?" he asked as I took it.

"Oh, um, nothing. Thank you," I told him.

"Then why do you look like you've seen a ghost?"

"It's probably my nerves," I took a drink, making sure to lick some of the chili powder on the rim to add a little heat to the mouthful of sweetness. The look he gave me said he was none too convinced, but he didn't push the issue, either.

I looked back out over the crowd, hoping to see where the uneasy feeling stemmed from. The possibilities were endless. Knowing it was pointless, I tried to concentrate on the conversation the others had delved into without looking as lost as I felt.

"But if we don't know who we are looking for, what's the point?" Tia was asking.

"A few of us know some of the other shifters," Eli responded, "and didn't someone say there were familiar scents here last week? We might get lucky and be able to put faces with those smells."

"It's sound thinking, but no guarantee," she argued back.

"Of course, it's no guarantee, but it's better than what we've got to go on at the moment, unless you just want to try and raid the warehouse?" Kendrick added.

After Tia's unsuccessful argument, the talks became menial. Discussions turned to the music the DJ played, the decor, food, and whatever else could sound like normal conversation between friends out for the night. I don't know if the subject shifts were intentional or if there was nothing left to say on the matter.

I kept my eyes roving over the party goers, not quite able to shake my discomfort. I guess it was noticeable after a while because Bobby came to sit next to me. "Hey, Cookie Dough. You alright? You've barely touched your drink and you're not talking."

"That obvious, huh?"

"Yeah, kind of."

"I just had this weird feeling earlier and I guess it stuck with me."

"What kind of weird feeling? Like Deja vu or like gas station burrito, weird feeling?" he joked.

"You've been hanging out with Miguel too long," I rolled my eyes at his lame joke. "I just picked up on a vampire sig earlier and it got under my skin a bit."

"Did you pick it out on purpose?"

"Yeah, I was tapping different sigs to see what all I could feel. I wasn't paying attention to whose I was picking out, so when I picked up on it, it kinda gave me the willies."

"And why would it give you a bad feeling? Did I miss something? Did you recognize it?"

"I guess because there were vampires who came in with the shifter and Selby when Mila was kidnapped. Wait a minute," I told Bobby, then shouted, "Mila. Selby. Come here for a minute."

They made their way over, fresh drinks in hand. "What's up?" Mila cooed as she sat down.

"Last week when you guys came back, Miguel came over after you disappeared—"

"Whoa, love. Slow down. When we came back or when I disappeared, start at one of those timelines, but not both," Mila patted my leg.

"Okay," I started again, "When I got home from work, the back door had been broken and the kitchen was a mess. I called Miguel to come help because I knew he would be able to smell them. The sigs were nearly gone, and so were the scents. However, we were able to pick out a few. I got the sig of a vampire and he smelled two vampires and two shifters. We vaguely touched on your kidnapping when you made it back home. Though, Selby all but admitted, with a guilty look, to being part of it, but neither her scent nor her sig were there. What happened and who was at the house?"

By the time I was done with my descriptive question, everyone had gathered around to listen. "As I'm sure you could probably tell, I was cooking when the back door crashed in. There were four of them, Selby included," she tilted her head in Selby's direction. "There were two vampires, a shifter, and Selby."

"Hold up," Miguel said, "I didn't smell her. I smelled two shifters. How is that?"

"I was forced to wear Dom's clothes," Selby answered. "They knew Mila befriended a bunch of supernaturals, so they took precautions to throw anyone off who has an excellent sense of smell."

"So, they know about us?" Alex asked.

Selby bobbed her head, "Yes," she sent me an apologetic smile, "Mira somehow knows all sorts of things that no one knows how she finds out, but they weren't sure if she would be alone. So, I had to tag along, holding the device, but still had to hide my smell. When whoever realized she was missing, if it was soon enough after, they would think exactly what you thought."

"Who was the shifter?" Cason chimed in.

"Dominique," Selby and Mila answered in unison.

"If you were using Dominique's clothes to mask your scent, and he was present, that would explain his scent being there, but not the other shifter I smelled," Miguel argued, "where did the other scent come from? Whose was it?"

"I don't know. There was only me, Dominique, and the two vamps."

"Do you know who the vampires were?" Tysen asked, rubbing his hand along his chin.

"No. I have never seen them before and they were very careful not to use names. They had their bloodlust under control, so they couldn't have been younger than five years, but they didn't have an air about them that screamed ancient, either. I would say they were probably somewhere between fifty and a couple hundred years old."

"What makes you guess such an odd range? Even though it's a wide range, it's kind of specific," Kendrick put in.

Selby shrugged a shoulder, "Just their mannerisms, I guess."

"What kind of mannerisms?" Tysen asked, still running his hand along his chin.

Her nose scrunched in thought, "Speech, for one. The words they used aren't received well in today's society, words like 'behest', 'catpurse', and 'affeared'. One of them constantly tapped his fingers, like he was always anxious. The other was always tugging on his long sleeves. I know it's not really much to go on, but..."

"That doesn't narrow anything down, truthfully," Eli stated flatly, "vampires usually talk funny when they are forever old. And there are quite a few of them." He tipped his head towards the first floor, as if to prove a point.

"How long do we want to stay?" I asked.

"We should probably hang out for a couple of hours. It's still early," Kendrick answered.

"I don't think we should limit our searches to just the club," Selby added, "there are other places open 'til the early hours. I think we'd probably have better luck trying out other smaller bars. There might be too many people in a place like this. It's too new."

"She's got a point," said Cason. "As much as I dislike the idea of the hole in the wall bars, we'll probably have more luck with the regulars. The older or more local they are, the more apt to stick with what they know, and we'll have a better chance of overhearing something with less background noise."

"I say we give it another hour. Everyone needs to get out and mingle. We won't be hearing anything all crowded up here in the corner, I'm gonna grab another beer, who wants to come?" Eli walked away, setting his empty beer bottle on the tray as he passed by a waitress.

I stayed in my little corner while most everyone dispersed. Cason, Tia, Eli, and Kendrick made their way to the bar. Jake and Selby found themselves a booth within eyesight of our little corner while Tysen, Mila, Miguel, and Alex found themselves a place on the dancefloor. Bobby leaned back against the wall and signaled the waitress for another drink.

"Want anything?" he asked.

"Nah. I'm nursing this one," I held my half full glass up for show. "What do you think about all this mess?"

"Well, when you said you had a little bit of trouble, I didn't think conspiracy theory kind of trouble. If this is as big as everyone thinks, and I am not saying it's not, but if it is, it will get a lot worse before it gets better," he admitted.

"I have a feeling you're right. And I don't like it one bit," I said as I warily glanced around the second floor. "I know they suggested to stay for another hour but clubbing really isn't my thing. There are too many people to block out here. I think I am going to go out front and get some air. I'll probably still be there when everyone is ready to go."

Bobby stood with me as I put my glass on the table. "I don't think any of us need to be out alone. I'll come with you."

"I'm good. I've been alone all week. I think I can handle a few minutes by myself outside. You go ahead and grab your other beer." I said, walking away.

I was on the steps back down to the first floor when the uneasy feeling settled in the pit of my stomach. I pushed my back against the wall as a big guy with linebacker like shoulders pushed past me. I released a breath I hadn't realized I was holding when I finally got to the bottom of the stairs. I was never going to make it outside by myself and I knew it. I got to the hallway leading to the bathrooms at the other end of the room. I sidestepped a couple standing in the middle of the doorway making out. Like most single restroom establishments, the line to the ladies' room was nearly as long as the hallway. I stood at the end of the line hoping, against all logic, the women ahead of me were not in there telling ridiculous stories about their hookups and redoing their lipstick. Unrealistic, I know, but hey, I could always wish.

The line was moving painfully slow when the big guy from the stairwell was back in front of me, "Hey, you mind if I wait with you?"

My face scrunched, "In the line to the women's bathroom?"

"Well, yeah. The line for the men's is moving faster, but there's no one to talk to over there," he thumbed at the line behind him.

"Wouldn't you get to the beginning of the line faster if you *stayed* over there?" I pointed down the hall where the line to the men's room was indeed moving horrendously faster.

"Probably," he flashed what he presumably thought was his most impressive smile, "but then I wouldn't get a chance to talk to a pretty lady for as long."

I leaned forward and swiveled my head to look at all of the women standing ahead of and behind me in line, "Imma call bullshit. There are plenty of pretty ladies up there," I thumbed to the other end of the hall, mocking him, "and back there. Why me?"

"Why not you?" he asked without missing a beat.

"Because she didn't come alone," came Bobby's gruff, and welcomed, voice from behind me. The guy looked me up and down, shook his head and walked away.

"Guess it's taking longer than anticipated to get outside for some fresh air," Bobby commented.

"Seems that way," I responded in kind.

"Well, the hour's up. Everyone's out by the sidewalk waiting to find a place to grab a bite to eat."

"Seriously? I've been in line for an hour?"

"Almost. Bathroom lines will make a person lose track of time real quick," he said with what was becoming his signature wink.

"Shut up. You really have been hanging out with Miguel too much. What did you two do this week, go on lunch dates every day?"

He belted out a laugh, "No, but I am either really good at picking up small details because of what I am or I'm just that awesome."

"Ha! Aren't we humble? Let's go," I said, giving up my place in line, "I can pee later. I'm hungry now."

WE MET UP WITH EVERYONE AND started walking. I guess they had already decided where to go before we came out because no one said anything to us about where we were headed. Which, in all honesty, was fine by me. I was starving, so as long as we got some food, I didn't care.

After walking about three blocks, we abruptly stopped. A cold voice flitted from the shadows and at the same time my skin felt mixed sensations from sigs too close for comfort. First, the tingly numb feeling I get with vampires around spread over my entire body and as soon as the threat registered, the pins and needles feeling of the shifters prickled, overriding the numb sensation.

"Look who we found. It's the mad scientist, the unpredictable captive, and a plentitude of odiferous animals," came the cold voice as a tall, pale couple stepped out of the shadow the whispers had originated in.

"I'm going to take a shot in the dark that these are the old geezers who can't quite get with the times," Cason deadpanned.

"Yeah, this would be them, but where are the other morons in question?" Eli responded when Selby nodded her head.

"Who the fuck are you calling a moron?" said a deep voice from behind us.

Half of us spun around to get a view of the new comers and the other half kept their eyes in front. The voice from behind sounded familiar, so I turned to see the big guy from the club had followed us with a few of his friends.

REFLECTED

I tapped the flaring sigs as energies spiked from pending excitement, fear, anger, and confusion. I found Miguel's sig, tugging it immediately. I was most familiar with his and how to manipulate it to get the desired results. Tingles washed over my arms. Long claws pierced my fingertips as they erupted. My forearms bulked up, burning with thickening muscles. Growls from the shifters came in low warning tones.

"Damn, Dom. You really have gone off the deep end, haven't you?" Tysen said, stepping up between Dom and the rest of us.

"Me? How in the hell can you say that when you've turned your back on the pack?"

"I've done no such thing. I've been the one there throughout the mess Darrell left, putting the pack back together from the divide he created."

"Bullshit! You created the divide with your self-righteous shit," he bit back.

"No, I stood up for what's right. You've lost it if you think it's okay to kill and torture innocent people for amusement or money."

"Stop it, you two. I don't want to have to separate the bad puppies," the smaller vampire interjected, "we need the scientist and the former captive. Allow them to leave or there—" A sickening crunch interrupted him mid-threat. I craned my head around to see Kendrick stepping back as the vampire held his hands to his face briefly before resetting his broken nose.

"No one is going with any of you," Kendrick said as he placed himself in front of Selby.

A flash of movement to my left caught my attention before all hell broke loose. I turned to see what the movement was and body slammed to the pavement. My newly formed claws found soft flesh in the body above me. A high-pitched screech followed as the force from a punch landed in my ribs. I shoved hard on the body and rolled right, pulling myself out from under the heavy weight. I was surprised it was a woman just slightly bigger than myself. She seemed much larger when she was on top of me, but then again, she put me on the ground with the force of a truck without me seeing her, so knowing what to expect kind of flew out the window.

Within seconds she was launching herself at me again. Since I could see her, the surprise was gone and I was able to counter her lunge with a quick shift to the left, pushing her as she dove past me, raking her own claws against my midsection. The drag of her claws against my stomach barely registered as I threw myself on top of her. I grabbed her head, throwing my momentum forward, slamming her head into the ground. Her eyes rolled back into the back of her head while I quickly righted myself, stepping back to get a view of the melee around me.

So many bodies and movement made it hard to track my people, let alone get a grasp on where everyone stood in their own fight. Miguel, Alex, and Tia were partially shifted and trading blows with four other shifters. Where in the hell did all these people come from? Bobby and Selby were fighting back to back with what looked like cat shifters from here. I was solidly impressed with their fighting skills. I stood for only a moment longer to try to find... someone, anyone, but someone found me.

"Whatcha waitin' on?" Eli asked as he gently elbowed my arm.

"Fuck me, where did everyone come from?" I asked, bewildered at the sight before me.

"I'm not sure. That's Dom, the psycho from our pack we've been looking for, but the others I guess were sent in by Bossman. He seems to want those two pretty badly," he nodded towards Selby.

I grunted in response to his assessment as I ducked a swing from another shifter to my right. I thrust my clawed fist (which is hard to make by the way) upward into the stomach of the burly man now in front of me. Eli had engaged in his own fight by the time I was knocked back to the ground with a solid punch to the face. I kicked out hard and connected with a knee. A howl rent the air as the shifter's knee buckled forward, causing him to fall next to me. I elbowed him as hard as I could while I had an opportunity to because, well, when he got back up, he was going to be pissed. I scrambled away on my hands and knees as the big lug started to get back up. The sound of bones popping sent shivers down my spine.

I found a little bit of cover underneath a nearby bush so kindly placed for my chickenshit needs, okay, we both know that isn't true. But still, I hid like a scaredy cat, partially concealed under the shrubbery planted next to the building I somehow ended up next to. I caught a flash of blue light and a sweep of mist flitting through the air on the other side of the street. I knew then Mila had left, but whether she was okay, I couldn't tell you.

I scanned my surroundings once again, barely able to distinguish friend from foe. Grunts and flesh hitting flesh noises from the fight carried from around the corner of the building I was hunkered down next to. Doing a mental count of who all had been with us, I could see fewer than half my friends. Mila was gone, Eli was still fighting the same shifter, Bobby and Selby seemed to be holding their own with complicated looking moves I couldn't begin to name, Cason limped from around the corner, half carrying Tia, who looked to have a nasty gash across her thigh, exposing her femur. Tysen, Kendrick, and Miguel were nowhere in sight. I spotted Alex kneeling on the ground next to a limp form, blood pooling underneath her. She looked up, craning her head around, stopping when she made eye contact with me. The look of horror on her face jerked me from my thoughts. I shuffled my way out from under the bush, fear coiling in the pit of my stomach. I barely made it out from underneath the bush when a sharp, piercing pain lanced through my skull. Alex laying Jaykob's head gently on the ground was the last thing that registered in my mind before the world went black.

20

The pains that ripped me from unconsciousness were beyond unbearable. My shoulders felt like they were being torn from their sockets. The muscles in my neck, chest, and back were stretched so tight I couldn't breathe. If I had a breath, the scream that wrenched from me probably would have been glass shattering. Tears immediately sprung into my eyes, causing my vision to blur. I couldn't tell exactly how much of the blurry vision was due to crying and how much the pain attributed to it, not that it mattered.

I tried moving a little to see if I could possibly get out of this horrendous position. With both arms stretched out, chained too close to the wall, my feet barely touching the floor, every tiny movement sent agony throughout my body. When I attempted to put my feet in a good position to adjust myself, I jostled my shoulders and chest. The confusion from the strange, disconnected feeling of my lower half made me move quicker than I intended, creating new waves of pain that rippled through my body. I stupidly tried to pull my hands out of the cuffs. The result of my idiotic idea was excruciating spasms shooting down my arms and into my chest and back so intense I passed out again.

When I awoke the second time, the agony was not less, but different. I was no longer chained to the wall, but lying on the cold, hard floor. The coolness of the floor did soothe the pain some, but not enough to rejoice over. My shoulder joints burned like they were on fire, my head was too heavy to lift. My chest, back, and arm muscles ached as if I had attempted to move a fire truck like the guy I saw in the toughest man contest on a viral video.

A small whimper escaped through my lips as I tried to move. My body had regulated my breathing as it's supposed to while I was unconscious, but it was still rather difficult to pull in a full breath without pain. I tried to ease myself up off the floor to a sitting position several times before finally succeeding.

Sitting up, I could more fully take in my surroundings. I was in a cell; as in a real jail cell. The abandoned police station was old and had shut down about twenty years or so ago. The city planning committee didn't take into consideration which way the city had to expand due to the historical district and natural terrain, which meant I knew where I was! Jake, Miguel, Alex, Tia, Cason, and I had spent many a teenage evening here drinking and playing stupid games like truth or dare, spin the bottle, and hide-n-seek.

The thought brought excitement that was immediately quashed by the thought of Jake lying on the ground bleeding. How was he? Was he still alive? How injured was he? What day was it? What fucking time was it? Who in the fuck brought me here? How the fuck was I supposed to get out? These thoughts bombarded my brief clarity, making me anxious. I was alone, my brother was dead or dying or injured badly. I had no sigs to tap. However long I had been there was plenty long enough for the energy to have dissipated. The more these thoughts ran through my head, the more my chest constricted. A panic attack was in my near future if I didn't get my shit together.

I looked around the outside of the cell to see if there was anything close enough to use to get out of here. Yeah, I know, useless idiot seeing if someone left keys in reach. But hey, I didn't know what kind of people I was dealing with. They could have been dumb enough to leave something, though I didn't set my hopes on it. Which was a good call on my end because there was nothing I could use. There was no furniture; no desks or chairs, no coat racks like you see on tv and in the movies, not even scraps of trash from people having been here playing around anymore. Nothing. I turned to the place where a cell cot should have been. The only thing in its place was a slab of steel bolted to the floor and attached to the wall. The chains I had hung from were not in there, telling me I had been transported from at least one other location. Would one of the shifters be able to follow my scent? Fuck! How long had it been? Would it even be worth it to try at this point?

I was in one of the rooms in the centermost part of the building. I knew this because there were no windows. I was not sure how old the building was, but whenever it was built, they thought to put the booking cells in the center, closer to the offices to make it easier to process arrestees. And it sucked some serious monkey balls for me.

I don't have any clue how long I stood rooted to the floor, mulling over the different thoughts bombarding me. I was still lost in thought when I heard a timid voice call out.

"Hello? Is anyone here?"

I was jerked from my musings with disbelief. "Hey!" I shouted back, "Hey! In here! I'm in here!"

"Who's there? Where are you?" the voice called back.

"I'm in here! Follow my voice! My name is Lyssandra and someone threw me in one of the cells. Help! I'm locked in!"

"Keep talking, I think I'm almost there," she said.

"Yeah? Good! Can you describe where you are? I might be able to guide you here?"

"No. It all looks the same, but with a few useless intersections."

"Oh, yeah. I forgot about those. My brother and friends and I used to come here when we were teenagers."

"Yeah? Why? There's nothing here."

"Because we were stupid teenagers," I responded sadly. The last image of Jake flashed in my mind.

"Oh. Speak up, I'm at another one of those stupid intersections. I think I took a wrong turn."

"Ok," I said a little louder. She was close enough to not have to shout like I had been, but still far enough I had to put effort into getting my voice out there. Normally, it would have been no big whopper, but my chest still hurt like a mofo. Shit, I picked up Alex's jargon. Ooh! I could probably pick up her sig from this distance. I tried to locate her sig, which seemed to get slightly stronger as, I presumed, she moved forward. "Do you have a name?" I called out.

"Well yeah," she said it as if I were an idiot, which at this point, I wasn't completely inclined to disagree with, "I'm Whisper."

"Whisper? That's pretty. And unique."

"Thanks. My parents thought so, too, I guess."

"You don't like it?"

"I like it well enough. Almost there, I think. At another intersection, say something."

"You sound young. How old are you?"

"Hey! I found you," a scrawny, pretty, blonde girl said as she walked down the hall. "I'm fifteen."

"Hey! You did! Do you have a phone? Can you call and get help for me?" I asked as I tried to get a read on her sig. She had a *familiar, but don't know why* feel about her, which was slightly disconcerting. She was definitely not a normie.

"No, I don't have a phone," she said as she tugged on the hem of her neon green shirt, coming to stand in front of the cell. "How did you get in here?"

"I don't know. I woke up in here. Is there anyone outside?"

"Nu-huh," she gave a head shake, "just the birds."

"Well, damn." I sighed. I watched her as I tugged a few strands of her sig. In the short time I had been practicing, I had learned quite a bit. I learned most sigs are built the same, you know, like anatomy in general; the heart pumps blood, the lungs pull in oxygen, kidneys filter … well, you get it, anyway. I tugged a few strands, curious to how her energy was composed. Her energy was extremely strong. It left a gritty impression, letting me know she was an earth elemental like Selby. "What are you doing out of school? You meeting some friends and skipping?"

It was her turn to give a sigh, "No school today. And I don't really have any friends. I guess I'm in that awkward stage I heard about."

"Oh. Sorry to hear. So, what are you doing here?"

"Well, coming to give you a message, of course," she smiled tightly.

"What? What do you mean a message? Who are you? Who sent you?" I blurted.

She raised her hands in the universal 'calm down' gesture, "Slow down, one question at a time. I already told you, my name is Whisper. I was sent in here to give you a message. I had to memorize it before they would let me out, so here goes—"

"Wait! Who sent you? Let you out of where?" I asked, shrieking a little.

"That's two questions. But it's doable. I was sent by the vampire. He said he's not run into many of your species. He would like some of your blood. He wants to know what you are capable of, not to drink, though if you are not opposed, something can be arranged I'm sure. I mean, vampires do drink blood, so I guess he'd go for you giving him a drink. He said you will get food and water, but you're on your own for the rest of your needs. When he unscrews himself from whatever he's dealing with and comes to you, volunteer to give up some blood and he'll let you out. Until then, you're shit out of luck. Well, that's pretty much the message. I changed the wording a bit because it sounded way too 'grumble, grumble, bark' and I figured being nice about it would help sway you to do what you need to get out of here. I mean, I would prefer nice instead of nasty. So. Did I answer your bazillion and one questions? What are you, by the way?"

I stood shocked thoroughly to my core for several moments. A child, CHILD, was sent to tell me I have to cooperate or I will be left to rot, or worse. This child was sent by a vampire, probably the same one we'd been looking to find a way to bring down. She said she had to memorize the message before she would be let out, meaning he held her captive, too.

"How long have you got?" I asked as thoughts to find a way out of here started.

She gave a shoulder shrug, "I don't know. I was dropped off a few blocks away at a gas station and told where to go. I guess they thought it would look less suspicious than just dropping me off at the old police station."

I nodded my head in agreement. Whoever we were dealing with weren't complete idiots and thought about covering their tracks some. "What day is it?" I asked.

"Oh. It's Sunday. About noon. How long have you been here?"

"I don't know. I woke up in here a little while ago." I looked down at myself. I was still in my clothes from Friday night, albeit they were absolutely disgusting. At some point, probably more than once, I had pissed on myself and it had already had the chance to dry. I was still bloody and dirty from the fight and hiding like a fraidy cat, my shirt was ripped where claws had torn through. I had been left on the floor to come to. "I was kidnapped Friday night. We were attacked by a group of vampires and shifters. Do you know if they took anyone else? Am I the only one you were sent to give a message to?"

"Oh, that sucks. I don't know if they got anyone else or not. You were the only one I was supposed to talk to. Maybe you are the only one they brought back," she gave a tiny shrug, looking down. "I hope you're treated okay, though. It could be way worse."

"Did they hurt you?" I asked, already knowing she spoke from experience.

"I don't want to talk about it. Here," she said as she pulled an energy bar out of her pocket, "I snuck one for later because I didn't know how long they would let me out, but you probably need it more than I do."

I took it carefully, trying not to make any sudden movements for her benefit, and mine. Oh, good gods, I hurt so badly.

"Sorry I don't have anything to drink, I can go see if the water faucets still work," she started to turn away.

"No!" I called out a little more strongly than intended, "Um, no. Please stay here. I don't want to be alone."

I sat down gently on the floor, slowly unwrapping the bar. I took a bite, moaning as the crunchy goodness fell apart in my mouth. After I swallowed the first bite, I devoured the rest of the bar without thought. A sharp twinge hit my stomach, causing me to feel nauseous for a few minutes. I kept still for another few minutes to let the food settle in my stomach. Whisper watched intently the entire time like she'd never seen anyone eat before.

I wiped the crumbs off my face, "Sunday, around noon, you say?"

"Yeah, I know it doesn't make you feel better. Probably more confused or mad or something. I'm sorry." She said as she sat down in front of me.

"So how will you know when it's time to go? Is someone coming to get you?"

"I don't know. They didn't say. I guess they will. Maybe they'll just pick me up when they bring you food," she shrugged again.

"So, you're a what? You aren't a normie, are you?"

A laugh bubbled out of her, "A normie? What's that, like a normal person or something?"

I chuckled, "Yep. A normal, everyday person with nothing supernatural going on with them."

"Yeah, no. I'm not a normie, I'm an elemental. I like your word. You did make it up, right?"

I nodded, "Uh-huh. An elemental, huh? I know a couple of elementals. What is your element?"

"Earth."

"Oh nice. I have seen some cool stuff an earth elemental can do. Are you able to do a lot?"

"Nah, not really. I mean, I can do some stuff, but apparently when bad stuff happens, I forget I can do stuff at all."

"That's normal. Don't beat yourself up about it. What kind of stuff can you do?"

230

"Oh, um. Just the usual stuff I guess. I can lift dirt, make tree branches move, help plants grow, though I am not too good at making things grow."

"That's cool. When you make tree branches move, are they still on the tree or do they have to be off, like fallen limbs?" I asked, genuinely curious.

"Both. It's harder when they are on the tree because other forces are at work, like the wind and the energy naturally in the tree. But if the tree knows I'm not like, trying to rip off its arm or something, it will be more likely to work with me."

I let out a giggle, "Yeah, I can see it not wanting to cooperate if you are trying to rip its branch off. You know, I would ask you to go to the gas station to get help, but I have a feeling it would get you in trouble and me no help. Do you have any ideas how I can get out of here? I mean, I really don't want to give anyone my blood. And I certainly don't want to wait for someone to come feed me. I'll have to use the restroom at some point."

She sat quietly for several minutes thinking. While she was off in La-La Land, I grabbed onto her sig. I tugged a few strands, pulling on the most solid one. I concentrated on a spot behind her on the wall, trying to shift the miniscule particles that made up the concrete. I thought if I could move them around some, I might be able to do so where the bars met the floor or ceiling. If I was lucky, it would convince her to help and we'd both be out of there in no time. The idea was a good one, but either I was really bad at manipulating her power or I was just too weak because nothing happened. Not a crack.

Exhaustion took me and I found myself lying on the floor, eyes heavy. "I think I'll let you sleep," she said quietly as I slipped out of consciousness.

I was awakened who knows how long later by a couple of bumbling idiots. I typically use the word 'idiots' carefully, but there is no way I could with what I woke to.

"I don't know," a gruff male voice said.

"What do you mean you don't know? Wasn't you listening?" the other one responded.

"You were there, too. You should know what she is," he chastised his partner.

"Yeah, I was listening, but it don't mean I know what she does. I bet he said to stay out of there cuz she can set us on fire with her subsconces."

"Her what?"

"Her subsconces. You know, the thing in your head when you sleep that keeps you breathin' and stuff. Subsconces."

"I don't know what you're talking about. There is nothing in my head."

"I can attest to that," I said groggily, "and yours, too." I gave them a tight smile as I pushed myself up on my elbow. "I'm only kidding, you guys," I quickly added when they glowered at me.

"Well, what would you know about what's in our heads anyway?" the gruff one asked.

"For starters, you have what everyone else has, I assume." Placating seemed to be the best way to handle these two, "You both have brains in your head, and what you're referring to is what is called the *subconscious*. It's part of your mind that you aren't aware of that tells you how to think and feel about something."

"Ho, you dummy! I told you, you didn't know what you were talking about!" the younger one said, elbowing the other one in the ribs.

"You did not! You said you didn't know what I was talking about, not I don't..." he stood for a minute, looking lost before starting back up, "You didn't know what I was saying, not me not knowing what I said. Did that come out right? It sounded funny in my head."

"I know what you meant," I told him, giving a scornful look to the young one. "What are you guys doing here? Did you bring me food? Whisper said someone would be by later with food."

"Uh, yeah, we have food for you. But first we're s'posed to ask what's your answer," the younger one asked.

"Oh. Tell him no thanks. What did you bring me?" I bat my eyelashes, hating how degrading I was being to myself.

"Sandwich and water," Young One said as he thrust dry bread and cheese through the bars.

"Thanks," I said eyeing the food warily, taking the sandwich. "What are your names? Mine's Lyssandra."

Nuh-uh," the younger one said, "I'm not getting all sweet with you. You're gonna get us in trouble."

"Oh," I replied, "I'm not trying to. I'm sorry. Water?" I held my hand out expecting a bottle of water, not the zip-lock bag of water Gruff handed me. "Um. Thank you," I said, probably sounding as puzzled as I was.

He nodded and leaned in to whisper conspiratorially, "I'm Sal."

"Is it short for Salvatore?" I asked, equally as quiet, though I don't know why since the younger guy was still standing right there giving disapproving looks.

"No. Salamander, because I'm a Salamander shifter," he toted with his chest puffed out.

"Oh. Well, it's... fitting," I told him with the fakest smile I could muster.

"Well, there ya went and dunnit," the young one protested, "you done gone and went and made friends with the enemy. Now she'll kill us all with her fire powers, or whatever!"

I choked on the dry bread as I spluttered, "Fire powers? Where did you hear I have fire powers?"

"From Bossman," he seethed, "he said you'll burn our asses and run away if we went in there with you."

I couldn't help but laugh, which garnered more glowers from young one. "First of all, what are you? If you are a shifter, you can smell me and see I don't have fire powers," I bluffed, I didn't know if he really could or not. "Second, I am just a plain Jane human. I don't know what he, Bossman, would be talking about. And third, I have to pee really badly. Could one of you take me to the bathroom? He said you couldn't come in here, but didn't say you couldn't escort me to the bathroom, right?"

They shared a look before Sal shrugged a shoulder, "She's right. He didn't say nothing about not lettin' her use the bathroom."

While they had a brief staring contest, I quickly tapped their sigs. Both were shifters, though without actually tapping the sigs, I couldn't tell you what kind. Luckily dumber one already told me what he was. I didn't want to chance a partial shift by tapping the other one and end up with wings or cute, tiny paws.

"Damn. Women are always right," the young one deflated. "Mom always said to listen when a woman talks because she will tell you all you need to know in one sentence if you listen."

I covered my mouth, pretending to be choking down the last bite of the sandwich. I didn't really need to pretend the sandwich was horrible. I put the corner of the bag to my mouth, hoping I didn't pour the water all over my face. Yeah, I'm sure I could have used a wash, but not with the only water I had available to drink. I gulped the water down, dribbling it down my chin and neck, but not caring in the slightest.

He fumbled around with the keys as I crossed my legs to put on a little more show of having to use the restroom. When he finally unlocked the door, I waited until Sal motioned for me to step out of the cell because the last thing I wanted was for them to perceive me as a threat after the 'I'm innocent' show I'd just put on.

As soon as I was out of the cell, Young One grabbed my arm and all but dragged me down the hallway. He would stop at various intersections, trying to figure out which way to go. I tried to tell him, but was shushed every time. I had little choice but to follow wherever he went. Finally, after completing the circle, Sal pointed up to the signs giving direction. It seemed to make Young One even madder because his handling became much more aggressive.

We pulled to a stop outside of the bathroom and he shoved me up against the wall to readjust his grip. "Go make sure nobody is in there to help her out," he told Sal as he held me still.

Sal was in and out, "It's clear. Ain't no one in there. Let 'er go."

I jerked away as he released his hold and rushed into the bathroom. I turned on the first faucet I came to and cried for joy. I didn't know why the water worked after all these years of the station being abandoned, but I wasn't about to question it.

I scrubbed my hands the best I could with cold water and no soap. Working in the medical field for as long as I have had ingrained how it's supposed to be done, and this wasn't it. While I was washing my face one of the guys, Young One to my guess, started banging on the door telling me to hurry before he came and got me himself. I took a quick look around the bathroom, after gulping down a few handfuls of water, to see if there were any windows. Being as short as I was in comparison to the stalls, I could only see the edge of the frame of one at the far end of the wall. I went to the nearest stall to relieve myself. Before I was finished, the bathroom door banged open and Young One barreled in yelling. Sal was on his heels saying something about 'giving her privacy for a minute'.

"Hey! I am still urinating!" I yelled at the stall door he began banging on.

"Stop talkin' so smart and hurry up in there," Young One called out.

"I can only pee so fast, for crying out loud. I washed my hands and face before I came to the stall. I'll be out in a minute. I am going to finish my business, wash my hands, and be in the hall before you know it. Please leave," I said, pleading at the end of my miniscule tirade.

"Better hurry," with a bang on the stall door was what I got in response.

As I was coming out of the stall, I could hear them arguing in the hall about how nice they should or should not be to me. I turned on the faucet again, drowning them out. I quickly went to the window. Seeing the night sky beyond, I pushed on it to see if it opened. It wasn't a large window, but maybe big enough for me to climb out of if I had to use it as an escape route. It never hurt to be too prepared. It creaked as I pushed it ajar, which made me pause to listen. The guys outside didn't seem to notice, so

I was giddy with anticipation and nerves. I hustled away from the window and back to the sink. I gulped a few more handfuls of water. Not knowing when I would get any more, I filled up the bag and left, leaving the semi-semblance of privacy behind.

I came out, mid-argument, it seemed. They both stopped, Young One snapping, "What are you lookin' at?"

I held up my hands in mock surrender, "Nothing. I didn't mean to intrude." I turned and walked in the direction of the cell. They scrambled after me, I assume realization dawned, their prisoner had walked off without them.

"Hey, wait up," Sal said, huffing.

I stopped and waited for them to catch up. I stood there for a few beats really wishing I knew what kind of shifter the other one was. I was pretty sure I could handle a lizard, but not knowing what Dumber Two's animal was kept me from doing anything drastic. The way my luck plays out, if I tried to shift something of his animal, I wouldn't get big scary teeth, but something weird like fish lips. If I tried to run, he would probably be some big, fast cat. Ugh, sometimes life sucked too much.

We made it back to my cell in less than half of the time it had taken him to drag me in circles to find the bathroom to begin with. Young One slammed the door behind me. I jumped from the sudden, loud bang.

"Hey, were you guys the ones who brought me here?" I asked, hoping to stall them a little longer. I really needed to find out what his animal was.

"I was one of 'em, but he was doing something else," Sal pointed toward Young One.

"Ah. Ok. So, I hate calling you the name the I'm calling you in my head," I tried again for politeness.

"What you callin' me? You know it ain't nice to be callin' folks' names?" Young One got huffy.

"Well, I was calling him Gruff, because he has a gruffy voice," I said pointing at Sal, "because I didn't know his name."

Sal smiled broadly, "It's not a bad name. I kinda like it."

"Well, I have to call you something. Since I didn't know your name, I started calling you Young One."

"I'm not young!" he protested. "You've got to call me something else!"

"I'm sorry. It's stuck. I will just call you Young One from now on. It's no disrespect to your mother, by the way. I would love to call you the name she gave you. I'm sure it's a wonderful name," I said, internally rolling my eyes.

"Lucas!" he yelled at me, "My name is Lucas and she picked a good, solid name."

"Sal and Lucas. I like it. I like you guys. You've been courteous gentlemen, under the given circumstances," I nodded, taking a seat on the floor. "Oh, speaking of courteousness, is Whisper still here? She's such a lovely girl."

"That's awfully nice of you," Sal said, "yeah, she should be here somewhere. Did you want to talk to her one more time before we leave?"

"Please, if it won't get you guys in trouble," I nodded my head like an enthusiastic child, although the muscles in my neck and shoulders protested with sharp pains.

"Nah, it shouldn't be a problem. I'll go get her," Sal said as he walked off.

"I hope you aren't trying to pull anything slick," Lucas said, giving me the evil eye.

"Wouldn't that get me killed? I'm a human and you're a what, tiger? I wouldn't make it ten feet before you shredded me with your claws or big teeth," I said as innocently as I could without it seeming too much. I hoped.

"I'm not no tiger," he pouted.

"You're not?"

"No. I am not," he enunciated each word clearly.

"Oh, I thought you might be. I'm sorry. What are you?"

"You just won't stop, will ya? Not until I tell ya what I am, huh?"

Smiling the biggest fangirl smile I could, I shook my head, "Nope."

He rolled his eyes at me, "Fine. I'll tell you, but you have to promise not to laugh."

"Laugh? Why would I laugh? I can't turn into anything. I can't do anything with fire, like you were led to believe, but it would be too cool if I could," I said wistfully.

"Well, if you promise not to laugh," he hedged.

I crossed my chest with my finger in the universal 'I cross my heart' motion, kissed my fingers, zipped my lips and threw away the key.

It seemed to please him, so he mumbled, "I'm a bhihfd."

"A what?"

"A bhuidks," he mumbled again.

"Alright, if you don't want to tell me after I promised not to laugh, that's fine. Just don't ask me to keep any other secrets," I tried the childish tactic again, since it seemed to work on him the best.

"I said, 'I'm a boar!'" he finally yelled.

I flinched back at the tone of his voice, "Oh. Why would I laugh about that? That's incredibly unique."

"What? No pig jokes?" he asked, tone snide.

"Uh, that would be a hard no. No pig jokes. Boars are ruthless. I don't know who would be so stupid as to make fun of a boar shifter." I could think of about a hundred jokes, but they wouldn't have done me a damn bit of good in my situation.

He nodded his head and stomped off, "I'll see if I can find Sal and the chick."

I sat on the cold floor for several minutes running through all the options I could imagine. Since sigs are energy signatures, they linger for a bit after a person has left, but just like many resources, once you use it, it's gone until whoever comes back and replenishes what you've used. I could theoretically use all their sigs to get myself out of this mess if

I used the leftover energy sigs smartly. But how in the fuck was I supposed to do that?

Lucas and Sal came strutting back down the hallway with a moping Whisper trailing behind them. I looked between the three of them to see if they were the reason for her current mood. I shook the thought off, it wasn't my concern. My concern was getting my shit together and getting the fuck outta Dodge.

"Thank you, guys. I know you don't have to play nice with me. I really appreciate the kindness you all are showing," I said as they approached.

"You better be thankful enough not to screw it up for us," Lucas scorned.

"Oh, absolutely. I wouldn't dream of it. Are you guys going to be the ones to come back to bring me food and water?"

"Prolly," Sal answered, not looking too convinced at his own words.

"I don't know if he'll let me come back," Whisper said.

I nodded, trying to look lost in thought. When I finally spoke, I made myself sound as pitiful as I could, "I really hate to ask, but have any of you got a jacket, or sweater, or anything really I could use for a pillow or maybe a blanket? It gets cold on the floor and even colder on the metal table in the air." I nodded to the cot table in hopes to pull their sympathetic strings.

They looked at one another for several minutes, mentally debating the pros and cons, by the looks on their faces. Finally, Sal pulled his shirt over his head and handed it to me through the bars. I gave him a grateful smile, "Thank you, Sal. How did you ever come into a job where you aren't working for the good guys?" Without saying anything further, the three of them left, Sal leading the way with a pensive expression on his face.

I sat still, listening to the echoing sounds of their footsteps fading, then the sound of the vehicle they drove off in. When I was sure they were gone, I began tugging on the sigs left, pulling at the elemental strands first. I noticed even though Whisper was fairly strong in energy, hers faded the fastest. It was already dissipating.

I pushed her energy, gently at first, to the floor where the bars sat in the concrete. If I could loosen them, partially shifting into a boar for strength may do the trick to get out of this damn cell. I was at a loss as to what I could use the salamander abilities for, but I'd figure it out if need be. Or so I hoped.

With a few pulls and twists of Whisper's sig, I could make the bars wiggle. Not much, but more than not at all. I had just a little bit left of her sig to use, so I put all my concentration into as many of the bars as possible. A brief jolt of elation shot through me as the concrete shattered next to one of the bars. I closed my eyes, tilted my head back to let the moment sink in, hoping that it wouldn't be short lived. When I opened my eyes, my hopes were quickly dashed. I don't know how I let it slip my mind that the bars would have been embedded into the ceiling as well.

I tried to renew my joy as I reached out for the other sigs. Lucas's sig was still strong and heady. Sal's was strong, but slowly fading. I pulled Lucas's sig and put my own energy to work. I didn't want to shift, but have the strength. Unfortunately, when tapping a new sig, there is no choosing what you get. Once you get used to the sig, you have more control. Sometimes you get to pick what parts of you do shift. Since I had never tapped either one of their sigs before, I wasn't sure of what I was going to get.

I was beyond happy when I pulled his sig and no discernable weirdness happened. I did feel stronger. I grabbed the bars at the bottom, put my feet on the bars next to them and pulled as hard as my limited strength allowed. The groan of the bars and scratching of the concrete on metal urged me on, like my own personal cheering squad. I stopped to look at my progress. I was sorely disappointed in how little the bars moved. I took another deep breath, grabbed the bars once more and yanked hard. A loud crack resounded in the empty hallway, sounding much more productive than it probably was, but I didn't dare stop to look again. I wanted to feel my arms further away from my starting point before checking again. Lucas's sig was quickly being used up and I had to get as much done as I could with it while it lasted. My arms and back were already aching, my palms were sweating and finally, one of the bars gave way underneath my hand. I let it go, putting all my efforts into one bar. It took less time for the second bar to give than the first one did. I quickly scooted to my left and worked on the next bar until my strength finally gave out. I pulled one last time. My sweaty hands slipped off and I fell flat on my back. I was hurting and aching so much I didn't move. I just lay there, inhaling the musty smelling air of the forgotten building.

While lying sprawled, I thought of all the uses a salamander could have. To be honest, I was coming up short. I studied human anatomy, and most shifter anatomy, for work, but I can't be truthful and say I ever studied amphibian biology or anatomy. *Salamanders are amphibians, right? Or are they reptiles? Um. See? I couldn't even tell you which class they were in. I'm pretty sure they're amphibians. I think.* Anyway, the mental debate had to be put on hold until I caught my breath. I couldn't do anything if I couldn't breathe.

As I wheezed in the foul stench of my own smelly fumes, the dank air, and quite possibly part of my lungs, a thought hit me like a ton of bricks. Jake was uh-may-zing at manipulating sigs. So much so, that if he chose to, he could shift into the entire animal sometimes. He said it took all his concentration and was exhausting, but it could be done. I thought back on Bobby's words. Bobby told me in order to change into someone else, I needed to concentrate on the outer appearance and the internal stuff would fix itself as necessary. I wondered if I put all my concentration into it, could I shift my entire body? A salamander is tiny, so it seemed logical that it would take less energy to change into and maintain the form.

I sat up, took out my water and drank almost half. I forced myself to zip the bag and put it down. If this didn't work, I was going to need my water to last who knows how long.

I didn't want to fuck my clothes up if this worked, so I stripped down to nothing, setting them next to the bars. The cool air made me shiver and goosebumps rise. I shook my arms out, mentally prepping myself. "I can do this," I chanted to myself several times. I held completely still, grabbed Sal's sig and wrapped myself with it from head to toe. I put all thought into what I imagined was a tiny salamander. I closed my eyes one more time and imagined a fire salamander, which was the only one I had any kind of knowledge about, limited as it was. I pictured a tiny little black body with bright orange spots. The smooth body, I remembered, glistened in the light if it was wet. I held the image for several beats, letting the physical sensations pass before I braved opening my eyes. The tingling started on my arms and shoulders, then spread all over my body. You know the tingly jolt you get when you stick your tongue to a 9-volt battery? Imagine that all over your body, and lasting about as long. It didn't hurt, but it wasn't exactly comfortable, either.

REFLECTED

I slowly peeled my eyes open, one at a time. I felt kind of silly, like someone expecting to be hit in the head by a falling toilet or something, but went on with it. The bars in front of me looked larger than they had a few minutes before. They were thicker and spaced further apart. As I took in my surroundings, I realized I was viewing everything from the floor. I tried to look down at my body, but my head wouldn't turn right. I couldn't lift my hand in front of my face either. I began to panic a little when it dawned on me that it had worked, I did it! I shuffled, rather ungracefully, through the bars. The viewpoint was strange. I had never really paid attention to how high up my little body was in comparison to a tiny animal like this. I could see for a long distance, but the further away, the blurrier the image. I could see just fine up close, huh. Who knew salamanders were nearsighted?

I closed my tiny eyes again and put all my focus on letting go of Sal's sig and returning to my normal, everyday, naked self. As much as I would have loved to explore all there is to being a salamander, I was desperate to get out of the building. And Sal's sig was nearly gone. I would have ended up using it all up and probably getting stuck somewhere I couldn't get my curious self out of when I returned to my normal size.

I snatched my clothes off the floor through the bars and hurried to put them on. I grabbed the bag of water and Sal's shirt, and ran in the direction of the bathrooms. I wanted to get a few more gulps down before I attempted to squeeze through the window. I wasn't too keen on trying to sneak out the front only to be caught by someone watching. Remember me mentioning my luck? Yeah, that's how it would go.

I pushed the window open, not caring if it made noise. I was the only one around who would hear it. I hoped. I pulled myself up and shimmied my top half through. As I was edging myself out, the front of my pants got hung on the lip of the frame. My button up fly popped back open as I forced myself out. I put my hands out to catch myself, to no avail. The strength I had built up before tapping all those sigs had been drained. I was surprised I hadn't passed out already.

Landing on my face, I lay there in the cool night air hurting and exhausted. I knew I couldn't stay there, no matter how much I enjoyed the soft grass on my face. The longer it took to get my ass moving, the closer I was to getting found and thrown back in the cell, or worse. No fucking way was I laying there and letting it happening again. I took several gulps of fresh air and pushed myself up.

I scoped out my options. The buildings nearby were semi-close together and I could easily run into one of the surrounding ones, but most were abandoned. I would only be killing time, as well as giving them a trail to follow. I knew there was a school about twelve blocks northeast of the police station, but considering it was Sunday, and night time, I didn't think I would get too lucky finding someone there. I racked my brain for a minute, trying to remember if Whisper had said which gas station she was dropped off at. I was almost positive that detail had been left out.

Heading off in the direction the school was in, I kept looking over my shoulder and around at every little crackle, snap, and movement. The further away I got, the more my anxieties kicked into gear. You would think relief would have washed through me, but no. I knew I was not in the clear. Not as long as I wasn't home or in the safe, well, safer, company of my friends. I also couldn't help but be worried about the last thing I saw before I was knocked out. My chest started constricting, making it harder to breathe. I pushed my legs faster and harder. I knew I wasn't running as fast as I could have been, my body already having been put through hell. My mind was telling me to go faster, push harder, but my legs were screaming to slow down. Chest pains, sore arms, and the stitch in my side weren't helping to encourage my body to move any faster, either.

I ran blindly through bushes, between trees, behind buildings and cars for what seemed like forever, but was probably more like a block or two. My body finally yelled 'no more' as I collapsed on the ground in someone's backyard. Not only did my body give up, but I believed my sanity had fled as well. I belly-crawled to a nearby playset, curled up in a ball underneath the slide and cried— ugly-snot, bawling like a teething baby, can't catch my breath, sucking wind, cried.

The horrible sounds coming from me at my momentary breakdown must have caught the attention of the family dog living in the house. The patio light flicked on, the squeak of the back door opening and a loud, deep 'woof' caused me to freeze, fear gripping me tight. A few seconds later a cold nose pressed against the back of my neck. The dog let out a whine and bark making me jump and curl further into myself. I let out a quiet whimper, praying the owner would just call the dog back in and leave me to my misery. Then it dawned on me, maybe he or she could and would help me, but I was too terrified to move, let alone call out for help. My brain and body were seriously out of sync and I didn't know how to get them back on track.

I didn't have long to wait to find out how the owner would respond. "Hey. Are you okay? Shit. You're not okay. Here, let me help." Warm hands roved over my arm and back as she tried to help pull me out of my ball.

I was reluctant to move, not sure what to expect. Fear, pain, exhaustion, relief, anxiety, all battled to take the forefront emotion. When I unfurled myself, cramps and tears took control, leaving jerky movements in their wake.

"Oh, honey," the lady said as she knelt beside me, "can you get up?"

I shook my head, then nodded, then shook it again, whimpering and crying uncontrollably.

"You're in shock. Okay, this is what we're gonna do," she gently pushed the hair out of my face, "I'm going to go in and get a warm washcloth. I'll be back to help you clean up a little. When you can, we'll go inside to get you something to drink and maybe something to eat if you can stomach it. Shadow," she pat the dog on the head, "sit. Stay here with her."

All I could do was nod my head in acknowledgement. Shadow eased down beside me and slipped his big, fluffy head into my lap. I absently stroked his head as I waited for his owner to come back.

"I'm coming," the woman called as she crossed the yard. "I'm here," she said as she sat down on the cool grass next to me. She began wiping my face with the warm rag, then moved to my neck and arms.

My sobs slowed as I began to catch my breath. "Thank you," I told her as she finished wiping my arm.

She looked startled for a moment, like she was surprised I knew how to speak. "You're welcome," she replied kindly. "Do you want to go in now? I started a kettle of water. We can get some tea and try to get you something to eat."

"Yeah," was all I could manage.

We got up and went inside. She closed the door behind Shadow and led me to the dining room. "My name is Abigail. Make yourself comfortable. I'll get the tea. Do you want chamomile or peppermint?"

she asked as she pulled out two cups from the china cabinet.

"Chamomile," I said, sitting at the end of the table closest to the door.

"Alright. I'll be right back with the hot water, sugar and honey. The tea is in the middle compartment of the tea box on the table. If you decide you want another flavor, they're labeled, so feel free to look through them all."

I was mildly amused because she offered me the choice between chamomile and peppermint, then switched the offer to whichever I prefer from the many choices in the box. As a trained professional in the medical field, I knew this was an appropriate action to take. Making the person engage their brain to pull them out of shock was crucial for many reasons, but it was strange being on the receiving end of the process. I allowed the thought to roll into thinking about doing an injury check. If she was a nurse or worked in the field, there would be an upcoming question or two about my physical condition.

I had placed my hands in my hair and was feeling for knots or bumps when she came in with a big tray loaded with everything she said she would bring, and more. My stomach rumbled at the sight of the crackers, fresh bread slices, half and half, jam, butter, cheese, and other goodies on the tray as she sat it on the table.

"Oh, honey," she cooed again as I grabbed my stomach, grimacing at its announcement. She poured the hot water in my cup, handed me a tea bag, and slid a small plate over in front of me, "Help yourself to whatever you want. I thought you might get hungry, if you weren't already. What's your name?"

"Lyssi," I replied as I untwisted the string on the tea bag, dropping it in the water. "Thank you."

"It's no problem. Do you have any injuries? I can get the peroxide and some bandages if you need them."

"I don't think so. I'll be alright, but thank you." I said as I put bread and crackers on my plate. "But, umm... Do you have a phone I can borrow? I can call my brother and have him pick me up."

"Oh, sure. Hang on a sec and I'll get it for you," she got up and went through another door at the other end of the room.

I busied myself with cramming food in my mouth while she was gone. I had scarfed down four slices of bread and jam by the time she made it back and set a phone on the table next to my plate. I picked up the phone, input Jake's number then paused. I didn't know if he was okay or even alive. Would he be able to answer my call? I quickly hit the back button, dialing Miguel instead. I didn't want my anxiety to kill my thought processes if Jake couldn't answer. I also wanted Miguel to be with me when I learned what happened, just in case my fears were confirmed.

"Hello," Miguel answered in a weathered voice.

"Miguel," I whispered, too choked up to say anything else.

"Lyssi?" he asked, excitement seeping in.

I cleared my throat, "Yeah, Guel, it's me. Come get me."

"Yeah. Of course. Where are you? Are you okay? I'm slipping my shoes on right now. Bobby has been hanging out here, I'll bring him with me. Do we need to bring back up?" the words rushed out of his mouth almost too fast for me to keep up.

"No. No, I'm okay. I don't know where I am, exactly. Hang on," I pulled the phone away from my face and asked Abigail for her address. She rattled it off and I repeated it to him, "I'm okay, but please hurry."

"On it, Lys. I know where that is, so I should be there in ten to fifteen. Just hang tight." He hung up and I handed the phone back to Abigail, thanking her for letting me use it.

"It's no problem. Do you want some fresh clothes before your brother gets here? I'm sure I have some sweats that will fit. They might be a little long in the legs, but the waist should be fine," she offered.

I looked down at my clothes, "Oh, no, I couldn't take your clothes. He'll be here in ten or fifteen minutes. I'm sure I can wait another few minutes before getting out of these. Besides, I would love a shower or long hot bath before putting on fresh ones." I took a sip of the hot tea, relaxing a little at the warmth spreading through my body.

Abigail and I sat in silence, Shadow lying in between us dozing on the floor. After a few quiet minutes I asked, "Would it be alright to use your restroom?"

"Sure, come on, I'll show you where it is. It's on the way to the living room anyway, so we'll just go in there when you're done. I'll bring your tea."

She showed me to the bathroom and pointed towards the living room to the left of the foyer as she flipped the light switch on for me. I closed the door, washed my face and hands, and leaned on the sink to catch my bearings. I quickly used the toilet, washed my hands again and met her in the living room. She handed me my tea and asked, "Do you mind telling me how you ended up in my backyard? I don't mean to pry, but do I need to call the police for you?"

"Oh. Uh, no ma'am. I can handle all the formalities. I will give them your name and address if they need it, though, if it's okay with you." I knew by the look on her face she didn't believe me, but she didn't want to argue about it. Which I appreciated immensely.

"Alright, but if you change your mind, again, let me know."

Before I got a chance to answer, the doorbell rang, sending Shadow into a frenzy. Abigail grabbed his collar and they led the way to the front door. I followed behind quietly. She reached for the doorknob, readying to open the door when I put a hand on her forearm. "Wait," I said, anxiety starting to inch back into my mind, "ask who it is first. If they don't say Miguel or Bobby, run."

The look of disbelief I received let me know then that I may have put this kind woman and her loved ones in danger by letting her help me. "What? What do you mean 'run'?"

"I was kidnapped. I could have been followed," I answered being as vague as I could. I hadn't had the energy to tap her sig, so I didn't know if I was dealing with a normie or another supernatural. But if I was being helped by a normie, there was no way she would be safe from the jackasses who would soon be on my trail, if they weren't already.

She pulled her hand away from the knob and called out, "Who is it?"

We waited in tense silence until the doorbell rang again. "Who is it?" she asked louder the second time.

"Hi. My name's Bobby. Lyssi called earlier and gave us this address to pick her up. Is she still here?"

Before she could answer, I pushed past Abigail, threw the door open and hurled myself into his arms. He caught me effortlessly as if he had expected my reaction.

"Hey there Cookie Dough, we've been worried about you," he whispered, hugging me back just as tightly. "Are you alright?"

I pulled my head back to look him in the eyes, "Yeah, I'm okay. Let me say thank you and we can go."

He nodded and let me go. I turned around to face a misty-eyed Abigail watching quietly with her hand over her mouth. I stepped up, gave her a quick hug, "Thank you, so much, for everything."

"No need to thank me, hun. You get home and rest. You need it. Have your boyfriend there run you a hot bath. You should be good to go in no time," she tipped her head towards Bobby when she said 'your boyfriend'.

"My boyfriend?" I asked, a little shocked.

"He certainly isn't your brother. And by the look on his face when you swung the door open, well, let's just say it's all I needed to see to know how he feels about you. Why? Don't you see it, too, dear?"

I looked back at Bobby, who had shoved his hands in his pockets and was looking down sheepishly. I thanked her again, gave Shadow a quick rub on the head and walked with Bobby to Miguel's waiting car.

Bobby opened the passenger door for me and I got in. I looked around, confused. When Bobby got in the driver's seat, I asked, "Where's Miguel?"

"He'll be back in a minute. He said he smelled something when we first got here, so he went to check it out."

"What did he smell?"

"I don't know. He didn't say, but it put him on edge a little. He said he'd be back in less than ten, so we have a few more minutes to wait."

"What if he doesn't come back?" panic flooded my voice when I asked.

Bobby leaned over and pulled me into him, "He'll be back. He's just sniffing around."

"But you don't know that! You don't know who could have followed me!"

"We do know, remember, we there when you were taken. He'll be okay," he spoke reassuringly.

My breathing had hitched and was slowing back down as he was rubbing his hands in circles on my back. He was right, if anyone would be okay, it was Miguel. He was a jaguar shifter and a shaman. But after the weekend I just had, I was having a hard time coming to grips with safety.

"Bobby?"

"Hmm?" he asked back.

"How's Jake?" His hands stilled for a few heartbeats and then resumed their circles.

He let out a breath, pulled me back to look him in the face. His hand found my cheek, while he looked past me out the window. His thumb slid across my skin, back and forth as he gathered his thoughts. I was taking none of this as a good sign when he finally looked me in the eyes and answered.

"He didn't make it out of the fight," he whispered.

Shock tore through me. Everything stopped. I couldn't speak. I couldn't breathe. I tried to wake myself up from this excruciating nightmare that wouldn't end. Not Jake. Not Jake!

"No. No. No, you can't be right," I said, tears welling.

"I'm so sorry, Cookie Dough," he said, trying to wrap me in another hug.

"No!" I shouted, shoving him back, hitting him repeatedly. "No! You're lying! You have to be! This isn't funny!"

"No, it's not. I wish I was lying, but baby, I'm not. I'm sorry."

I shoved the car door open, jumped out screaming and ran. Nothing mattered anymore. I had to get to Jaykob's house to see for myself he was okay. He was still alive and breathing. Bobby had played a cruel, sick joke.

I hadn't made it far when I was tackled from behind, landing face first in the dewy grass. Strong arms held me while I thrashed and fought to get away. Bobby's gentle timber flitted through my hair, "Shhhh. Lyssi, please stop. I've got you, but please stop fighting me. You don't have the energy for this."

I stilled my body while the sobs flowed freely. Bobby relaxed his hold, keeping me in his arms as he tried to comfort me, running his fingers through my hair. A cold, wet nose and warm, wetter tongue slid up my face as I cried for the second time that night. I pulled my head back into Bobby's chest to see Shadow stood over me once more, followed by Abigail's voice. Again.

"Lyssi? Are you okay?" she landed on her knees beside us, pulling the dog out of my face. "I heard you scream. What's wrong? I'm calling the police," she stood quickly when she saw the bear hold Bobby had me in and turned back to the house.

"No!" I shouted, as I slid myself out of Bobby's grasp. "No, please," I said quieter, barely above a whisper, "don't call them. There's nothing they can do."

She stood there watching, eyes darting back and forth between Bobby and me. He stood up and seemed unsure of what he was supposed to do next.

"Tell me why I shouldn't call the police," Abigail demanded.

"It wasn't his fault," I gestured to Bobby, who had moved to stand behind me. "I'm sorry for the extra scare," I sniffled like a child. I slipped my hand into Bobby's and tugged him up against my back again. He slid his arms around my waist, leaning his head down to mine so we were cheek to cheek. I took a deep breath, as tears pooled in my eyes, unbidden.

"Do you want me to tell her? She still doesn't look convinced that I'm not trying to hurt you," he whispered for my ears only.

I shook my head, then nodded, "Please."

He kissed my cheek and stood up straight. I put my hands over my face while he told her what had happened, vaguely, of course.

She let out the familiar 'oh honey' and ushered us both back to the house. We sat outside on her front porch while we waited for Miguel to come back in somber silence. None of us seemed to know what to say. I was fine without the sympathetic and pity-filled talks.

A short time later Miguel appeared from behind one of the neighbor's houses. I found myself running to him as if I were drowning and in search of a life raft. When we met up in the street, he yanked me off the ground in a fierce hug, spinning in circles.

"Holy fuck, Lys. You're okay," he said, tears silently wetting my cheeks again, his and mine.

"No, Miguel, I'm not. Jake…" I trailed off, not able to say anything more.

"I know. I'm so sorry. It's not the same without him," he whisper-cried.

We stood still in the middle of the road for a long time just holding each other. He had been my brother's best friend since we were kids. He was obviously taking it as hard as I was.

"Where is he?" I finally found the courage to ask.

"Here. In town. We haven't called your parents yet. Alex and I decided we would try to find you first. There was no way either one of us wanted to tell Aunt and Unc they lost both kids the same night."

I nodded my head, pulled away from him and dragged him towards the house. We stepped up to the porch and I introduced him to Abigail. They shook hands, then we politely excused ourselves and left.

The car ride back to Miguel's house was silent. Before I learned about Jake, I thought I would have been bombarded with questions. I probably would have been had Jake been alright. The silence was both welcome and unnerving. It was nice in the respect that no one thought they had to say something to try to make me feel better. It was unnerving because Miguel was never quiet. He always had jokes, was singing some ridiculous version of the newest hits, or just rambling to hear himself talk.

The strange stillness in the air came to a stop when we pulled into Miguel's driveway. Alex, Tia, and Cason came out of the house, Tia and Alex running full force. I stepped out of the car and was immediately slammed into the side of it when both women jumped on me. The air was knocked out of me and I fell to the ground, pulling them both with down with me. The three of us sat crying for long time.

Miguel, Cason, and Bobby eventually helped us all up, Cason engulfing me in a strong hug of his own. I pulled away, having had enough of the emotional outpours and went inside. I tried to tell everyone I was alright, but I knew they could see through the lies.

Bobby followed me to my room. (Yes, my room. I've had a room at Miguel's since he bought the place. Perks of being the best friend's sister since childhood. It was a three-bedroom, Jake got one of the rooms and Alex and I shared the other.)

"Can we talk for a minute?" he asked timidly.

REFLECTED

I went in the room, closing the door after I gestured for him to come in. I sat down on the floor, resting my head on my knees, waiting to hear what he had to say. He sat down beside me, not saying anything at first.

"I really am sorry," he started. When I looked up and opened my mouth to let him know how confused I was, he put a finger to my lips, "I'm not in here to pity you. I'm in here because I want to take care of you, for a little while, if you'll let me." He pulled his hand away when I closed my mouth, "I want you to talk to me about what happened this weekend and let me know who it is I have to kill. I don't necessarily want anything romantic from you right now. I know you can't. I understand that. I respect that. But I'm not walking away from you tonight, without you knowing I will be here when you need me. I've found a family here with you and your friends and I don't take that lightly. One of my family was killed and another was kidnapped this weekend. I was helpless while you were gone. We couldn't find you after the shifters and vampires left and we looked and called for hours. I don't think any of us slept. I can't begin to fathom how you feel right now, but I am asking you to let me help."

His admission curled itself around my heart. It latched on for dear life and left me speechless. He stood up, took my hands and pulled me up with him. He left me standing while he rummaged through the drawers for clothes. He pulled out everything I would need then headed off to the bathroom down the hall. I heard the water turn on a few minutes before he returned. Taking my hand in his, he guided me to the steamy room, closing the door behind us.

I looked around, surprised by what he had laid out. There were fresh towels on the table by the bathtub, my clean clothes next to them, my favorite soap, shampoo, and conditioner sitting on the lip of the tub, and unlit candles by the sink. He walked to the candles, pulled a lighter from the drawer and lit them.

He turned back around to face me. "Alex helped pick out your favorite scents," he gestured to the candles. "We know you can't go home and figured you wouldn't want to stay at Jake's. But we all wanted you to be able to rest and take the time you need to recover in comfort. And I needed you to be able to take the time to let it sink in that you have me as long as you need me." He stepped up, wrapped his hand around the back of my neck, settling his fingers in my hair. He leaned down and kissed me on the forehead, my cheek, and softly on the lips. He pulled away slowly, then reached down and turned off the water.

"I'll leave you to relax," he said, as he kissed me on the cheek again before turning off the light and walking out the door.

I sat in the tub until the water turned cold. I let it out, refilled it, and washed my hair probably about fifteen times, scrubbed my body until it was raw, let the water out and refilled it again. When I finally stepped out of the tub, there was no hot water left in the water tank. I got dressed and padded back to my room. I curled up on the bed, begging my mind to let me sleep.

I lay awake, crying off and on for a good few hours before the bed dipped down from the weight of another body. Alex curled up behind me and never said a word. I could feel her tears trickle down the back of my neck occasionally, but she never made a noise. She lay there just holding me, like I imagined a sister or mother might do. She stayed with me for about an hour, then left as quietly as she had come in.

I must have dozed off because when I turned over there was a glass of water, aspirin, and toast sitting on the nightstand. I sat up, took the aspirin, drinking half of the water at once. I left the toast and padded softly to the bathroom. I could hear voices speaking in low tones from the kitchen, but I ignored them. When I was done in the bathroom, I started to head back to my room, but stopped when I heard Bobby talking.

"No, Alex. I will not push her. I know you mean well, but she'll either come to me on her own terms or not at all."

"Bobby. Bobby, Bobby, Bobby," she said. I could picture her with her hand on her hip, pinching her nose with the other and shaking her head as if she were talking to a stubborn teenager. "I'm not tellin' you to push her, ya goofbutt. I'm telling you to go check on her. She's gonna need all the people she can showing her support right now."

"I get it, but if I just pop in randomly it'll push her away. I don't want to upset her. She has enough to deal with without thinking I'm trying to get into her pants. I don't know what happened to her. She could have been sexually assaulted or raped for all we know, and I could have already screwed up by kissing her."

"You what?!" Miguel's voice boomed down the hallway.

"I know, Miguel. I probably shouldn't have—"

"You're damn right you shouldn't have. You don't need to be putting your mouth anywhere near her, asshole," Miguel seethed.

Well damn. As flattering as it was, I didn't need Miguel to be trying to step in where he had no business stepping. I turned away from my room and went to the kitchen. I expected to see everyone there, but the only people there were Miguel, Alex, and Bobby. I stood in the doorway watching their dynamics for a few minutes. They seemed at ease with each other, even though tensions were high. Bobby didn't look to be offended by Miguel's rant, Alex didn't seem anymore flustered than she usually did, which was hardly at all, and Miguel just looked tired.

"Hey guys," I said quietly.

All three of them stopped to look at me, looking guilty for talking about me.

"No need to send Bobby in to check on me. Obviously, I'm alright," I shot a look to Alex. Turning to Miguel, I said, "And you don't need to worry about protecting my virtue. That ship sailed a long time ago." I walked up to Bobby, kissed him on the cheek, then got myself a glass out of the cabinet behind him. Alex always had a bottle of wine on hand, so I grabbed it out of the fridge and poured myself half a glass. I set the bottle on the table and motioned for them to join me.

"Sorry, Lys," Miguel started to say, but stopped when I waved him off.

"Nah, no need to say you're sorry for anything. I need to tell you guys what happened and I would rather not wait until tomorrow. I may not want to repeat it again, but I am pretty sure one of you can do it for me when Mila, Tia, Cason, and whoever else needs to ask 150 thousand questions."

They all took a seat around the table, Miguel to my right, Bobby to my left, and Alex straight across from me. "So, before I start, is there anything else I need to know about? I want to get it all out of the way to be able to process it to get it done and over with."

Everyone shook their heads no, so I began. I started at the point in the fight when Eli and I separated and finished at the part where Bobby rang Abigail's doorbell. I had long finished my wine off and was finally starting to feel sleepy. I waited for them to start asking questions, which took them awhile to get to.

"You don't know who originally took you?" Alex asked.

"Nuh-uh. I was under the bush, I saw Jake, scrambled out, and that's it. I woke up chained to a wall, and I don't know where I was kept at the time."

"The only people you saw were the salamander shifter, boar shifter, an earth elemental and a woman who none of us know what she is, right?" Bobby asked.

"She was human," Miguel said, "Abigail's a human."

"Well, still. Human, shifter, centipede, mannequin, whatever she is, it has not a damn thing to do with what happened to Lys," Alex put in, "but I want to know a few things. First, who the fuck knocked out our girl and snatched her right out from under our noses? Second, where in the hell did they take her and why did they not keep her in the same spot? It almost sounds like they were afraid to keep her there for some reason. What would the reason be? Third, what in the blue hell they think they gonna do with her blood? I can see a shifter or vampire blood bein' useful, but a reflector can't change like them."

I knew there would be more questions coming to flesh out any potentially hidden information, but I was too tired for it. I had already caught myself nodding off a bit while Alex was talking. It was almost daylight and I was beyond ready for this night to be over with. I stood up and grabbed

Bobby's hand. He gave me a surprised look when I pulled him to his feet.

"We'll finish talking about this later. It's too late. I am sore and exhausted. I'm going to bed," I called out over my shoulder as I headed to the bedroom, dragging a shocked and speechless Bobby with me.

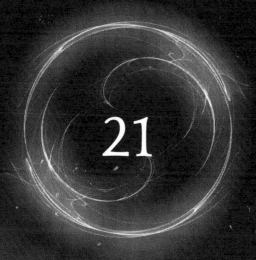

21

Sal and Lucas stood in front of the cell, eyes bulging. The bars at the bottom had been pulled inward, concrete pulled up around the base of the bars, and the timid, friendly female was missing from the cell.

"She was so nice and kind," Sal said in disbelief.

"I told you not to try an make friends with her," Lucas spat.

Whisper stood behind them laughing. "Oh, you two are so screwed," she wheezed.

"Shut up," Lucas told her as he bent down to inspect the bars.

"Hey," Sal said, "Wasn't there supposed to be someone outside all night?"

"Prob'ly. Wanna go look an see if they're still there?" Lucas looked up from poking his finger in the hole where the bar should have been.

"Not really," said Sal as he turned around and walked away.

Lucas sat back on his heels, looked around aimlessly, scratching the back of his head. "How in the hell did she get out of here?"

"It looks like she bent the bars, dummy."

"I can see that, but how? She weighs, what? A buck o'five? She didn't look like no Superwoman to me."

"I don't know. But looks can be deceiving, you know," Whisper crossed her arms and jutted a hip out. "I mean, look at you. Who would have thought you could form a complete sentence?"

"For real, if you don't help try to figure this out, I'll let Bossman know exactly how much help you really are."

"Oh, like that's supposed to scare me. I don't give a damn if you tell him or what you tell him. What else can he possibly do to me? Huh? He's already taken everything from me. There's nothing more he can do to make me hate him more." She turned on her heels and stomped away.

"Let her go, Luke," he told himself, "rationalizing with a pissy teenager had never happened before an it won't start happenin' now."

He bent back down to look at the damage done. After several minutes of looking at the hole, he heard Sal announce, "Ain't nobody out there. You think they even showed up last night?"

"How am I s'posed to know? I left when you did."

"I don't know. I thought maybe you'da seen 'em when we left," said Sal as he pulled the keys out of his pocket. "Move yer fat head outta the way so I can open this door."

"Watch who you're callin' a fathead," Lucas said.

"I didn't call you no fathead, I said you *have* a fat head. There's a difference," Sal rolled his eyes as he opened the door. They looked around the cell for a few minutes before they determined it a lost cause and left.

"You think she had help?" Sal asked as they walked back to the front of the building.

"The bars were bent in, not out. I don't think they could have been pushed in like that if someone helped her. They would hafta pull them, I think. Why? Who do you think coulda helped her?"

"Well, the guard isn't out front. Maybe we have a traitor in our misted."

"Midst, not misted. I don't think no one is dumb enough to betray Bossman, not after him killin' them other two the way he did. Man, that was rough to watch," Lucas shivered.

"I guess it's why the other one hasn't come back yet. If Bossman ever gets his hands on that Dom guy," Sal ran a thumb across his neck.

"Yeah, I don't wanna be that guy."

"You think we both need to be there when he finds out she escaped?"

"I'm not going in there alone! You better bring your big ass in there when he calls or you'll end up just like that Dom guy will."

"I don't want to end up like those other two, either," said Sal.

"I think Whisper's right. We are so screwed." Lucas dropped his head as they walked back outside.

22

Bobby was gone when I woke up. His spot was cold, so he'd been up for a while. I thought about what happened after we went to bed. I was thankful he didn't take advantage of my emotional state. I crawled into bed, he kicked off his shoes, pulled off his shirt, slid in beside me, engulfed me in his arms and let me cry myself to sleep on his chest. He didn't give me false placations and assurances, either.

I got out of bed and stretched. I found myself some fresh clothes, trudged to the bathroom to brush my teeth and shower. I walked into the kitchen where it seemed everyone under the sun decided to meet up. Cason, Tia, Mila, Selby, Tysen and his entire pack council, if I remembered them correctly, had somehow squished themselves into the tiny space.

The conversation slowed when I walked in. They didn't stop completely, which helped to not make me feel like an exhibit on display.

Tysen was the first to address me, "Afternoon, Lyssandra. I'm glad to see you're ok. I'm sorry about Jake. He seemed to be a great guy."

I nodded, not quite wanting to face reality yet. Mila walked over and handed me a plate fully loaded with some of my favorite comfort foods; Dutch bitterballen, Hungarian goulash, khachapuri, and a few raspberry filled sopaipillas piled high on the plate, making it heavy. She kissed me on the cheek then cleared a pathway to the table so I could eat.

I sat down, not hungry. I poked at my food, trying not to cry. I have always hated crying in front of others, but was having a difficult time not doing so. I shoved my plate away and put my head in my hands. I had to face all these people, but I didn't want to see pity etched into their faces. I wanted to see determination. I wanted to see resentment. I wanted to see a fire like they had never known.

I slammed my fist on the table, making several of them jump. "Alright. Let's get something straight," I stopped to make sure I had all of their attention, "I am not under any illusions that I am the only one who has lost someone here. I am also not under any illusions that I was the only one to experience cruelty underneath the psycho who kidnaps people and uses them for science experiments. I do not want, nor need, your pity. What I do want and need is your determination to find the fucker and bring him down. I want to make sure that sick bastard can never hurt another soul again. So, from this point on, I want ideas. I want information. I want details that will progress into a plan. Then I want that fucking plan executed. Now, who wants to go first?"

No one spoke for several minutes. They all either looked everywhere but me or looked me straight in the eye. A couple of head bobs from Selby and Tysen boosted my confidence, reassuring me my outburst wasn't unwarranted or inappropriately timed.

"Cookie Dough, I agree wholeheartedly. The first suggestion I have is to get you trained in physical combat. You won't be going into another fight ill-prepared if I have anything to say about it," Bobby announced.

"I think we all can use the extra practice with hand to hand," Shawn, I think his name was, agreed.

"Do we want to delegate responsibilities?" Eli asked.

"I don't think we need to go out like that. Not yet anyway. I think the best place to start would be to figure out what we already know and move on from there. Figuring out who would be useful doing what may be impractical if the situation doesn't fit," Miguel said.

"My pack has decided to accept me as the alpha. No one has challenged me for the rank, so I can make whatever calls are needed, and they'll be legit. We need to take care of Dom and whoever he has following him. Knocking them out of the game will help make sure Bossman has a few less people to send after anyone," said Tysen.

Everyone let the thought linger in the air. Alex snapped her fingers, asking "Who's going to be inside gathering info? We need someone who can let us know what's going on with those injections."

"I think Miguel is perfect for the position," Mila said as she stepped away from the stove, "he's already running the tests in the main lab. He's strong in his fighting, magic, and with his animal. He can handle his own if shit gets deep. The problem we need to work out is how to get him in the lab at the warehouse without raising suspicions."

"Well, it shouldn't be a problem, he's already started developing a paper trail he can bring to the attention of the couriers. He can let them know he needs to speak to the head tech to make sure they have been sending the right samples. The couriers are usually idiots for hire, so they won't know anything different. They'll let her know and she'll have them bring him in," Selby informed us.

"Parts one and two figured out," Kendrick called out loudly, clapping his hands, stepping over and sliding my plate back in front of me, "and you have to keep your strength up if you think you're going to be any use to any of us."

I looked around at the people gathered in the room. Several of them were nodding their heads in agreement, while others motioned with their hands for me to start eating.

"It's a pack thing," Marcus, again, if I remembered right, told me. "We wolves take care of our females. You need to eat, and there are seven of us here that will make sure no one bothers you while you do."

Miguel reached over to grab a sopaipilla off my plate and five different hands smacked his, two smacks accompanied by a low growl.

"Oh damn," he cried, "you weren't playing. Not that I really thought you were, but she's got plenty and won't eat it all anyway."

"Then you can have whatever is left when she's done," Marcus half growled.

"Alright, alright."

I picked up my fork and put the first bite of savory goulash in my mouth. My eyes rolled back and moaning noises couldn't be stopped. I realized how hungry I was and the shoveling began. I didn't even pay attention to the eyes on me as I gorged myself on Mila's yummy foods.

Eventually the kitchen started thinning out as people paired up to talk about what needed to be done. Tia, Bobby, and Selby stayed at the table with me.

"I know you don't want to talk about it yet, but we kind of need to," Tia hedged.

"Talk about what?" I asked.

"Well, you and Bobby have been using Jake's gym to train, but now with Jake gone..."

"I know," I said, putting down my fork. "You're right. I don't want to think about it. But whether I want to or not, I have no choice. Especially after the little speech I just gave."

"You do need to keep working out. We can do a few things," Bobby said, "we can go to the gym if we need to. Or you can come to my place and use my equipment. It's not nearly as elaborate of a set up as what Jake's is, but it still does the job."

"No, I think I need to keep going to Jake's," I said after a few silent minutes. "I need to be able to start moving forward. I need to feel his presence, smell his smell." Tears sprang up in my eyes, threatening to roll down my face. I refused to let them fall of their own accord, wiping them away.

"We can do whatever you need us to," Selby said. "Remember, I have been where you are. I will help in whatever way I can."

"You aren't alone," Tia reminded me.

"Thanks, everyone." I said as I got up and took my plate to the sink.

Bobby came up behind me, slid his hands on my waist and whispered, "We need a few minutes alone."

I peered over my shoulder at him, "What for?"

"Come on, you'll see," he replied, walking down the hallway.

I followed, curious as to what he would need to talk about. I really hoped it wouldn't be the awkward conversation that usually follows first nights spent together. My stomach balled up, a hollow feeling settling deep.

"I didn't think you'd want an audience," he said while closing my door behind me when I entered the room.

"Uh... for what?"

"I didn't want to say anything last night, you'd already been through enough, and you looked to be doing alright considering, but you have some injuries needing to be tended to. I can fix that." He reached out, lifted my hand up and rubbed the marking on my wrist from where I'd been shackled to the wall. "I bet these aren't the only injuries you got this weekend. I can heal them," he said as he lightly kissed my wrist, "all of them."

The hollow feeling in my stomach turned to flutters. My face heated as blood pooled in my face, brightening my cheeks. His eyes never left mine as I stuttered and stammered for something to say. "How?" was all I managed to accomplish with his searing blue eyes boring into mine, like he was trying to peer into the depths of my soul.

Slipping his hands onto my hips, he walked me backwards until my back bumped into the door. Standing less than an inch away, he leaned down and whispered, "I'm a biokinetic, Cookie Dough. May I?"

My brain only allowed a gulp and nod. He trailed his hands up my sides to my shoulders, and back down to my wrists, setting my sensitive nerves alight. He gently held each wrist, pulling my arms up to the sides. I could feel his power sink into them, making the tissues whole again. I wasn't tapping his energy, but it still left the tickly-bug crawling feeling. When he was done with my wrists, he slid his hands up to my shoulders, repeating the process all over again.

"Where else?"

"My. Um. My head."

He eased his hands into my hair, "Where?"

"The back and right side," I whispered back.

He slipped his hands in my hair, the crawly feeling spreading across my scalp. I closed my eyes to try to rid my mind of the image of bugs all over my head. When the crawly feeling stopped, I opened my eyes to see he hadn't moved an inch.

"Anywhere else?"

I tried to shake my head no, but it was hard with him holding it. Keeping his eyes on mine, he nodded once and eased his head down slowly, giving me time to stop him before connecting his lips to mine. A fire I had all but forgotten about for so long, erupted within me, melting the butterflies that had replaced the hollow feeling I walked in with. His lips brushed lightly against mine, spreading the fire throughout my body. His kisses became firm and assured, his tongue flicked out, gently stroking my lips. I opened my mouth, inviting our tongues to mingle in a slow, torturous dance. My hands found their way up his sides, over his shoulders, while I leaned forward on the tips of my toes. I gripped his shirt tightly as he untangled his hands from my hair, swept them gently down my back, placed them behind my thighs and lifted me. Thumping us against the door, he held me in place, deepening our kiss. My mind and body fought for dominance as my legs wrapped around his waist to pull him closer. I hadn't realized I was rocking my hips into his until a pained moan escaped his throat as his fingers bit through my flimsy pants, pleasantly digging into my ass. I stopped, pulling away from his kiss, letting my head fall back to thud lightly on the door.

"I'm sorry," I said breathlessly.

He trailed kisses from the corner of my mouth, along my jawline, to underneath my ear, "For what, Cookie Dough?"

"I—" my breath hitched as his warm tongue slid to my earlobe, where his teeth grazed the sensitive skin. "I don't know," I finally managed to say.

Following the same path back, he lined my jaw and cheek with kisses until our lips crashed together again like magnets refusing to be kept apart.

I lost myself in his kisses; forgetting about being chained to a wall, awaking on a cold floor in an abandoned police station, running for my life, and the pain of losing Jake. The only thing that mattered were his lips, hands, and body as they moved seductively, passionately with mine.

His kisses slowed, then finally stopped, "I should be the one saying I'm sorry."

I gave him a puzzled look, "Why?"

"Because I lied to you last night."

His admission made me freeze, "What? What are you talking about? What did you lie about?"

"When I told you I didn't want anything romantic from you, it was a lie. I still know you can't, not completely, but I want it. I want you. And I am willing to wait however long you need me to."

I traced my fingers lightly over his lips, red and swollen from our kisses. Tears rose unbidden as I tried to formulate my thoughts. I opened my mouth to try to tell him how much his words meant to me, to say thank you, but he stopped me with a gentle kiss.

"I don't need an explanation. I won't set a time limit. I haven't been so attracted to anyone in a long time. There's no need to rush. But," he turned around and walked us to the bed, stopping when his knees bumped the mattress, "we do need sleep." He threw me unceremoniously down on the bed, making me erupt with laughter. Crawling onto the bed, he settled himself in between my legs, "I can go home tonight or I can stay here with you and you can snot all over my chest like you did last night."

"Ew," I slapped his shoulder, "I did not *snot* all over you last night. I cried like a baby, yes, but I didn't snot."

"Oh, I beg to differ. You cried. You snotted. You drooled. And you snored." He added emphasis to his words with squirmy fingers in my sides.

REFLECTED

My hands immediately went to my face, a completely different kind of heat followed, turning my face bright red from embarrassment.

He gently pried my hands away from my face, "Have I told you lately you're cute when you blush?" He kissed the tip of my nose and lightly kissed my chin, then rolled away, taking his warmth with him.

I leaned up on my elbows to look down to him, "No, you haven't. I don't know if I like the compliment or not because it means possible embarrassments are in my future just so you can get your rocks off watching me blush."

He whipped his hand around my waist and pulled me on top of him, "Maybe."

"Ugh. That's not helping me lean towards telling you, you can stay," I cocked an eyebrow up.

"It's up to you anyway. If you want me here, I'm here. If you need time alone, I can go."

"You do put off an amazing amount of body heat," I said as I slipped off his body and over to where I normally sleep. "What time are we supposed to start training?"

"Usual time, Cookie Dough."

"Then you might as well stay. There is no way I will be getting up in time to head to Jake's otherwise," I winked as I slunk under the covers.

"Oh, so not only am I your personal heater while you sleep, but now I'm your alarm clock, too?"

"Yep. Don't you feel special?" I kissed his rugged jaw as he settled in on his side of the bed.

He reached over and turned the light off, wrapped his arms around me, and kissed the top of my head.

"I honestly do," was the last thing I heard before sleep took me for the second time in twelve hours.

6 AM CAME WAY TOO SOON FOR MY overall happiness, although my attitude towards working out had changed since Friday. The 'it won't happen to me' and 'I have time' mentality had drastically changed to 'not again' and 'not on my watch'.

Bobby had already been up for a while when he came in to wake me. I groaned, rolling out of bed, thumping my feet heavily on the floor. Since I shared this room with Alex, she had workout clothes I pilfered from her dresser. I hurried through my morning routine; brushing my teeth, throwing on her yoga pants and fitted tank top, eating a light breakfast.

I slid into the passenger seat of Bobby's car, asking him if we could swing by my house first. I wanted to pick up my car so I wouldn't be stuck without a ride if everyone decided to disperse.

The quick ride to my house was pleasantly silent. We seemed to have come to some sort of understanding the night before and didn't need to fill the air with awkward questions and weird sentiment. In the silence, I practiced tapping his sig, switching back and forth between taking on Mila's and Alex's appearance.

"You're getting good at that," he said as we pulled into my driveway.

"Thanks. You and Jake taught me a few helpful tricks."

"I'm glad they were useful. Maybe next time we can work on some other things, like how to mimic the funky hair colors Tia likes to sport."

"Yeah, that would be great. I don't really want to run around with pink skin again."

He chuckled, "I don't know, I'd be interested in seeing what you look like in a pink or blue."

"Ha! You did already see me in a pink or blue."

"No. I saw what Tia would look like pink. I want to see your body."

"Uh-huh. I bet you say that to all the girls," I laughed.

"Shit. That didn't come out right, but you know what I meant."

"Suuuure I do," I winked as we climbed out of the car.

I flipped up the false electrical outlet panel door and fished the key out of the hidey hole, unlocked the door and stepped in. Bobby came in right behind me, bumping into me when I stopped.

"What's wrong?"

"My lanyard is gone." I said, puzzled.

"Maybe you put it somewhere else. Is it in your room on your dresser?"

"No. I have a routine. When I come home from work, I drop my lanyard and keys in this bowl," I said, grabbing my keys and picking up the bowl, "and I hang my purse on the hook next to the table. Every time, without fail. I never move it because those things are expensive to replace if lost."

"Feel for sigs."

"Nothing," I said as I put the bowl back on the table.

"How far away do they have to be for you to lose it?"

"I can feel all a sig from anywhere in the house. It's a nice size house, but it's not too big."

"Alright, then it's been a while since anyone has been here?"

"Yeah. There are no traces from anyone having been here, nor is anyone here now."

"Ok, let's look around and see if anything has been disturbed. If you think maybe Mila, Miguel, or Alex might have grabbed it, just on the off chance of you returning to work, give them a call real quick," he suggested.

"I don't think they would have. I am pretty sure someone would have said 'oh, by the way', don't you think?"

"No, probably not. There was quite a bit going on this weekend."

"Yeah. You are probably right," I blew out a breath, knowing he was right. "Well, let's take a look around. I'll grab my phone from your car and be right back."

He went further into the house as I sprinted to his car to grab my phone. On my way back, I peeked inside my car to see if anything had been messed with in there. I was pretty sure there was nothing of use inside for anyone, not unless they wanted to steal my insurance card, but the likelihood was pretty slim. Then again, why would anyone want my lanyard? It's only a work badge allowing me into the building and into my lab. I mean, it tracks the hours I work, but it's useless to someone else, right? What would they care how many hours I worked in a week? Then it hit me.

"Bobby!" I yelled as I ran back to the house.

"What? What's wrong?" he called, tromping back down the stairs.

"They want my work information. They want to know what hours I work, when to expect me home and most likely times I'll be alone in the parking lot. If this goes up the chain of command like we think, they will be able to cross check my employee records and be able to place me and Mila in the same household, if they haven't already. Which will then connect Selby to me because she helped Mila escape. They'll know we are all connected and not just a random happenstance of me being with them Friday night."

"All the more reason for you to not come home. Cookie Dough, I know you want to take your car, but it might be a bad idea. It stands out on the streets. Not many people, if any, have a car like yours in town. They'll be able to spot it since someone has been here and seen it parked in the driveway. Word will spread through the ranks on key things that stick out, and that car of yours definitely fits the bill."

I crumpled, tossing my keys back in the bowl. Knowing he was right sucked. I wanted my car because things would return to some semblance of normalcy when everyone went back to work. Well, everyone except me. I couldn't go back to work because I was tied to now not only one person, but two people they had a target out for.

"Did you see anything out of place when you looked around?" I asked.

"I don't think so, but then again, I don't know where you and Mila keep all of your stuff."

"Point taken," I said as we got back in his car.

Bobby drove back to Jake's house with his hand in mine. Too many things had happened the last few weeks for every bit of my sanity to be intact, and I appreciated the gesture of comfort without the false bravado.

He eased the car into the driveway next to where Jake would have had his truck parked. I am pretty sure he didn't park in Jaykob's spot out of respect.

"Where's Jake's truck?" I asked, looking around wondering if it had been left at the club.

"It's at Cason's house. They said Cason lived closer to Effusion and it made sense to take it there instead of all the way back out here or over to Miguel's."

I nodded, not quite able to respond due to the knot in my throat. I sat in the seat long after he turned off the ignition. I caught myself looking around as if Jake would be running up to the car, like he sometimes did when I arrived. He loved to work outside doing yard work and connecting with the earth. I guessed it was a part of our heritage he was really in sync with.

Vision blurry from fighting back tears, I fumbled with the door handle, trying to get out to get some fresh air. Suddenly I was feeling claustrophobic in the tight confines of the car. Bobby gripped my hand harder, just for a bit of reassurance.

"We don't have to go in just yet. We can go somewhere else. You don't have to do this if you aren't ready,"

"I know. But I need to. It's just hard."

"We'll leave any time you want. Just say the word and we're out."

I gave him a weak smile as I finally found the handle cooperative. I got out of the car and noticed Miguel sitting on the front steps with his head hanging. I heard a few sniffles as I walked up.

"What are you doing here?" I asked when I made it to the steps, sitting beside him.

"I couldn't let you do this alone. I mean, no offense, Bobby."

Bobby held up his hands in surrender, "None taken, man. I know Jake was a great guy, but I had no significant place in his life. I was the dude he just met who was diggin' his sister. You were

291

family. And if you'd like, I can always go and come back in a few, ya know, give you time to do this."

Miguel looked to me, letting me make the choice to accept Bobby's offer or not. We held each other's gaze for a long while when I shook my head, "No, Bobby. You don't have to leave. But if you don't mind, would you give us a little while before you come in?"

"I'll do whatever you need me to. Both of you."

Miguel stood up, offered his hand, and they did the awkward handshake-bro hug thing guys tend to do. Bobby kissed me on the cheek and went back to his car. Miguel and I turned to go in the house, but neither one of us seemed to know *how* to go in. The door was unlocked, as always because Jake never locked the door. His philosophy was if someone wanted in badly enough, they would find a way in, locks be damned. It was better to let them in than having to replace what they broke as well as what they took.

We finally, after many agonizing minutes, mustered up the gumption to walk through the door. The moment we crossed the threshold, I lost it. I fell to my knees, my heart ripping from my chest. I could smell his cologne, hear his soothing voice, see his brilliant smile, feel his strong arms hugging me. Everything, all at once, and none of it at all. Miguel came down to the floor with me, though I was unaware he was even there.

I slowly became aware of my true surroundings again when Miguel let out a strange noise with a strangled, "Fuck! Lyssi, get a grip on yourself."

I dropped my head, wondering what he was growing about. Both of his hands were covered in blood from where my claws had sunk in deep, the blood dripping down. Gasping, I yanked my furry hands back and covered my mouth, accidentally ripping his arm like paper in a shredder. I scratched my own face as I quickly pulled my hands away, belatedly realizing mine were covered in blood, too.

I let out an ear-piercing shriek that brought Bobby running in the front door. Miguel had grabbed my face, telling me he was alright when Bobby tackled him, sending them both sprawling. My panic had cranked up a few notches as I watched them grapple for control.

"Stop!" Miguel shouted, laying back, hands up in surrender, "Stop! She partially shifted!"

"What did you do to her?" Bobby landed on top of him, holding him with his forearm on Miguel's throat.

Miguel tapped Bobby's arm, "Nothing. Get off me and I'll tell you what happened, but I don't think this is exactly helping her right now."

Bobby eased his hold, looking back to me, "Fine, but if you did that to her, I'm kicking your ass."

Miguel nodded, sitting up when Bobby let him go and moved closer to me. "She fell to the floor pretty much as soon as we walked in. She was crying and the next thing I knew, her claws were out and in my arm. She freaked out more and ripped the fuck out of my arm when she pulled back," he said holding up his quickly healing arm. "Her emotions are controlling her powers. She's not in control of them enough yet."

Bobby crawled over to where I was sitting, pulled my face up to inspect the mess, "Did you cut yourself?" His tone was calm, but I could see the concern written all over his face.

"I think so," I pulled away, ashamed of myself and the reaction I'd just had.

He let me go with no fuss, not saying any more. He helped Miguel off the floor and they both pulled me to my feet. Miguel went to the bathroom, brought out a wet towel, and started wiping blood off of the floor. "I got the water warm if you want to go clean up, Lys."

"Thank you," I said, darting into the bathroom where I washed as much of the blood off as I could. There wasn't anything I could do about the nice new gash on my cheek and chin, but I did manage to get it to stop bleeding.

I pulled myself together as much as I could, still decked out in jaguar claws and fur. My chest still hurt from the pain of coming into Jaykob's house and realizing he would never come home again. I was used to working with Miguel's sig, so making them disappear was nothing I couldn't do.

I walked out to hear Bobby and Miguel expressing their concerns about how my emotions seem to be ruling me and how to help gain control.

I was a bit peeved at hearing them talk about me while I was out of the room, but then thought about what I just did to Miguel and couldn't logically argue about it. I was a ticking time bomb when my emotions got the better of me. But it didn't mean I had to like it.

"So, what do you suggest?" I interrupted.

"Training," they replied in unison.

"Ya think?" I crossed my arms over my chest.

"I try not to," Miguel said, "it hurts."

"Ha. Ha," I said, "How are we supposed to train? I can't keep my shit together long enough not to hurt someone."

"Let's head to the gym room. We'll figure something out," Bobby said leading the way to the room at the end of the hall.

Jake's smell was overwhelming in the closed off room. It was a powerful trigger for the tears wanting to freefall again.

"Let's start with stretching. Miguel, are you joining?" Bobby asked.

"Yeah. She could use the support, but also maybe we can do some sparring and she can get a good look at how we move so when it's her turn she'll have a clue."

"Sounds good to me." Bobby led us through about thirty minutes of stretching before getting to the equipment. We each went to our own thing and began our workouts. They made it through several pieces of equipment each before I was done with fifteen reps of chin ups and pull ups. My arms were feeling wobbly already and I wanted to curl up in a ball on the floor. I didn't though, and I didn't complain. I knew that this past weekend could happen all over again and I was damn determined it wouldn't.

I started in on lunges and squats, panting like a dog having a heat stroke. (Okay, so I don't really know if dogs pant when having one, but you get the picture.) My legs and arms burned from the efforts they were not accustomed to, but I did find the workouts a little easier than when we originally started.

By the time I finished my few measly reps, the guys decided to have a throw down in the middle of the room. I was so caught up in my own little miserable world, I hadn't noticed when they were through with their exercises until I heard grunts and the sounds of flesh hitting flesh.

"You guys aren't protecting yourselves, and each other, with gloves?" I asked, disbelieving they were so careless.

"No need to, pint size," Miguel huffed out as he dodged a right hook. "I'm a shifter, so I heal fast. He's a freak who can heal himself."

They danced around the mat several times before Miguel lunged, kneeing Bobby in the side, then threw his elbow into his back on the opposite side. Bobby stepped back, dropped down twisting, sweeping Miguel's feet out from underneath him. I watched in awe as they got up, were knocked right back down, traded punches, kicks, leg sweeps and who knew what else. I wondered how they could keep going without healing themselves because they each were a bloody, bruised mess.

After several anguish-ridden minutes, for me mostly, they stopped to get some water.

"What did you see there?" Bobby asked.

"I saw you two beating the shit out of each other. Other than that, I couldn't begin to explain."

"Well, you're up next," Miguel said, squeezing a bottle of water in my face as he walked by.

"Oh no, I can't do any of that. I can go to the punching bag if you want me to practice hitting stuff."

"The bag won't dodge your punches, won't move out of the way of a kick, and won't hit back. You're up," Bobby raised an eyebrow.

I walked to center of the mat, not caring for the idea in the slightest. I took my stance just like if I were at the punching bag. Neither Bobby or Miguel corrected me, so I assumed I got it right the first time.

"First thing we're going to work on is blocking. It's pretty basic, and you have to know how to protect yourself without throwing a punch," Bobby announced.

I nodded, watching as Miguel stepped up, pretending to throw a punch at Bobby's face. Bobby stepped back to allow Miguel's fist to swing right by his face. "Avoid if you can before exerting any unnecessary energy. You of all people should know energy can be depleted, which can be the difference between life and death or just barely surviving and walking away relatively unharmed."

Miguel threw another punch at Bobby. Bobby shoved his forearm up to stop Miguel from connecting with his jaw. Bobby countered by attempting to jab Miguel's ribs. Miguel immediately dropped his elbow, letting Bobby's hit be absorbed by a less sensitive area.

They did a few more back and forths so I could see various forms of blocking and dodging. I stepped up and Miguel stood in front of me, fists up, ready to go.

"You better get ready, mamacita. I'm about to bring the paaaaiiiin," he teased.

Without thinking, I threw a quick jab and punched him in the mouth, "Oh shit! What the hell, Chica? I wasn't ready!" he whined.

"Oh, Guel, I'm sorry," I rushed up to his side to check him out.

He quickly grabbed me by the neck and put me in a headlock, "Don't ever feel sorry for your opponents," he chastised, while he gave me a noogie.

His childish behavior pissed me off, so I punched him in the back the hardest I could in my trapped situation, to no avail. He laughed off my hits, pissing me off more. I eventually weaseled my way out of his arm, but I was almost positive he let me go. We got back into position and all jokes seemed to stop. He threw a punch, connecting with my right cheek. 'Seeing stars' is not just a cliché. That shit really happens, as it did with his first punch.

REFLECTED

I stumbled back and landed on my ass, holding my cheek, trying to regain focus.

When I stood back up, Bobby came to stand beside me. He said most people have some sort of tell, letting you know when they are going to strike. He showed me where to look and what would be the most likely tell that would hint to what's coming.

For roughly forty-five minutes I got my ass handed to me by both of them. Every so often they would switch out, taking turns at knocking me senseless. I was tired and getting pissy about not getting a single one up on them when I sprouted claws and fur for the second time.

Miguel let out a low warning growl to let me know he was fully prepared to fight cat to cat, and it scared the shit out of me. I'd seen cats fight. Big cats. It's not pretty. No way in hell did I want to go toe to toe with Miguel sporting cat anything. He *was* a shifter. I just pretended to be one sometimes. I didn't think about whether or not he really *would* hurt me. I thought about not fighting with him in any part of animal form, which only brought on more panic.

I was standing there with jaguar fur on my arms and claws, scared shitless, listening to Miguel growl when the signaling pinpricks of a partial shift shot up and down my lower half. My legs buckled, making me crash to the floor. I looked down at my body to see them turning into the hind legs of a jaguar.

I wailed from the pain of bones cracking and shifting out of my control. Bobby slowly backed away from both of us, and I didn't exactly blame him. I wanted to back away, too, but my legs had another idea. By the time my bones stopped popping, cracking, and reshaping themselves, I was seriously disfigured. I had human arms and hands covered in fur, claws instead of fingernails, and jaguar legs preventing me from standing correctly, sending me straight to the floor each time I tried to stand. My head and torso had not changed, throwing my balance off more than I cared to admit.

Miguel let out another low growl and lunged. I shrieked and tried to scramble back, shredding the mat beneath all four sets of claws. He landed on top of me, face transformed, jaws wrapped precariously around my throat. He let out a growl every time I moved or twitched, applying more pressure without breaking the skin. My heart screamed that Miguel wouldn't hurt me, but my brain was yelling he had already lost it.

I doubled up my fist, as much as I could double up a clawed fist, and punched him repeatedly in the side. The punches were weak and didn't phase him. With each of my swings, his teeth dug a little further until he finally broke the skin. Blood tickled as it trickled down the back of my neck and dripping onto the floor. I pulled my legs up between his body and mine and shoved as hard as I could. He rolled away, landing on all four padded feet, fully transformed into a large jaguar.

REFLECTED

As I lay there keeping a close eye on the pacing cat, my heart raced while I tried to gather enough of my senses to turn my legs back into their true form. I knew I could spar with claws; Miguel, Tia, Alex and I had practiced several times, but there was no way I could fight with legs I couldn't stand on.

I evened my breathing, taking control a little at a time. Until Miguel leapt at me again, pinning my shoulders to the floor. I tried to kick at him again, but he moved to the side too quickly for my feet to gain purchase. He snapped his teeth inches from my face, then bounced backwards to remove himself from my reach, pacing again.

While he paced, I brainstormed all the possible ways to get myself out of this mess. Panicked thoughts were not kind thoughts. My legs tingled again with the telltale sign of another shift, but since my thoughts weren't controlled, there was no telling what they were going to turn into, sending my panic up several more notches.

I screamed again as the pains returned, bringing the sounds of snapping bones. Heart racing, I looked down at my legs, certain I was going to be horrified. And again, I was right. Giant bird legs. Not as in scrawny human legs people sometimes get teased about, but real bird legs; knobby kneed, ostrich or emu type legs and feet. I let out another panicked noise, thinking how the fuck did that happen? Miguel's animal was expected, he was there. How did I end up with an animal I wasn't even sure was a shifter species? Why did my legs not return to normal? Why was this crazy shit happening to me?

Miguel let out another guttural noise before the weight of his body land on top of mine once more. My shrill voice echoed in the room as I hit and kicked blindly in my panicked state. His claws raked against my still furry arms, as he fought to hold me down. A warm, wet substance slid down my stomach through my shirt as Miguel's body went limp above me.

His body was eased off mine and Bobby's face appeared above me, worry in his eyes. I pushed myself away from them as Bobby rolled Miguel, motionless over to his back.

"Is he dead? Is he okay? What did I do?" I cried.

"Shh. Concentrate, Lyssi. I need you to get your own form back so you can help me. He'll be okay."

I nodded, terrified I had just killed one of my best friends. Fear and rationality battled for control, making it hard to reign in my wayward thoughts.

Muffled, pained noises escaped the large cat, reassuring me I hadn't killed him at least.

"He'll have to stay in jag form until he heals, but he'll be alright. He's tough, Cookie Dough."

My legs and arms began to tingle in the familiar way, letting me know I was changing. I forced my fears down, focused on my own image, then let the change happen. I looked down to my own body, tears of relief, fear, and frustration pouring down my face. I crawled hesitantly to Miguel, afraid of what I would see. Relief won the battling emotions when I could see his steady breathing and twitching eyelids. I rubbed my hand gently over his muzzle and to his neck, burying my face in his coarse fur. Bobby got up and left us alone for a little while. When he returned, he had a first aid kit with him. I helped clean the wounds, Miguel stirring when the iodine hit the deepest cuts.

"Are you okay?" Bobby asked.

"I am now," I replied with a shaky voice.

"Alright. Go get some water. You need to rehydrate and he'll need it when he comes back around. Bring a bottle and a bowl for him so he'll have whatever he needs."

I knew it was a distraction, but the distraction was welcome, no matter how menial. I came back from the kitchen a little while later with a bowl and two waters in hand. Miguel was still on the floor, but his breathing had steadied and his groaning stopped. Bobby took the bowl and one of the bottles and set them aside. I handed him the other one, "You take it. I drank plenty while I was in there." He nodded and took the water.

"The thing about shifters," he said, "is when they're injured this badly, they won't shift back until they're almost completely healed. Since we don't know the extent of the injuries, we won't know how long he'll stay like this."

"I know. I won't leave him like this."

"No. You can go get a shower and get cleaned up a little. I'll stay with him and when you get back

303

I'll go shower, then fix us something to eat. Maybe he'll be back around enough by then to get some nutrients in to speed his healing."

I left the guys on the floor, feeling slightly better knowing it wouldn't take long, but still worried. I lost my brother less than a few days ago. I wouldn't survive losing anyone else.

23

Sal watched, fighting the urge to shift as Lucas flew into the wall behind them. Lucas landed with a thud on the floor. Carter's temper could be considered frightful at best. Whisper stood still watching, hoping Carter would leave her out of the punishments.

"You didn't get a single drop of her blood before she escaped! Do I have to do everything myself? All of you fuckers are incompetent!"

"Sir?" Whisper asked.

"What?!"

"In hindsight, it may have been preventable if we knew what she was. We still don't know what she is, so it makes prediction impossible."

Carter turned his death stare to her, making her shrink back a little, "That should have been disclosed to you when you were told what to do. Am I to guess it wasn't?"

"Yes, sir. We were never told. We were just told to go get blood from her, feed her bread and water once, maybe twice a day until she cooperated or until told otherwise."

"Let me take another guess as to who gave you these instructions. It was the vampires who brought her back in the first place?"

Whisper nodded, "Yes, sir."

Carter took a minute to consider the new information, "Go to the rec room. Tell everyone you see on the way there I am calling a meeting. You two," he said pointing back and forth between Sal and Lucas, "go get all the shifters, and I mean all of them. I am done fucking around with all of you."

"Emilia," he said into the phone as he slammed the door shut behind them, "you and those worthless vampires get your fucking asses over here. Playtime is over."

24

I showered as fast as I could and raced back to the gym. Bobby and Miguel hadn't moved since I left. I sat down next to them and thought better about asking if anything had changed. I could see nothing had.

Bobby leaned over and kissed my cheek, "Remember, he'll be okay. Talk to him. I'll be back after I shower, with something to eat."

"Okay. Will you call Mila, Alex, or Tia and have everyone come over?"

"Yeah, I'll call them before I shower," he said as he left the room.

Bobby was back less than fifteen minutes later, "Mila said she'll round everyone up and bring food," he said as he sat down beside me.

"That was fast," I told him.

"It helps when all your stuff is still here. Jake told me I could stay with him if I didn't want to trek back and forth between here and my house every day. At the least, I could leave some of my shit in case I needed it."

I nodded, knowing my brother was kind hearted enough for it to be true, "Did you tell her what happened?"

"I gave her the CliffsNotes. I hope you're okay with it."

"Yeah. I don't want anyone to be surprised when they see what I've done," I looked down at Miguel, remorse and shame overwhelming me.

"Hey," he said as he turned my face up to his with a finger, "it was an accident. Accidents happen and he will be okay."

I pulled my face away from his hand. "But I could have killed him. I panicked. I knew in my mind it was Miguel, but my heart kept racing and things kept happening that I couldn't control."

"Do you remember the first time we went outside to practice after Milena showed up?" he paused to let me think about it. "I told you, your emotions get the better of you and you let them control you too much. This is an unfortunate example of why you have to keep control. It's not only about being in control of your abilities. It's also about being in control of your actions when your brain says one thing and your heart says another. You did a great job of regaining control. And no one in their right mind is going to be mad at you for this, including Miguel. We are all here to help you through this hiccup, and we aren't going anywhere."

"Hiccup? You call almost killing my dead brother's best friend a 'hiccup'? What the fuck is wrong with you?"

"No, that's not what I meant and if you stop for a minute and get out of your emotions, I think you'll realize you know it."

I took a deep breath, to reign in my emotions. They bounced all over the place; from sorrow, to fear, to frustration, and everything in between. I knew in my head and my heart he was right, even though I didn't want to admit it aloud.

While I stewed on his words, the sound of running footsteps echoed from the hall. Alex rushed into the room and to Miguel's side, squeezing herself between me and Bobby. She stroked his fur for a couple of minutes before she turned to me. "What happened?"

I gulped, "We were sparring and he shifted. I panicked and couldn't control my own shifts. I did this. I almost killed him. I'm so sorry, Alex."

She turned to me, wrapped her arms around me and hugged me tight. "Get yourself together, Chica. This was not your fault. He knew what he was getting into, I promise you. He always did this kind of shit with me and Tia La Rosa when we were kids. You know he did. His stubborn ass is fine. He's gonna be up and his normal, jerk self in a few hours. You watch."

"I wish you two would stop calling me that," Tia said as she entered, "It's not my name and I am no rose."

"Eh, Chicana, you know we do it because we love you. Besides, you believe your shit smells like roses," Alex winked at me when she was done ribbing Tia.

"I do not. And even if I did, it's still no excuse to keep calling me that. I figured you would have learned your lesson by now. Do you remember when Tio Mateo came running outside in nothing but his underwear when he thought you guys were screaming for Tia Rosa? He thought something was wrong and we got a disturbing view no amount of eye bleach can ever remove," she shivered.

"Food's here," Tia and Alex said in unison to me and Bobby, who had moved to one of the workout benches to give us room.

Alex and Tia left to go get food. "Good gods, shifter noses are sensitive. Go get something to eat. See what Mila brought for Miguel while you're in there," I told Bobby when he didn't move.

He got up without a word, leaving me alone with Miguel. I apologized over and over while I ran my fingers through his fur. I snuggled up behind him, holding the enormous cat as he slept.

I don't know how long everyone left us alone, but the quiet helped me get my thoughts in order. I looked back at all my reactions leading up to my lying on the floor with an unconscious jaguar. The series of events unfolded in my mind and I noticed a pattern. It was like an epiphany. The things Bobby had been telling me all of a sudden made sense and everything was clear. I could see the point where I detached my emotions during the fight and after I woke up in the cell. When I thought about it all with a calm mind, my confidence raged and I knew practice was going to be the make it or break it for me in the long run.

MIGUEL WOKE UP LATER DURING THE night and confessed to scaring me shitless on purpose, pissing me off to no end. Although he did say he hadn't thought it would happen the way it did. How in the hell was I supposed to know my magic would tap Bobby's in my panicked state and do whatever it wanted? I remember clearly wishing I had more stable legs to stand on, but looking back on it later, I could see where I should have been more specific.

For the next six days, I trained relentlessly while he took the time to completely heal. I trained in everyday clothes, meaning my painted-on-looking jeans, a t-shirt, and whatever shoes I happened to wear. Fostering my anger at his stupid stunt, I allowed it to push more force into my hits and kicks. I learned how to put it aside, which led to being able to push the other emotions away with it, including the grief from losing Jake. My clothes and my emotions, I decided, would not hold me back from accomplishing what I needed to do.

Over those six days, I sparred with everyone, including Tysen and a few wolves from his pack council. Determination thrived within me like I never knew before. My contact accuracy and force of contact improved by remarkable strides. Sig tapping and manipulating, and emotional control became second nature. I didn't allow the breaks in between practices to result in relapsing back into a state of non-committal. I slept hard at night, too exhausted to let my fears of losing someone else take root.

Mila never returned to work after her kidnapping. With neither of us working, I didn't know where the money would come from to pay our utilities and other expenses until Mila shared her secret with me that funds would always be available. She offered to pay for things at Jake's house until I got back to work, whether at BTCL or somewhere else. Luckily, by the time we had the discussion, I had gained more control over my emotions or I would have been a sobbing mess by her offer of kindness.

Since my moment of clarity and Miguel's asshole move to get my emotional state in check, I decided I would stay at Jake's house. It made me feel closer to him, which in turn made it easier to get a grip on my emotions. Everyone argued with me about it at first because we were all still targets for the vampires and shifters Bossman had gunning for us, but when Bobby offered to take the spare room, all fussing about it stopped when I conceded.

The one time I allowed my emotions to rule me was the day we buried Jake. Mom and Dad tried to talk me into coming back to the rez for safety, which probably would have been the best thing to do if I weren't so set on helping my friends put a stop to the kidnapping and killings. I understood where they were coming from, but I didn't have it in me to let Jaykob's murder go.

Bobby knocked on my door, pulling me out of my musings about the changes throughout the week. "Hey, Cookie Dough," he used my nickname for the first time in days. "How you doin' in here?"

"Hi. I'm okay. Sore, tired, drained. All the usual, you know?" I waved him in.

"Yeah, I know." He sat at the foot of the bed, "I can imagine you are. You've been working hard this week. You've not given yourself any downtime to speak of. Any way I can help?"

I sat up against the headboard and pulled my feet underneath me, "Do you know if anyone has any more information on the group that attacked us?"

"That's what I came in here for, actually. Tysen called. He said some of his wolves were out doing a perimeter check on their property and found a few familiar scents lingering. They didn't find anyone, but someone has been out to their property scoping them out."

"Do they know who it was?"

"He didn't say. He did say the scents were familiar and none of them were part of his pack. He asked if it would be alright for a few of them to come by this evening. I told him I didn't see where it would be a problem, but I'd double check with you and get back to him. I thought about calling Miguel first, but decided you should make the call, uh, decision, too."

"Sure. I don't see why not. If they have information we could use, then yeah, get whoever over here that needs to be."

"Do you mind if I call them in a little while?" he asked.

"Why in a little while? And why are you asking me?"

He scooted up the bed until he was face to face with me, "Because I want time with you before anyone gets here. Once I make the call, it won't take long before they're all here making as much noise as inhumanly possible."

The sincere and pleading look in his eyes was more than I could handle. His expression asked me to make the first move. Our interactions had been limited since Miguel forced me to face my lack of control. I leaned and let our lips connected with warm familiarity. The passion in his kiss buzzed through my body. He grabbed my hips and pulled me closer to him, forcing a moan out that I'd been trying to withhold. The sound set him off, inviting his mouth to move past my lips and to my neck. His hands found their way up underneath my shirt, his firm grip resting on my sides. I untangled my feet and pulled them out from underneath myself, putting them on either side of his body. Threading my fingers in his hair, I let my head fall back to give him better access to my neck. My head thumped against the headboard, making us both chuckle.

"Let me fix that for you," he said between kisses.

He sat up on his knees, gripped the hem of my shirt and pulled upward. His eyes stayed locked on mine as I raised my arms over my head. A few seconds later my shirt was on the floor while our mouths found each other all over again. I pulled at the bottom of his shirt, not caring in the slightest if I was gentle with it. He helped pull it off, then settled me on the bed, sliding his body on top of mine.

"Better without the pesky headboard reaching up and smacking you in the back of the head?" he asked, giving me one of his seductive smirks.

"Aren't you Mr. Chivalrous?" I teased back.

"Well if you don't like Mr. Chivalrous, Mr. Rough and Ready can come out to play."

"Oh, so you have a split personality? They have meds for that, you know."

He tickled my side, making me draw my legs up in reflex. With him lying between them, the movement pulled him flush against me and all laughter died when I realized how *Mr. Ready* he was. The intensity in his icy blue gaze and his stilled hand on my side rekindled my fervor and our lips collided once more.

I wove my fingers through his hair again, pulling his head up to kiss his jaw. I licked, nibbled, and sucked along his stubbled jawline to the lobe of his ear, nipping the soft tissue of his ear lobe with my teeth as I started grinding against the hardness still locked in his jeans. He let out a throaty noise, sending a fire from my belly to between my legs.

His hand eased upward, settling on my chest. He moved his thumb in slow circles on the cup of my bra and slipped his fingers under the strap pulling it down, freeing my breast almost entirely. His feather soft touch became firm and assured when he skimmed my nipple with his fingers, making it pebble. Turning his head back to me, he found my lips with his then kissed his way down my neck and across my shoulder to my other bra strap, grabbing it with his lips to slip it off my shoulder. He lightly ran his tongue along the skin next to my bra at the top of my breast until he came to the center of the cup. Grabbing the flimsy material with his teeth, his hot breath crossed my nipple as he pulled down fully releasing my other breast. I gasped when his tongue flicked out, wetting and teasing my erect nipple. My hands, still entangled in his hair, clenched as I let out an approving mewl.

I arched my back, encouraging him as he moved back and forth, licking, sucking, and grazing me with his teeth. He trailed his mouth across my skin, moving down across my belly to the top of my shorts, leaving tingles in his wake. He looked up at me, kissing gently as he slid his fingers into the waistband, waiting for me to protest. When I didn't, he sat up on his knees and pulled my shorts off in one smooth motion. Staying on his knees, his hungry eyes roamed my body taking in the sight of my near nakedness, almost to the point of embarrassment. When he was done looking he returned to his spot between my legs, kissing from the top of my panties to the inside of my thigh.

"I think blue is my new favorite color," he said softly as he teased my core with his breath, running a finger along the lace.

I squirmed with each new caress across my skin from the tingles his touch left behind. It was nothing like anything I had ever experienced before. "Are you pushing your sig out?" I asked, breathless.

He stopped and looked up at me, puzzled, "Am I what?"

"Are you pushing your sig out? Or. Um. Using your magic?"

"No. I don't use my magic in the bedroom unless we've both decided beforehand how and what I'm going to do with it. Or without your consent first."

"Oh," I said, embarrassed I'd put a stop to the moment with a stupid question.

He crawled back up until he was laying on top of me again, "Why did you ask that? Was I doing something wrong?"

"Oh gods, no. You weren't doing anything wrong," I said, grabbing his head and kissing him quickly, "the exact opposite, actually. Remember how I explained what your sig feels like?"

"Uh. Yeah. It's not much of a confidence booster, by the way. Who wants to feel bugs crawling all over them?"

A laugh escaped me because of his dejected tone, "Yep, bugs. Crawly, tickly, bugs. But the strange thing about it that made me ask is when we are intense, and intimate, your touch leaves a tingle in its wake. It's never happened before, and Oh. My. Gods. is it amazing. I was just wondering if you were doing it on purpose?"

"Huh," he said, amusement tinging his voice. "No, I didn't do it intentionally. But you like it, you say?" He ran a finger over my left nipple, sending a shock through my body and straight to my core.

My pleasure-filled gasp must have been answer enough because his mouth found my hardened nipple again. He didn't take his time reclaiming his place between my legs, mouth teasing my center, much closer this time.

"Let me show you the difference between when I do use my magic and when I don't," he said as his fingers traced along the lace at my apex. "This is no magic." He moved his fingers gently along, barely applying pressure and a light tingling followed. Without warning, all the nerve endings in my sex came to life. I cried out in surprise, arching my back up off the bed. "And that, my Cookie Dough," he said as he kissed my center through the lace, "is with magic." The pressure of his touch hadn't changed, but holy hell at the sensations he sent through my body! It was phenomenal.

"With or without it?" he asked.

"Both," I breathed, trying to regain my train of thought.

He kissed his way back up to my mouth, unhooking and removing my bra along the way. "Are you sure? Not about the magic, but this. All of this. We can't go back to the way things were when we've gone through with it."

"I don't expect to," I said, giving him my most sincere look.

He kissed me hard, pulling me closer. I pulled away and pushed him up onto his knees. I unbuttoned his pants, glancing up at his face. I didn't recognize the expression on his face, so I stilled my hands until he nodded his head once. With his invitation, I unzipped his pants, freeing him from their constraints.

"Holy fuck!" slipped out of my mouth before I got both hands slapped across my mouth.

He laughed while he slid his pants down to where he could kick them off and onto the floor. "Not what you expected?"

"I hadn't really thought about what to expect. I mean, I could feel you through your jeans, but damn!"

He lay on top of me, bringing his lips to mine, "I'll be easy. Stop me if it gets to be too much."

I nodded with a promise that I would as he made a new pathway with kisses back down my stomach.

He didn't ask before he stripped my lacy blue panties off, tossing my them to the floor with the rest of our abandoned clothes. His tongue flicked in and out, between teeth grazes on the inside of my thighs, as he moved up to my center.

When his mouth found my sweet spot I almost lost all control. He slid a finger inside, and after a few minutes, inserted a second. He put an arm under my thigh, wrapping my leg over his shoulder, settling his hand on my stomach. He kept the delicious torture up; his tongue sweeping, fingers sliding in and out until stars burst behind my eyelids. When my legs started shaking, he extracted himself from the tangled mess we'd become and slid his body up mine.

He stopped at my entrance, waiting patiently for me to welcome him in. I rocked up to him and he took his cue, slowly sinking in, little by little until I was comfortable with his large size. He rocked slowly at first, picking up his pace only when I did.

Our slick, sweaty bodies took over and all else was gone. Nothing else existed but us. As hands and mouths roamed all over each other's body, all sounds ceased; the ticking of the clock in the hall, the birds outside, the TV that stayed on in the living room, everything except us silenced.

"Lyssi, I want to call you mine," he said in a whisper after we were through.

"I've noticed you do already."

"No, I was kind of joking around, using a term of endearment, or wishful thinking. I want to be able to say it and it not be in jest, a term of endearment, or wishful thinking. I want to say it and it be real."

"What does that mean to you? I know what it means to me, but I want to make sure we're on the same page." I told him.

"It means forever, Cookie Dough. I want to bond with you. I know it's fast. I know you've been through a lot, but that's just how it is for me and my kind. We are built a lot like wolf shifters when it comes to mating. We mate for life and when it hits us, there's no stopping it. When I saw you in Effusion that night, that was it. The urge to bond to you hit me with a force that knocked my breath out. Its only become stronger and I can't fight it. If you reject me, then you reject me. I can't and won't make you love me, but I'll never be able to move on. And it's what Milena was talking about when she said I haven't reached my full potential. A biokinetic reaches the peak of their abilities when the mating bond snaps into place."

"Wow. Talk about pressure."

"I don't mean it like that. I don't want you to feel pressured, but I do want you to know; I can't watch you with someone else. I can't support you if you choose to be with someone other than me. It's not me being a dick, but it's physically impossible. I can control all sorts of things with my abilities, but that's one of a few things I can't."

"Have you tried to bond with anyone before?" I asked, eyeing him out of the corner of my eye.

I knew what he was talking about. Reflectors were much the same way, if I were to believe the stories my parents told. Once we bonded with our mate, things like the tingles he left on my skin when he touched me became explainable. It was supposed to only happen when a couple bonded, not before.

"No. It's got to be a natural match. I can't just go bond with someone because I'm crushin'," he laughed. "It won't work that way, even if I wanted it to. It must be equally reciprocated. I haven't found anyone I felt the pull to bond with before. Until you."

"What happens to a biokinetic after they bond?"

"The same thing that happens to a lot of other species, I guess. We develop a bond connecting us to whomever we mate with. I mean, it isn't the type of bond that when one dies, the other one dies with them in that moment, but they'll wish they had," he said while he trailed a finger up my arm, leaving an electrical tickle in its wake. "It does give a significant power boost, but I'm not quite sure how that works."

"I'm not ready for a bond. I don't know what to say without sounding like a bitch. I mean, I'm seriously into you, but a life-long bond is not something I've thought about."

"I know. I didn't want you to be surprised if the part that's urging me to bond with you makes me do things I wouldn't normally do."

"Like what?"

"Not going home," he chuckled, "having to be around you more. I won't be able let you get too far without losing my mind. I don't mean like going to work, to the store, or anything that simple, but more like when you were kidnapped. Miguel and Shawn had to step in to keep someone from getting hurt when I lost my shit on Eli and Kendrick a few times. I probably would have got my ass handed to me, but they recognized it for what it was and took pity on me." He turned over, pain of the memories evident in his eyes, "I can't go through it again, Cookie Dough. It will get someone killed."

I let his words sink in, the fluttering curtain giving me somewhere to focus my eyes. "My parents talked about how reflectors bond and it sounds a lot like how it happens for biokinetics. Do you think it explains the aftermath of your touch?"

"It might. I don't know what happens to reflectors, you're the first one I've met that I know of. I don't know who to ask about it, either."

"I do, but I won't. I'd rather figure it out on my own. I do know it will happen when I am ready. And I'm not right now."

"I know," he kissed the top of my head and rolled away, picking up his pants, "and in the meantime, we have a group of obnoxious shifters to get over here. I'll call Tysen and Miguel if you want to go get in the shower. They'll know what's up, but I don't think you want my scent that strongly on you when they get here. I wouldn't have a problem with it, you're too cute when you blush." He gave me another of his heartbreaking winks.

I buried my face in my hands at the thought of Miguel and Alex giving me shit about it, "Fuck me, they are going to be relentless."

He pulled his pants on, gave me his flirty wink when I peeked at him between my fingers, "I would love to, but we might want to wait until after all the sniffers are out of the house. You'd never hear the end of it."

He bent down, kissed me hard, then left me to get ready. I got up and gathered my clothes from the floor and tossed them into the laundry basket. By the time I got my stuff together, showered, and made my way downstairs, Tysen and his counsel, Miguel, Alex, and Selby were all in the living room bantering back and forth.

"Ooooh, look at you glow," Alex squealed, bouncing over to me.

"Shut up, kangaroo," I nudged her when she got within elbow's reach.

"Ha! No way! It's been for-ev-ah since you've been serious enough with someone to give up the goods. I'm happy for you!" she gushed.

"Thanks. I think."

"You need someone. Especially now," the tone in her voice sobered, "and for the record, I think that crazy bitch sister of Mila's is playing both sides."

"What? Why? What makes you say that?" Eli asked.

"Well, for starters," she turned to address everyone, "she told Chica here she would need to learn to be alone. That's not true. Not entirely.

She has us, all of us, but she and Jake were close. Super close. They were closer than most siblings are, and that heifer is the one who sews dysfunction and obstacles for people to overcome, right? Well, she might've meant Lys would need to learn to live without Jake," she glanced at me with sorrow in her eyes, "and she could have been alluding to Lyssi's upcoming kidnapping. If coming to warn us about that kind of shit and causing it isn't playing both sides, I don't know what is."

Silence filled the room for several moments while everyone thought over the new realization that she could be right.

"But wait a minute," Kendrick said, "she doesn't cause death. That's the other wacko's job."

"You're right," said Miguel, "she didn't cause Jake's death, that was the warning part. She could've been behind Lyssi's abduction, though. That would be something to overcome," he flicked his eyes between me and Bobby, "for a couple of people."

Bobby shuffled his feet, jamming his hands in his pockets, "I already apologized. Give me a break."

Eli slapped him on the back, "No worries, man. We can tell when someone has lost his marbles because he's scared for his mate." Eli tapped his nose to hint at the secret.

"Hold up just a minute," I interjected in their camaraderie, "but I am not his mate."

"Says your mouth, but that's about it. Whether you want to admit it or not, you two have a thing.

Your pheromones kick into overdrive when he's around and so do his when you are. Not to mention that fucker", Shawn pointed an accusing finger at Bobby, "lost his marbles when you disappeared. Simple things set him off and he reeked of anger, fear, guilt, and all the other smelly emotions when he didn't know where you were. Which only happens to mates."

My face flushed and I busied my eyes everywhere except at another set of eyes.

"If Milena is playing both sides, then we should let Mila handle it," Tysen said, steering the conversation away from mine and Bobby's personal business. "What we need to handle is the trespassers on the property. They were the same ones in on the ambush after we left Effusion. They're stepping up their game and we need to figure out what do from here on. I can't let it go, but since they've already taken the life of one of yours, you have just as much to say about it as we do."

"I think it's time to take the fight to them," Selby said. "If we wait for them, they could pick us off one or two at a time until they have what they want or there are none of us left to fight back."

"She makes a good point," Kendrick chimed in.

"I think so, too," Eli nodded.

"Alright. Let's make some plans then," Alex said as she hopped up and down like a rabbit.

25

Four days later we stood at least fifty strong down the road from the warehouse Mila had been kept prisoner in. Tysen had brought most of his pack, minus the few staying with the elderly, children, and non-fighters. Miguel, Cason, Alex, Tia, Bobby, Selby, Mila, and I were all standing near the back of Tysen's truck. Tysen, Eli, and Shawn greeted us with nods and a few handshakes.

"Who's ready to do this thing?" asked Eli.

Selby was dressed in a red leather jumpsuit from head to toe. Strapping a rather nasty looking blade to her leg, she replied, "Let's shut this bastard down."

Shawn looked her up and down, smirking and told her, "Remember, there are shifters in there who know you. They won't hesitate to try and rip your pretty little head right off your shoulders."

"That's what I'm counting on," she said then blew him a kiss.

"Mmm. Cocky. I like it," he said, "let's hope it doesn't get you hurt."

"You just worry about protecting your pups. I got this." She walked away and leaned against the car in front of Tysen's.

"I hope she doesn't take this shit lightly," he said looking around at the group, "I'd hate to see her cocky attitude get her killed."

"I think she'll surprise you," Mila told him. To the rest of us she said, "Milena won't be here. She's never involved in the actual fighting. Mira, however, will be hiding somewhere in the background, if she's here right now. She doesn't like to get her hands too dirty. She'd rather wait until the end of the chaos to show up and steal the glory. I'll try to find her and deal with the mess she's bound to create. It will keep her magic out of the fight and keep her from influencing you directly."

"Selby said there are usually around fifteen shifters here at any given time. If that's true, isn't this a little overkill?" Tia asked.

"Not hardly," Tysen was the first to answer. "Yes, there are usually around ten to fifteen shifters guarding the gates and grounds, but there are more in the back with the people who have been experimented on. Then there are the experiments themselves. Who knows how far they've advanced the formula in the last week or two and who knows how those who were injected are reacting to them. If the tamers feel like they can corral them back up, they might let them out of the cages. We also know there are at least three vampires, maybe more."

"Does this Bossman ever leave? Is there a chance he's not in there?" Cason directed the question to the shifters.

"Yeah, he leaves sometimes," Eli answered.

"Did he have a schedule? Like was always gone on Tuesdays or some such craziness?" Alex asked next.

"Nope. He comes and goes whenever he wants to," Shawn said.

We stood around a few more minutes to see if there were any more questions. When none came, Tysen, Eli, and Shawn all pulled their shirts off. They turned around, walking to the wooded area, shucking shoes and pants as they went. Alex and Cason's eyes lit up in appreciation of the naked backsides disappearing into the woods.

"This is the part that's gonna suck the most," Alex whined.

"They won't be long. They're the fastest in the pack," Damien said as he walked up.

"I know. I just hate waiting is all."

He nodded, "I know the feeling. But you should be better at the patience thing since you're a cat shifter, right? Uh, better than a wolf, that is."

"Nice catching yourself there, bro," she narrowed her eyes at him, then flashed a smile to show she teased. "I guess so, but I never thought about it. It's different in cougar form. There's no real sense of time. There's just the hunt, ya know."

"Yeah, I get it," he said, looking over where the other three wolves had vanished into the trees.

"You're not in the bottom of the pack if you're a council member. Why didn't you go with them?"

"It won't take more than the three of them to do a quick perimeter check. The fewer, the better. They'll be slowed down if too many go out there. It's also reaffirming our places within the pack. We have a hierarchy and it's crucial to how well we function. Since Tysen is the new alpha, even though he isn't new to the pack, he still has to assert his dominance. It's his job to coordinate any plans and make sure we all know what our jobs are. If he fails to do those two things, the pack won't respect him and he'll have a shit ton of problems."

We stood in quiet contemplation as Alex and Damien talked about pack dynamics to kill the wait time. Tysen, Eli, and Shawn reappeared, with pants on, fifteen or so minutes later.

"The structure looks to be the same. Guards at the gate, a few milling around outside, but not paying any attention to their surroundings. It looks like we won't have an issue until security sounds the alarm and by then, hopefully most of the damage will be done already," Tysen announced as he walked up.

"Are we still on for the original plan?" asked Miguel.

"Yep. I need my guys who walked away from Bossman with me. Mind going and getting 'em, Shawn?"

"Not at all," Shawn said, jogging off to find them.

"Give us five to get there and in the door. It shouldn't be a problem since we left things up in the air. I'll have a couple of the guys shift and howl if we run into problems."

Miguel and I nodded. Selby came to stand with us after Shawn jogged off. "I'll go to the lab, Miguel do you want to come with me?"

"Yeah, I do. I want to get my hands on as much stuff in there as possible. It'll help to know what the fuck we are working against," he replied.

Three other shifters walked up with Shawn in the lead. "We're ready," Shawn told him.

"See you on the flip side," Eli winked before turning away and running off with the five other shifters.

Alex hopped in place, grabbing onto Cason's arm, "I know why you've been going out to the pack's territory so much. You and Eli are crushing!"

"Shut up. We are not," he denied, turning red in the face.

"Oh, you totally are," she squealed. "Nothin' wrong with it. He's a sweet guy. He's funny and hot as fuck. You go, boy!"

Miguel elbowed me and nodded at Cason, "At least she's moved on from you and Bobby, huh?"

"Oh, hell no," she pronounced it 'heyell naw', "I am not done with those two. They may release pheromones when they are together, but it ain't the only thing they been releasin'."

"Oh gods," I hid my face in my hands again, "she really has no shame, does she?"

"Not a bit," Tia and Mila said in unison.

"Time to start grabbing sigs, Cookie Dough," Bobby said, reminding me I needed to get my head in the game.

"Why do you call her 'Cookie Dough'?" Alex asked, "That's a strange nickname."

"Wouldn't you like to know," he shot me a wink making the fire return to my face.

"Don't encourage her, you ass," I told him.

Selby stepped over to me and put her elbow on my shoulder, "Ignore them. Alex is just jelly cuz ain't nobody tryin' to tap that." She stuck her tongue out at Alex and gave me a smile.

"Speaking of 'tapping', whose sig do you guys suggest I tap?" I looked around at all of them, hoping to get a break from the teasing.

"Who are you most familiar with?" Bobby asked.

"Probably Miguel, Alex, or Tia."

"Well, try to figure out which one you're most efficient with real fast and use that one," Tia said.

I focused for a few moments, sifting through all the energies surrounding me. There was no shortage, that was certain. I reached out for Miguel's vibrant energy. Figuring there were enough canines going in, using Tia's coyote would be a bit much. Alex's cougar energy was still, after all these years, as unpredictable as she was. I knew what I would be getting with Miguel's.

The comforting waves of his sig wrapped around my hands and arms first. The pins and needles sensation had softened over the years of practicing with his abilities. I wish it worked that way with everyone else's sig, but alas, maybe with more practice.

Claws extended from the tips of my fingers, making the sensations amplify a little. Fur pricked its way out of my skin, up my forearms to past my elbows. My muscles thickened, flexing with each popping noise.

I let out a sigh as the changes happened, relishing a new wave of strength washing over my entire body. I didn't have to move to know I would be able to run at the speed of a souped-up jaguar. Flexing my newfound muscles released a tension I hadn't noticed I carried.

Pulling myself out of my internal musings, I looked up to find all my little clique staring at me, "What?"

Variations of 'nothing' came from all around.

"It's time," Miguel announced.

One by one we all turned and walked up the road to the warehouse where we would find one of three things; answers, revenge, or death.

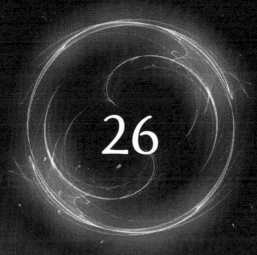

26

Heavy tension in the air settled on my shoulders. Energy whipped from the small army approaching the gates, amping up Miguel's energies, boosting mine further. Men and women began shifting as we ran, cracking bones adding sounds to the crunch of gravel beneath our feet. Musk from the wolves infiltrated my nostrils when the breeze skimmed over my face. Yips, howls, and growls reverberated off the trees, feeding the palpable waves of energy.

Three guards at the gate scrambled back and forth with confusion, fear, and panic etched into their features as they tried to figure out what to do about the oncoming hoard. Miguel, Cason, Bobby, Mila, Alex, Tia, Selby and I went straight for the gate and guards while most of the shifters jumped the four-foot fence with ease.

Selby pulled her knives from the sheaths, spun around and shoved one knife to the hilt in the jugular of the largest guard. Pulling the blade out quickly, she turned, thrusting her other knife upwards in the chest, under the ribcage of his comrade who tried to grab her from behind. Cason intercepted the third and final guard with a power punch to the temple, dropping him like a rock. I stopped mid-step in fangirl-awe, seeing Cason throw the punch and keep walking like nothing had happened.

Selby wiped her blades clean on the dead guards and nudged me as she walked by, "Come on, maybe we'll get to see his badass punch again when the rest of them come running."

I hustled to catch up with everyone as the doors at the front and side of the building burst open, animals and people alike pouring out. The melee had officially begun.

A white streak darted by on my right before I hit the ground with a bone-jarring thud. A large white snow leopard dug claws into my back and chest when it pounced, pulling my attention away from the open doors. I rolled over to my back to keep it from being able to sink its teeth into the back of my neck. Growing up with Miguel and Alex afforded me some reflexes and knowledge of large cat hunting tactics many people don't readily know. I kicked its soft stomach hard enough to throw it off me, thanks to the pumped energy I was still drawing from Miguel. The cat rolled and popped back up onto all four feet in seconds. Standing, warily eying each other we circled, sizing one another up. I faked left and spun to the right as the leopard lunged, raking my claws down the tough hide on the side of its neck and shoulder. The pained (or pissed) yowling noise it cried out made my insides cringe in dread. One of us would be dying, there was no doubt in my mind about it. What I did doubt was my ability to be the one to walk away. It swiped a large paw towards my face, missing me by a hair's breadth. I'm not gonna lie, I think I peed myself a little.

Trying not to trigger any more instinctual hunting reactions, I backed up a step to put some needed space between us. The muscles in its hind legs twitched in anticipation of the fight. Fighting back panic, an absurd image of it doing the 'buttwiggle' like the tiny cats in funny kitty videos flashed in my mind. A nervous and scared laughter erupted from me, causing the animal to falter a second, probably thinking I'd lost my mind.

I regained some of my wits and sprang forward, twisting myself so my body was flat against its side when I dug my own claws into its chest and throat. Sinew, blood, and fur came away with my claws as its limp body fell to the ground.

Horror at what I had just done roared through me. I took a life. I ended someone's future. I killed a powerful and beautiful creature. I looked down at myself, covered in blood, some of it mine, most of it not. Dizziness swept over me and I collapsed to my knees.

So self-absorbed with the atrocity I had committed, I didn't see the blow coming to connect with my left kidney, the sharp pain piercing my side, throwing me face down. A strong kick followed, rolling me to my side with an iron-like force. Gasping for breath, I tried to get a view of my attacker but my vision was hampered by the dust still afloat. Another kick found my chest, knocking the air I had managed to suck in right back out. Thick hands pulled me back up to my knees by handfuls of my hair, only adding to the agony already coursing through my head. The split second I was afforded to get a peek at anything was squashed by a rock-hard knee connecting with my face. Cartilage in my nose made a cracking noise, salty tears sprang and loosed, and a metallic bitterness filled my mouth. Searing pain tore through my skull as my hair was released and I fell backwards. Darkness filled my vision and silence followed.

Bobby's panicked voice filled my ears, "Cookie Dough, you have to wake up." Rough patting on my cheek stung, bringing me a little closer to my senses. "Lyssandra, wake the fuck up!"

I groaned, my head still swimming from being used like a soccer ball. Most of the pain had vanished, but the disorientation remained. Sounds of fighting began to filter in and I tried to blink but my heavy eyelids wouldn't cooperate. Breathing was easier than it had been a moment before, though my mouth was still dry from sucking in dust. "Bobby?" I choked out, voice cracking.

When he didn't answer, I forced my heavy eyes open. My eyes followed the sounds of flesh on flesh to see Bobby and a huge lizard grappling on the ground only a few feet away.

"Bobby! No!" In agonizingly slow motion, I pulled myself up off the ground. I watched helplessly as a large tail swung from behind the huge lizard and hit Bobby in the stomach. He flew back several feet from the impact, landing on his side.

Fearing for both, I shuffled in between the two. "Stop!"

"Lyssi, move!" Bobby cried out as the enormous salamander approached.

I spun around, the salamander's round blunt snout less than a foot away, inhaling. "Sal?" I raised my hands, palms down to show I had no intention of attacking. Stepping back to Bobby, I offered my hand to help him up, keeping the lizard in view. Bobby took my hand and stood up, but didn't let go. He eased his arm around me, not willing to take his eyes off the lizard, either. After a few more moments of staring each other down, the salamander turned and ambled off.

"That was weird," Bobby said.

"No. That was Sal," I corrected him.

"The shifter you mimicked to get out of the cell?"

"Yeah. That's him. And I feel jipped. He's fucking huge. I was like two inches long."

Bobby hooted with laughter while I took inventory of all my limbs. I realized I no longer sported claws and fur as I found the holes in the front of my shirt from the leopard pouncing on me. All the grief I'd been sidetracked from when I was struck in the kidney flooded back with the memory of killing the leopard shifter. Tears rolled down my cheeks while I watched the slow-motion replay in my head.

"What's wrong, Lyssi?" Bobby asked, pulling my face up so he could look me in the eyes.

"I killed it. Bobby, I killed the snow leopard that attacked me," I sobbed.

"I know. I saw. And I am so proud of you."

My face twisted in disgust, "Proud of me? How can you be proud of me when I took someone's life? That is just wrong."

"No, Cookie Dough. It's the way the fight went. It was you or him. He was fighting to the death and had you not killed him, he would have killed you. I was fighting off someone when he attacked, I came to help after the leopard went down and I was tackled by someone else. When I saw the asshole, the one who kneed you in the face, I fucking lost my shit," he said as he kissed my forehead. "There are three fewer shifters to worry about right now, but the fight isn't over. Mila couldn't find Mira, she said she's not here. Miguel and Selby headed off to the lab as soon as they could. No one else is really here."

"What do you mean 'no one else is really here'? How do you know all this? There are more shifters than we anticipated, blood is everywhere, bodies are everywhere. It's chaos," I looked around at all of the shifters still fighting.

"Bossman and Mira are both gone," he clarified, "Tysen came out after the fighting started. He, Eli, and Shawn were able to somewhat clear a path to the other end of the building where Miguel and Selby needed to go. He said he couldn't get into the security room before the call was made to warn everyone we were here. When Miguel and Selby get out of the lab, we're going to try and get out of here. Can you hang on long enough for them to get a few samples and get out safely?"

I bowed my head, knowing I had no choice but to say yes.

He kissed me on the head again and engulfed me in a tight embrace, "I was so scared. I didn't think I would get to you in time."

"But you did. Did you heal me?"

"Yeah, I did. And yes, I couldn't bear to see you hurting."

I bobbed my head, "Thank you."

"I told you once nothing would happen to you as long as I was around and I meant it, Now, come on," he pulled me back to where some of the fighting was dying down, "we have family to help. Grab some sigs, love. You have a badass bitch to be." He bent down and kissed me hard before letting me go.

When the head rush from his kiss passed, I opened my senses to find a sig. I found the strongest and closest one and pulled hard. Tingly waves wrapped around my body, warning me shifters were not the only ones in the fight.

"Bobby! Vampires!"

Bobby waved a hand to show he heard me and I pulled my attention back to the building where Miguel and Selby were running out the front door.

"I gotta go!" Miguel yelled as he ran past.

"There are vampires, Miguel," I called back to him. "Where is everyone?"

"I don't know," he yelled back, not stopping.

Selby did stop. "We decided on the way in if we got any samples, he would get them out of here since he's faster and can outrun almost everything here."

"That makes perfect sense, but where is everyone else?"

"Don't know. Just got out here."

"We have incoming," I told her as switched my attention back to the door.

She turned to face back the way she came, readying herself for a fight. Three vampires walked out, a broad-faced woman with a stocky build leading them. Someone was being drug between the two vampires in the back, pink and black sneakers struggling to walk upright.

Coming to a stop outside the door she announced, "If you want anyone else to stay alive, I suggest you call off your dogs, mutt."

Tysen called his pack and together they all came to stand beside me, Bobby, and Selby, taking up most of the fenced yard. Alex and Tia limped over to where we all stood crowded, waiting for the crazy lady to speak again. The shifters we had been fighting with stayed where they were, either standing or lying on the ground, not making any effort to support her or draw her attention.

"You aren't Bossman," I called out with a shaky voice, tired of waiting for her to speak. "Where is he?"

"No, I am not Bossman," she answered in a bored tone. "He is unavailable at the moment. And he will not be pleased when he comes back to find the mess you've made."

"Well, that sucks for you," I steadied my voice, despite the nerves, "release whoever that is behind you, and we'll leave so you can clean up as much as possible before he gets back."

An amused twinkle lit her eyes, "Oh, I recognize you. You're the quiet little mousy thing we brought back a week or so ago. You look an awful lot like the tall guy with the dark hair whose throat I ripped out. He didn't turn, did he? I don't think I got enough venom in him to make one of my little play toys, but if you have a baby vamp locked up somewhere, you'll soon regret it."

At the mention of my brother, my thoughts fled. Anger and grief battled for control, rage taking the forefront, "You? You were the one who killed my brother?" I let out a bitter laugh, "Yeah, no baby vamps for you. Not him and not another one ever again."

With the speed the vampire sig offered, I ran hard and fast. I was on her in seconds, black nails extended deep into her neck. In one swift motion, I caught the surprised woman's head in my other hand, jumped, putting my feet on her body and jerked hard. Her head came away from her body with a sickening, crunching, pop.

"Whisper!" Selby and I screamed together.

"Go to lockdown," the largest of the two remaining vampires shoved Whisper into the small one, "and take the freak with you."

"Noooo!" Selby screamed.

The smaller guy pulled Whisper back into the building while the larger guy advanced on me. The scuffling noises from behind me were almost too distracting and the screams coming from Selby was almost too much to bear. The vampire dove towards me, reaching for my throat. I swung the head I hadn't yet dropped at him and a gross, smooshy thump resounded when the disembodied face smashed into his. He staggered back a step or two and I lunged for him. I sank both hands into his hair and pulled. His head must have been screwed on a little better because it didn't budge. He wedged his elongated nails into my arms as he attempted to pry me from his upper body. I let out a screech, releasing his hair, and drug my nails down his face as I slid down the front of his body. His arm pulled back, delivering a hard backhand to my face. I ignored the pain spreading from the point of contact to the back of my head as images of Jake flashed through my mind while I stepped back to regroup, fueling my determination. He seemed to be wary of fighting with me, like he had fought someone of my stature before and learned that we smaller people aren't to be taken lightly. No pun intended. His eyes followed me closely as I paced in front of him.

I let my mind go blank as I prepared myself. Words Bobby had given me finally settled in, "You let your emotions control you. They control your actions and reactions." In that moment of complete understanding, my confidence soared. It was one thing to have an epiphany after tragedy, like with the incident with Miguel, but it was another thing to have one smack you in the face in a desperate situation, when it's needed the most. To see the enormous (in comparison to me) vampire watch me like I was the dangerous one was a massive eye opener.

"What's the matter, big boy? Got something against smaller people? Someone do you wrong and then kick your ass?" I teased, hoping I could get him flustered enough to make a mistake.

"Yeah, spiders are little and they can give a nasty bite," he said.

"You. Worry about spiders? You're that big of a pussy? You are a fucking vampire and you worry about getting bitten by a spider. What the fuck is wrong with you? Did your brain matter ooze out with your blood when you were turned?"

"What? What are you talking about? I have blood."

"Mhmm. Is that what you call the blackish goo you're seeping? Honey, it's not blood. It's dis-fucking-gusting, is what it is. I work with blood all day long and what you have is not blood," I flicked my fingers in his direction.

"I still bleed," he raised his voice like a petulant child.

"Then show me," I braced for impact, knowing this moose-brain was getting more and more pissed.

I tugged the energy sig closer to my body, making sure when he did move, I still had the vampire speed and strength needed to counteract his attack. I didn't have to wait long. He tried to blend into the shadows, but having the sig of the vampire, I could see where he was. As he jumped at me from the side, I twisted the top part of my body only, to meet his. When he crashed into me, surprise flashed in his eyes. I twisted back, pulling his heart out of his chest. His cold ikor oozed between my fingers, dripping down to the earth beneath my feet. I threw his heart down, not wanting to forget I had it in my hand like I had the head earlier. His body disintegrated and turned to ash before the heart hit the ground, the vampire energy I had tapped into, instantly depleted considerably.

"Someone needs to get that bitch's body burnt," I announced to the entire yard, pointing at the headless vampire still on the ground a few feet away.

Bobby ran full force, picking me up after he cleared the yard in seconds. "You were fucking amazing!" he said as he kissed my face over and over.

I laughed, "Maybe a little," I said as he put me down.

"No, for real. You did amazing. I could see when your demeanor changed. What happened?"

"You did." I took his hand in my ikor-free hand and we walked back to the rest of my clique that waited for us. The shifters scattered around the yard watched in silence as we all walked away.

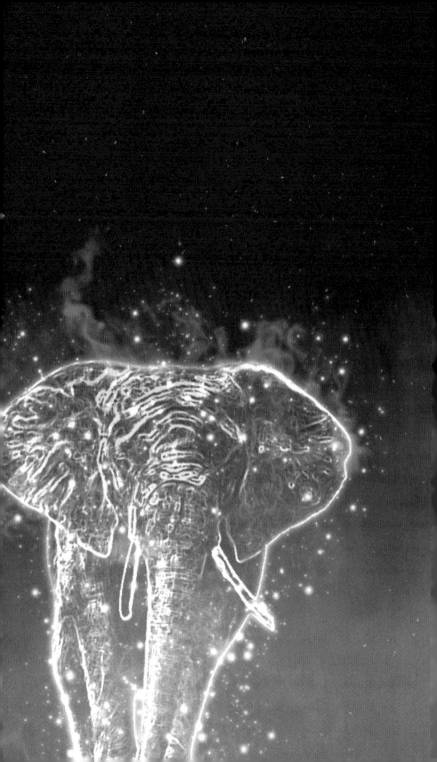

27

We all sat around Miguel's kitchen; every one of us were beaten, bloody and sore. The mood in the room was not excitement, but it wasn't exactly somber either. Tysen, Kendrick, Eli, and Shawn came back with us while the rest of his counsel went back home to make sure everyone else was okay.

"Did we lose anyone?" I looked around at the faces, covered in dirt and blood.

"He has Whisper," Selby spoke low at first. "He said she died. That sorry bastard told me she fucking died!"

"I know," I said, "I met her when I was captured. I didn't know she was your sister. I'm so sorry. And I think I know why he told you she died. He thought you would be easier to control if you weren't fighting to get her out of there. If you thought she were gone, there would be no reason for you to try to escape with her."

She turned her hate-filled glare to me, "I will get her back. I won't let them have her. They will regret my name ever falling from their lips."

"And we'll do anything we can to help," Mila told her.

"I don't need your help," Selby said as she stormed out the door, slamming it behind her.

"Cason," Eli gripped Cason's arm when he pushed himself off the counter to go after her, "let her go for a little while. She probably just needs a little bit. Let her have her few minutes, then go check on her."

Cason's hurt was palpable in the air. He looked at all of us, then leaned back against the counter.

"Miguel, what did you find in there?" Alex asked.

He sighed, "I don't know yet. I pulled as many bottles, tubes, and vials as I could. I got blood samples, a couple of stabilizers, and a few other needed odds and ends we don't keep in the main lab. I can go to the school and borrow their equipment, I have a few friends who'll keep it on the DL. I don't think it'll be wise to show back up to work now I've shown myself to be connected to you guys. No offense," he added.

"None taken," I responded, "I can help you whenever you go. I need something to keep me busy, and maybe with both of us working on it, we'll get the compounds figured out faster and know what those poor people are getting injected with."

"Dom wasn't there," Shawn said, throwing off the conversation a little. "That may not mean much to you guys, but it's going to mean a lot to Selby. It means her sister's still in serious danger. It also happens to mean our pack is still going to be involved. The one who took Whisper back in the building was one of the bastards lurking around our property. You, by the way," he said pointing at me, "are a badass. You ripped that bitch's head right off of her shoulders and tore the other fucker's heart out without batting an eye."

I didn't know how to respond to that. I didn't feel like a badass. I felt like a broken me. My brother was still dead, Whisper was still in the clutches of a psycho. Two psychos if we were to believe Domonique was still there. My heart ached because I missed my brother like no one would believe. I wanted to see his happy smile, to hear his teasing voice calling me 'Lab Rat', to be wrapped in one of his crushing-brotherly hugs that carried his earthy smell. I could only imagine how Selby felt. Her sister was still alive, but out of her reach right now. She had already witnessed her brother's death, and to know her sister could be getting tortured this very minute- it had to be beyond gut wrenching. No, I didn't feel like a badass. My heart ached as if it were empty and defeated.

"If you all will excuse me, please," I said as I left the room lost in thought and headed to the room Alex and I shared.

"Cookie Dough," Bobby tapped on the door as he entered the room right behind me, "you don't look so good. Talk to me."

"What's there to say, Bobby?"

"I don't know. How about starting with what's going on in that pretty little head of yours," he gave me one of his signature winks.

I cracked a small smile. "I think Shawn has it all wrong."

"Shawn? How does he… Oh, I get it. So, you are thinking he's wrong because Whisper turned out to be Selby's sister."

"No, I don't think you are—"

"Stop, Lyssi, just stop. You're trying to lie to me. Don't try to make this into something smaller than what it is. You didn't know Whisper was Selby's sister. Killing the one who was responsible for Jake's death didn't make you feel better because Jake is still gone. There are still people being used as test dummies, and we didn't save them. Well, let me tell you something. You *did* stop a few bad people from being able to hurt anyone else. You *did* show those bastards what they're doing is not acceptable and will be stopped. Maybe not today, but soon. You *did* protect yourself when your life was threatened. You came out on top. Not once. Not twice. But *three* times," he emphasized each number with a kiss on my face. "We aren't done with this fight. We have a long way to go, I think. I would be worried about you if you enjoyed the kill. I would be more worried about you if you didn't feel bad about taking someone's life. It means you have heart, Cookie Dough. It means you are a good person. Don't let someone's admiration for how you accomplished those difficult tasks take away from knowing you did the right thing."

I was left speechless again. How was he so accepting of everything? How did he keep his positive attitude when the world seemed to look like shit? I was not fighting my attraction to him anymore, but why was I fighting my heart to let him in? Was it because of Jake?

Studying his face, I saw nothing but love reflecting back at me. His eyes had softened since his speech. His touch, gentle. He leaned down to kiss me, raising my face with his finger under my chin to meet his. He placed soft kisses on the corners of my mouth before stopping to kiss my lips.

"Hey, Cookie Dough?" he whispered.

"Hmm?" I answered, caught in his trance.

"Go shower. You smell like a cat."

"Ugh," I slapped his arm, "for fuck's sake do you know how to break a mood."

He laughed as he kissed me on the temple, then walked around me to the door. Grabbing the doorknob, he turned and said, "I know how to fix a mood, too. I'll see you in the shower."

He walked out the door whistling a tune I didn't recognize. I shook my head and gathered my things to go shower, wondering the whole time if he was serious about getting in with me. He didn't leave me to wonder long after I got in. His large frame slid in behind me, his calloused hands moving from my back around to my stomach. He leaned into the hot water with me, his cool body flush against my back.

"I was wondering if you were kidding," I said, leaning into his chest.

"I would never joke about showering with you," he replied as he trailed soft kisses across my shoulder.

"How did you know I wouldn't throw you out?"

"You didn't tell me I wasn't allowed in the shower with you," his tongue traced circles underneath my ear.

"Mmm, is that all it takes?"

"Maybe."

"And if I kicked you out now?" I asked.

"Are you thinking about it?" he eased his hand up my stomach in between my breasts.

"I was," I teased.

"Oh? And now?"

"We'll see," I turned around to face him, running my fingers up his wet chest, "if you break any more moods, you're gone, buddy."

He gave me his sexiest smile and wink. "Sounds reasonable. But for the record," he leaned down where he could whisper in my ear, "it's not the mood I intend to break."

The kiss he followed the comment with was hard. He slipped his hands down to my ass and picked me up. He turned and put my back against the wall, stepping almost completely out of the water stream. My hands went into his hair as our kisses became more desperate. His tongue danced against mine, soft, yet firm. He readjusted our position, holding me up with one arm underneath me, his knee and elbow holding us in place. With his other hand, he smoothed my hair away from my face.

He pulled his mouth away from mine, resting his forehead against mine, "It's not about the sex, Lyssandra. I don't want you to think it is. The sex is a bonus, but I want you. All of you. I want your mind, your heart, your soul, and your body."

"Well, you just sounded a little creepy," I joked, "my soul? That's some next level shit, Bobby."

He chuckled, "I guess it was, but you know what I meant. I'll wait as long as you need me to, but I *will* bond with you. You are an amazing woman and it'll kill me to lose you."

I kissed his nose, his cheeks, his chin, and finally, his lips. Running my tongue across his full bottom lip, he opened his mouth to let me in. I couldn't tell him with words how much his admission meant to me, so I showed him with my body.

I wiggled my behind until he loosened his firm grip slightly. I pushed myself down his body until he was lined up with my core. Keeping my eyes locked on his, I eased myself onto his shaft, taking him all at once. His deep groan joined the sounds of the water hitting the floor of the shower. Bliss, love, devotion, elation, desire, all flooded my body as he took control, lifting me up and easing me back down in time with his thrust. Our momentum increased, passion pouring from one into the other. He lifted me up off him and put me down. I turned my back to him, relishing the slow movements of his hands across my ass and back. He placed his hand between my shoulder blades, eased me forward, and slid back inside me. He was slow and easy at first, but soon picked up speed as I rocked back harder onto him.

"Mr. Rough and Ready?" he asked, through gritted teeth.

"Yes, oh gods, yes."

His right hand gripped my hip while he twisted my hair at the base of my head in his left hand. I braced myself on the wall as his thrusting became harder. "I'm going to use my magic. Are you okay with it?"

I could only manage an incoherent mumble.

"I need an answer, Cookie Dough," he said as he released my hip and smacked my ass.

"Fuck! Yes!"

He slowed his pace, untangled his hand from my hair, eased his left hand around the front, pulling me back from the wall against his chest. Sliding the fingers of his right hand between my legs, he sent a little jolt of magic into me. My legs turned to jelly as my nerves lit up. His grip on my upper body tightened, holding me in place.

His breath was cool as it caressed the skin under my ear, "Do you like that?"

"Uh-huh,"

"Do you want more?"

I responded with a single nod.

He chuckled, rubbing me faster, kissing my ear and my neck as he sent another zap into me. I cried out in ecstasy when as my orgasm seemed to rock the foundations of the earth. He wasn't far behind me in finding his own release with a roar of his own. He gently leaned us against the wall, both of us completely spent.

"My ass is frozen, Cookie Dough," he brought me out of my euphoria with his words.

"What?"

"We lost the hot water some time ago when you were on the wall," he breathed.

"Oh," I laughed, "well, I suggest we wash up fast."

And we did. We dressed in a hurry, picked up our dirty clothes and left the bathroom.

"Holy fucking hell!" Alex called out, "That sounded hot as fuck!"

Heat shot through my face, but I'd had enough of her embarrassing remarks, "Do you want me to buy you a dick, Alex? I can probably find you a real one if a silicone one won't do."

'Oh!', 'Snaps', and 'Damns' came from everyone in the kitchen, but Alex didn't say another word. She bobbed her head and shot me the two-finger salute.

Bobby patted my butt as he walked by to get a couple of bottles of water out of the refrigerator.

He brought one to me, kissed me on the cheek, and went to lean against the door frame.

"So, what now?" I asked, cracking open the bottle, relishing the bite of cold water gliding down my throat. I shot Selby a confident smile when I realized she was back in the kitchen.

"We go home and make sure the pack is alright," Tysen said, gesturing at himself, Eli, Shawn, and Kendrick.

"We," Miguel pointed at those of us who worked at BTCL, "figure out what the fuck is in the serum they have been injecting those people with."

"What do we do?" Tia asked, motioning to herself, Cason, and Mila.

"We do what we're good at," Mila said. "I'll cook, you'll do hair, and Cason will fix cars and bikes."

"Oh," Tia huffed, crossing her arms over her chest, "so we don't do anything."

"Oh, yes we will. There were too many shifters at the warehouse for some of them to not go out to eat, go to a beautician, or a mechanic. Someone will slip up and say something they shouldn't. We'll be the ones they don't know are working against them. We have the perfect jobs. We blend," Cason agreed.

Mila pulled several cold dishes out of the fridge and placed them on the table in front of the shifters. Cason grabbed plates, bowls, serving and eating utensils and handed them to Selby, who set them on the table. Everyone dug into the food, talking about everything and nothing all at once. Voices carried over one another, removing any chance of silence, but carrying a peaceful harmonic chaos.

Bobby slipped his hand into mine and tugged me back to him.

"We need a few minutes alone," I whispered.

We snuck out of the kitchen and down the hall to the bedroom. I closed the door behind me and butterflies erupted in my belly.

"What did you want to talk about?" he asked, voice low.

"I didn't think you'd want an audience," I said as I gently pushed him against the door.

"For what?" he asked.

I concentrated a moment on his sig. A soft tickle floated across my skin as his nervous and excited energy coiled around me. I filtered my thoughts, curling my fingers around his wrists. Lifting his wrists up to my mouth, I laid gentle kisses on them. With my lips close to his wrist, I looked up at his curious blue eyes. "You've been worried. Much more than you should be," I kissed is wrist, pushing them to his sides against the door. "I can fix that."

He gave me a puzzled look, "How?"

I intertwined our fingers, stepping up to him, less than an inch away. I leaned in, standing on my toes, brushing my lips against his, I whispered, "Bond with me."

THE END

AUTHOR'S NOTE

Hello, dear readers. I first and foremost have to say thank you for giving me a chance to be a part of your lives for a brief time. Thank you for taking a chance to get to know the people and creatures I've created, and ultimately, some of the inner workings of my mind. It's been a ride so far, with both ups and downs, but I think that's to be expected anytime you venture off into new territory.

This story has been super fun to write. I hope that you have found something worth enjoying within and come back for more when my other characters have to face their own personal dilemmas while trying to stop Carter Droden, starting with part two of The Coverton Chronicles: Grounded, Selby's story.

Again, thank you so much for taking me with you in your daily lives. Do me a favor and leave a review where you picked up the book so I know I am going in the right direction to make work that you'll enjoy.

Until Next Time,
Ariz

FOR THE HISTORY LOVERS:

I do want to mention a few interesting things about the book. First, there are a few splashes of historical facts that were woven into the prologue. For starters, although there are some historical truths in story, most of it was complete hogwash made up to give the story life.

In Norway, there was in fact (according to some of the lazy research I did) a real man named Guthorm Haraldsson Halfdan, who had a few brothers, one of which was named Eirik (or some variation of that spelling, which changes depending on where you look) that was married to a woman named Gunhild. The brothers did battle for territories sometime after their father abdicated his throne. There were attempts made to kill one another, one of which was by poison, and from what I could tell, was how Guthorm really died. The way it all went down, I made that up to give my character, Carter, life. I don't know how Gumma died, but since she was supposedly behind the real poisoning, I felt she could get a little dose of her own medicine. Pun totally intended.

The scene with the sisters arguing in the cave is a real place in the Bulgarian mountains. Battles were held for years in that region and I thought it would be nice to see a snippet of an 'aha' moment with them. They are finally realizing that the world is changing and the people that believed so heavily in them before are getting consumed by the fighting between two of our major religions today, making the old gods and goddesses more or less fall to the wayside.

And the last piece of truth hidden in the prologue is how the start of World War One came to happen. No, it didn't start with a vengeful vampire out to kill a few goddesses, that part was nonsensical and fun to come up with. It did however start, by many historians' belief, by Archduke Franz Ferdinand and his lovely wife, Sophie, being shot to death in Sarajevo, Bosnia while checking on imperial armed forces and checking on a region that was previously claimed by war. I won't get into the political details, in case you are a reader that finds history boring, but if you are not, and you don't know the story, look up Archduke Ferdinand and you will have no shortage of interesting information. And finally, the same holds true for the Black Hand, which was a Serbian secret military society that was instrumental in the deaths of the Archduke and his wife. The man, Captain Dragutin Dimitrijević was real as well, and although the events and dialogue with Carter are not real, he did have a direct connection to the events that did kill the royal couple.

Made in the USA
Lexington, KY
30 September 2018